THE DAR[illegible]

There are places in this worl … angels fear to tread.

In book 2 of this gripping thriller, Cain Haight — a drunk ex-soldier, his opportunist ex-wife, her redneck mother, and a sweet Amish woman are on a mission to rescue two kids from the rebel soldiers who kidnapped them. But they have to survive journeying across the Tennessee landscape filled with nightmarish creatures. The words of Cain's grandmother echo in his ears. "There are places in this world where even angels fear to tread." But that's where we're headed, straight into Hell.

THE DARK 2, by *Wall Street Journal* bestselling author Christopher Greyson is filled with jaw-dropping secrets, a colorful cast of characters, and so many thrills that you need to buckle up before you read it.

Praise for Christopher Greyson's
The Dark

You can't shackle talent like Christopher Greyson's. He finally stepped out of his comfort zone and wrote one of the best dystopian novels I have ever read. I really enjoyed the terror and the suspense. I am certain you will too!
— Dan Santos — Author of the Insurrection Series

If you're captivated by a novel that launches surprises and eerie happenings with practically every turn of the page, this is it! Wild, so filled with never-ending twists and turns that it's impossible to put down! Once again, Christopher Greyson has written a thriller that will have you on the edge of your seat for the entire page-turning ride!
— Robert Tolich — Amazon Review

Mr. Greyson gifts readers with a frightening window into the ramifications of the enduring isolation of a global loss of power. With unexpected twists, our reluctant hero tackles unknown creatures, corrupt leaders, diabolical plots, and so much more in this edge-of-your seat, white-knuckle visit to the Highland Plateau town of Ridgecrest. — Micki Wiersma — Amazon Review

ALSO BY CHRISTOPHER GREYSON

The Girl Who Lived 1

The Girl Who Lived 2

One Little Lie

The Woman Beneath the Stairs

Pure of Heart

The Detective Jack Stratton Mystery-Thriller Series

Kiku - The Rogue Assassin Series

The Dark - A Post-Apocalyptic Thriller Series

The Adventures of Finn and Annie - A Mini Mystery Series

I'd like to thank Kathy Lombardo for all of her help. It's wonderful that people like her take the time to assist people in need like me.

THE DARK 2

WALL STREET JOURNAL BESTSELLING AUTHOR

CHRISTOPHER GREYSON

GREYSON MEDIA

1

YOU'RE SMOKIN' HOT

Cain Haight

I'm gonna kill someone today.

The muscles in my shoulders burn as I paddle downstream, but I won't stop. My oar slices through the water, each stroke moving me closer to my goal — saving my little girl.

Picturing Bri drives me on. Fen and Nicholi are hours ahead of us, but I'm gonna catch them. They took Bri and Jacob and headed for Fort Burgess in Leiper's Forge. Before the Dark, it was a fifty-mile drive. But we can't take the highway. To stay out of reach of the monsters, we've gotta stick to the Pintail River. The water keeps the beasts away. It's a natural barrier. The Pintail twists like a corkscrew, so who knows how long it will take to catch up to Fen, but one thing's clear, I'm not stopping.

I haven't seen any mutant wolves on the banks, but I've heard them. I glance back at Lucy and Sadie paddling in the canoe behind us. Lucy, my ex-wife, is riding in front. She angles her head and lifts her chin toward the left shore. Then she flashes me an open hand three times.

I hope she's wrong. One bone wolf is bad news. They're twice the size of a regular wolf, and it takes high-caliber rounds to put one down. A pack of fifteen might as well be an enemy army jogging beside us.

I'm glad I decided to leave Copper with Matt. Leaving my dog behind didn't sit well with me, but the thought of heading to shore so she could go to the bathroom was worse. The river is the only thing between us and whatever is in the woods.

I get back to paddling. All four of us are hell-bent on getting to those kids. Sitting in front of me, Mercy hasn't said a word in two hours. She's paddling just as hard as me. She swore to protect Jacob, and from the set of her jaw, she's determined to do just that.

Here we are, a drunk, my ex-wife, my redneck ex-mother-in-law, and the daughter of an Amish farmer on a mission to save two kids from communist soldiers as we try to avoid a host of creatures that eat the bones of their victims. I doubt there's ever been a rescue team like us. We all have skin in the game, but I plan to take out Fen and Nicholi. But before I kill them, I've got to catch them.

I paddle faster.

Less than a week ago, I only wanted to get drunk, drown my sorrows about my ex-wife getting remarried, and forget all about the Dark. The Dark started a year ago. It wasn't an attack. At least no military operation that you could see. A few people believe Russian hackers brought life as we knew it to a screeching halt. Others think it was a solar flare. Booth Gentry still claims it was aliens, but Booth ain't right in the head.

On Sunday, June 20th, at 8:57 in the morning, anything with a computer chip, the electric grid, all modes of communication, and every modern convenience stopped working. Without electricity and the internet, the town of Ridgecrest, population 1,023, perched on top of the Highland Plateau, went dark. Maybe the entire world did. We still don't know.

The Sheriff and two different groups of men left. I thought none of them came back, but I was wrong. Jesse Picket did, and Mercy's father, Amos, found him. The thing is, Amos didn't tell anyone. I'm still trying to get my head around that. I liked Amos. I thought he was a friend, but now that I've discovered he lied about Jesse, I'm not so sure.

As if reading my mind, Mercy glances over her shoulder. It looks like she is about to say something, but she focuses back on the river ahead.

I raise my hand, open my fingers, and whisper to Mercy, "Take five."

Mercy lays the paddle across the canoe, and her shoulders sag. Being Amish, her simple light blue dress is intended for modesty, but I doubt she thought about wearing it while rowing down a river in June in Tennessee. Her back is soaked with sweat, and it's sucking the fabric of her dress to her body in a way that leaves little to the imagination.

I glance around the canoe for something to take my mind off thinking about Mercy and say, "Give me that old pistol you brought."

"What for?" She asks as she reaches into a pocket on her dress and hands back a Colt Single Action Army revolver.

"If you're keeping watch, you need a working gun." I eye the weapon and relax a bit. What I first thought was rust turns out to appear more purplish. I hold it up and quietly call over to Lucy. She's the reigning champ of the county cowboy shoot and knows guns like Julia Child knows cakes. "You ever seen a purple shade on a six-shooter?"

"It's a mistake in the factory bluing. The solution was too cold. I'd swap out the ammo. That thing is older than her."

I spin the cylinder and pop it open. It's loaded, and the ammo looks new. I sniff and smell fresh powder. "This gun is well treated and recently used."

"My father uses it on critters." Mercy takes a deep breath. "You know, he probably has a good reason for not telling you about Jesse," her voice is soft, and she doesn't look at me.

"Maybe. Does he also have one for not telling me Jacob showed up after the Dark started? Or how about him taking that woman I found?"

"He said Ani is Jacob's mother. He probably didn't say anything about her because of him."

"You know they were fixing to hang me, right?"

Mercy swivels around and stares into my eyes. "They were going to hang you because they believed you killed Gunner."

"They thought I was lying about not killing Gunner and finding Ani. If your father had told them about her, they might have believed me about Gunner."

"I'm sure he would have before they put the noose around your neck." Mercy sits up straight and nods like that settled it.

I shake my head and reach for the wattle bottle. "There's more Amos didn't tell me, like about the wolves and someone killing the preppers."

"He didn't tell me either. When we get back, you should ask him."

I smile. She didn't flinch, and she didn't say she'd talk to her old man for me. Maybe that's her way of telling me to man up and ask him for myself. She also said, when we get back. Not if.

The girl's got grit. But everyone has their limits. "How are you holding up?"

"Fine."

I believe her. Besides sweating, she doesn't look beat. "You're in great shape."

Her eyes widen, and her cheeks flush.

"I'm not talking about your body.... I guess I am, but I meant you're fit, not sexy or nothing. I mean, you're smokin' hot, but I wasn't saying that." Mercy's turning all shades of crimson now, and I'm trying to figure out how to back out of this conversation. "Is there some secret gym on the farm?"

Mercy clears her throat before she speaks. "Farming is a workout in and of itself. Between churning the butter and carrying feed, it's a great deal of exercise."

I nod, figuring the best way to keep my foot out of my mouth is by keeping it closed.

Mercy grabs her water bottle and takes a long swig. "Ready?"

I tilt my head to the canoe behind us. "Lucy and

Sadie aren't used to this. We should give them two more minutes."

Mercy opens her mouth, closes it, and starts to turn toward the front of the boat.

"Hey!" I say a little too loudly. "Quit doing that, would you?"

"I have not done a thing." Mercy's eyes narrow.

"Don't go getting all uppity. All I meant is that you always start asking me something and then don't. It's driving me nuts wondering what you want to say."

Mercy straightened up. "A person should take every thought captive and control their tongue. I was going to ask you something, but decided against it."

"Well, do a better job of not letting me know you were gonna ask me something. Now I'm gonna be staring at your back and wondering what you were gonna say."

Mercy's lips pressed together. She thought momentarily and said, "I wanted to ask you about Betsy Weber. She used to buy my pies at the farmers market, and I made blankets for her children. Is she really dead?"

I take a swig from my thermos, cursing myself for not shutting my mouth. "The Mayor thinks she is."

"What do you think?"

Mercy's question tells me she doesn't think very highly of Martin. "I don't know. I didn't find a body. And I don't think Ben Pickett acted alone. Matt and Allen are going to keep looking for Ben's accomplice. If Betsy is still alive, I hope they find her."

Mercy nods and turns around. She's quiet, and I can't make out exactly what she's saying, but from the way her head is tilted forward, I'm guessing she's praying. I'm not in any position to ask God for any favors, so I'm hoping Mercy is praying for my little girl, too.

2

SANDCASTLES AND SCREAMS

Betsy Weber

Betsy stood in the knee-deep water and stared out at the sea. The beach was crowded with people laughing and playing in the water and on the sand. Her husband Carl knelt on the shore beside their daughter Nadia and son Daniel.. The three made a giant sandcastle, and Nadia placed a little plastic flag atop the highest tower.

Betsy was dreaming, but she didn't care. Carl was dead, the kids were missing, and she hadn't been to the beach since she was a kid.

A wave splashed against her waist, knocking her sideways. Over the ocean, a storm was rolling in. Long billowing clouds filled the horizon in both directions. Lighting crackled, tearing bright blue and white jagged lines in the black clouds.

Someone on the beach screamed.

Betsy turned to stare in horror as people disappeared into the sand. All along the beach, holes opened up.

"CARL!" Betsy screamed, but he and the kids were gone. Their castle lay smashed and sinking into the water.

The sand in front of her started to shift. A whirlpool formed, and a deep hole appeared.

She stepped forward and peered into the darkness.

Yellow eyes glared back at her. They weren't human. Whatever the creature was opened its mouth, revealing wicked teeth that gleamed bone white.

~

Betsy jerked awake. The room slowly came into focus. Her hands and ankles were bound. She lay on the hard cement slab in her cell. The memory of her escape slammed into her mind. The room spun, and her stomach flipped. She pulled herself to the edge of the slab before she threw up.

Her head settled against the concrete. She'd

failed. Tears filled her eyes. Somehow, she'd made it out of the compound and through the woods to Nancy's house. Her stomach flipped, and she vomited again.

What drug had Nancy's brother Gary given her? How long had she been out?

She turned her face toward the ceiling, but there was no metal grate with a view of the sky. This ceiling was solid cement. This wasn't the original cell they had locked her in. They'd taken her someplace else. Where? Why?

Betsy stared at the ropes binding her hands in front of her. She pulled and twisted her wrists, but the knots were tight. She raised her hands to her mouth and clenched the rope between her teeth. It didn't budge.

Fear ripped at her spirit, and despair seeped into the wounds. She'd be punished for her failed escape. The horrid memory of Gabriela's hand and the little girl's missing fingers made Betsy close her eyes.

Fresh tears fell, not for herself but for Camila. She would have her baby any day; if it were a boy, their captors would kill the infant.

"Oh, no. Please, Lord, no." Betsy sobbed. She bawled like a child and curled herself up, pressing her back against the cold wall.

Outside her cell, there was a sound. Faint at first,

it grew louder until Betsy realized what it was — laughter. On the other side of the door, a man laughed at her and her despair.

Deep in her breast, anger burned like she'd never known. White hot rage swept through her. She bit her lip and tasted blood. She straightened her body, every muscle tightening against her restraints. The ropes cut into her ankles and wrists, but the pain only fueled her rage.

The laughter grew, and so did Betsy's anger. Something wet and warm ran down her wrists. Like Sampson from the Bible, she imagined herself breaking the rope shackles and charging the door. Her arms shook, and the fire inside her slowly cooled.

Betsy sagged against the cement slab, gulping in air. She failed again. A fresh wave of despair swept over her and dragged her down into its pit. Camila's son would die, and it was her fault.

Once again, Betsy closed her eyes, but the words to her prayer wouldn't come. What was the use? Was there even a point in crying out when God wasn't listening anyway?

In a world gone mad, she felt her sanity slipping away.

"Please?" Betsy whispered. "Please?" She clasped her bloody hands together, and the ropes that had cut into her flesh sagged against her wrists.

Betsy's eyes snapped open.

Her struggle hadn't been in vain after all. The ropes didn't break, but the knots tightened, creating slack in her bindings. With her wrists slick with blood, maybe she'd loosened them enough. Ignoring the pain, Betsy pressed her hands together and pulled.

The rope slid down her wrist and almost over the first knuckle of her thumb. Wiggling and turning her hands, she fought against her bonds. She lifted her arms and clamped her teeth down on the rope already damp with her blood.

She snarled and thrashed like a fox caught in a trap. Her left hand slipped free. She chomped down on the rope to stifle the cheer wanting to burst from her lungs.

She may have been free of her bonds, but she was still trapped in her cell with guards standing outside.

Betsy's mouth curled into a determined bloody grin.

The seeds of a plan had begun to grow roots.

3

YOU SMELL

Bri Haight

Bri sat in the bow, trying to catch a glimpse of Jacob riding in the canoe in front of her. Nicholi's broad back blocked the little boy from sight. She hoped Jacob was okay. He had been bawling and fighting so much, Nicholi forced some pill into Jacob's mouth. Jacob had been sleeping since then. Bri felt like crying herself, but she wouldn't. Daddy always said if you're gonna cry, wait until you get out of trouble to do it.

Bri took a big breath and clasped her hands together. The plastic charms on her bracelets bounced against her wrists. Daddy had given them to her for her birthday. If he were here right now, she'd be hanging over the edge with her hands in the water, begging him to let her go for a swim. But her father wasn't paddling this canoe — Fen was.

Bri scowled. The Chinese soldier was beautiful in a Maleficent kinda way. But Bri imagined the cold woman's heart was as black as her eyes and buzz-cut hair. Fen even tried to kill her Daddy's friend, Goose, and all poor Goose had been doing was fishing. The rifle shot would have hit him if Bri hadn't rocked the boat. Afterward, Fen smacked her. Bri rubbed the back of her head.

"Don't be a baby." Fen snapped. "You're lucky I only hit you with my hand."

Bri wanted to turn around and spit in her eye. That's what Memaw Sadie would do. At least she always said that. But Mom would get mad if Bri did. Not 'cause it was gross and rude but 'cause it violated Mom's rule — never let them see you're mad unless you're ready to fight. And Bri wasn't ready to fight just yet.

Her shoulders slumped. She was only nine. What could she do against Fen and the giant in the other canoe without a weapon? Nothing!

A bush along the bank of the river shook.

Fen stopped paddling.

Bri held her breath. Her eyes burned as she stared unblinking at the shore. Earlier this morning, she'd seen one of the wolves. It was a quick glimpse, but it was huge. Bigger than the ones in *Beauty and the Beast.*

Fen began paddling again. "What's your name, kid?" She asked Bri for the millionth time.

Bri crossed her arms.

"You know, we only need the boy. I could toss you out now and make it easier for me to paddle."

Bri swallowed. She believed the wicked woman. "Bri."

"That's a pretty name. Mine's Fen."

"Like the marsh?"

"It has a different meaning in China — Perfume."

You smell like a yucky marsh.

Bri glared at the bottom of the canoe. Getting mad wasn't gonna solve anything. Neither was crying or being scared. She needed to be smart if she couldn't whoop Fen in a fight.

"What's your last name?"

Bri's lips mashed together. She didn't like her new last name, but her momma said she had to use it. "Green."

"Like the Mayor? The Mayor's your father?" Fen asked, then quickly continued. "No. He's too old. So, your father is the mayor's son, and your mother's name is Lucy?"

Bri crossed her arms. She didn't like her momma's new husband, Evan, either. She didn't like Fen calling him her father either.

"I'm glad I didn't toss you out of the boat. Being the mayor's granddaughter, there may be a use for you."

Bri was going to give Fen what for and let her know who her real daddy was, but instead clamped her mouth shut. The last thing Bri wanted was to get dumped out of the boat.

"I bet your grandfather would do anything for you, right?" Fen asked.

Bri nodded quickly.

"Do everything I say, and I won't hurt you. Do something stupid, and I'll feed you to the Xiǎo móguǐ."

"What's that?"

"Bone Rats." Fen laughed. "Little demons that will eat you up."

"Not if they eat you up first," Bri said, then bit her lip.

Fen laughed harder. "You have a temper, little girl. I like that."

They floated down the river in silence for several minutes until Fen began peppering Bri with questions. Most, Bri didn't know the answer to. How many guns did the town have? What kind? How many fighters? But then Fen asked a question that made Bri's heart speed up.

"Do you know the man named Cain?"

Bri nodded before stopping herself.

"How?"

"He, ah," Bri's eyes darted to the riverbank. If Fen thought she was the mayor's granddaughter, she was safe. She didn't know what the mean woman would do if she found out Cain was her real daddy. "He comes over to my Memaw Sadie's house."

"Memaw? Is that your grandmother?"

Bri nodded.

"Why does Cain go there?"

Bri shrugged.

"Do you ever talk to him?"

Bri shook her head no.

"Why not?"

"He's mean!" Bri blurted out. "And scary." Her daddy wasn't scary or mean. He was the nicest, sweetest person she knew.

Fen chuckled. "Others have told me the same thing."

Fen was right. Her daddy was good to Bri, but other people in town feared him. They said he was mean and crazy. Momma called him stubborn as a mule, wild as a tornado, and as dangerous as lightning. But he loved Bri. He would come for her. She just knew he would. But to do that, he needed to know where she was.

Goose! Goose saw her. He'll tell Daddy. Then Daddy would come.

Bri looked over her shoulder at the river, half expecting to see her father paddling after them.

"What do you want?" Fen asked.

Bri said the first thing that popped into her head. "I'm hungry."

Fen reached down and tossed a plastic bag at Bri.

She caught it. Something inside crunched. Bri smelled the peanuts before she opened the bag. The sun was high in the sky, and she hadn't eaten anything since yesterday. She broke open one shell after another and hungrily devoured the nuts.

"You're making a mess," Fen said. "Pitch the shells over the side."

Bri scooped up the shells littering the floor and tossed them into the water. The charms on her bracelets bounced against her arms. She grabbed another handful from the bag, and her eyes widened as she watched the peanut shells float like little boats on the water.

Fen continued to paddle.

Bri's heart pounded in her chest. She looked at the nuts in her hand. How long would they float? Not long.

Tears stung her eyes. She tried to hold them back, but they came anyway. Big drops rolled down her cheeks and landed on her hands and bracelets. The plastic charms glistened and sparkled.

Bri gasped.

Plastic floats!

She grabbed the charm of the little pink elephant with white glitter stars and clicked it off the bracelet. Holding the elephant and a couple of shells, she threw them as far away as possible and held her breath.

Fen continued to paddle.

Bri noisily crunched a mouthful of peanuts as she pulled off a penguin charm, then flung it way out toward the middle of the river. The shells caught the wind and did go far, but the plastic charm flew further.

Bri chanced looking back. Behind them, floating on the water, the little pink elephant sparkled. Bri smiled. "Thank you for the peanuts, ma'am. They're just what I needed."

”

4

AS BAD AS IT GETS

Matt Browner

Sheriff Matt Browner sat in the uncomfortable chair in front of the Mayor's large desk. His head throbbed. Doc Harmon had bandaged him up and given him some medicine, but his headache was epic.

The mayor, Martin Green, stood at the bar pouring another glass of dark liquid. Martin looked like a spooked horse. Panic rounded his eyes, and his nostrils flared. "This is about as bad as it gets, Matt!" Martin took a long swig from his drink and topped it off. "What are we going to do?"

"It's not your fault."

"Frank Pickett isn't going to think that!" Spit flew

from Martin's mouth and clung to his bottom lip as he stormed back to his desk, carrying the drink in one hand and the bottle in the other. "Fen told Frank that Jesse was alive and in Leiper's Forge. Frank believed that. You saw it yourself. Frank cried."

"We don't know if that part was a lie." Matt exhaled. "But it does call everything they said into question."

"Everything!" Martin flopped onto his high-backed chair, the leather crinkling beneath him. "They may not even be heading to Leiper's Forge. Leiper's Forge could be in ruins for all we know!" Martin's eyes hardened, and his trembling hand holding the glass steadied. "Why did they take those children?"

Matt wanted to point out that one of *those children* was now his granddaughter, but poking the bear wasn't a bright idea. "Hostages?"

Martin shook his head. "None of this makes sense. Why come into town with this story of helping us only to take off with two kids? What am I supposed to tell everyone?"

"Tell them the truth — you don't know."

Martin scoffed and sipped his drink. "And come off like a dunce? No thanks. The people elected me because I said I had answers." He closed his eyes and pinched the bridge of his nose.

Matt sat there in silence and crossed his arms. Once again, he pictured Cain and three women rowing downriver, determined to get those kids back. Their courage shamed him into speaking. "We need a plan." He grabbed a yellow notepad and pen off the Mayor's desk and pulled his chair forward. "Someone should talk to Frank Pickett. I'll do it."

Martin set his drink on the desk and slid his hand down his face. "I'll handle Frank. I need you to do something else for me. When Frank finds out that Fen and Nicholi hightailed it out of town, he may go after them. If he does, he's going to gather up his clan, and that includes Ben Pickett. But Ben's dead."

Matt froze. Cain confided that Ben Pickett had murdered the Weber's and Nancy Long. When Cain confronted Ben, Ben went for his gun, so Cain killed him. Cain also said that Martin didn't want Matt to know, so Matt sat there, trying to look unsurprised. "How did he die? One of the wolves get him?"

"Cain killed him. It was justified. Cain's dog tracked the woman to Ben's house. They're dead, but Cain hid Ben's body at the farm. I need you to find it and make sure no one else does. Understand?"

Matt wrote:

1 — Martin talks to Frank.

2 — Find and hide Ben's body.

"This is good." Martin tapped the notebook and took another sip. "We need to let people know, but I'll be dipped in wet manure if you think I'm calling another town meeting. Send out your brother to let people know."

"Allen can't reach everyone by himself. I'll send Josh Pierce and his boy Kenny, too."

"Tell Allen to speak to Amos, and he'll let all the Amish know." Martin straightened up. "Where is Amos? Considering Fen took his grandson, and his daughter went after them, I'd have thought Amos would be breaking down my door to talk to me."

"He came into town earlier with Cain and Mercy. Maybe he went home to let Sarah know. Do you want me to get him?"

Martin shook his head. "I bet you're right. Once Amos tells Sarah, I'm sure he'll be coming here. Besides, I need you to go straight to Ben's and get rid of that body. I'm already worried about what Frank is going to do. He'll go ballistic if he discovers Ben's dead and Cain killed him. And don't go telling anyone. Not your wife and not your brother."

"I didn't plan on it, and I won't. You know Ben may have been working for Frank Pickett when he robbed those preppers? In the least, I'd figure that Frank knew something."

"I've got enough on my plate telling Frank that Fen and Nicholi may have been lying about his son being alive. I'm not going to start accusing him of anything right now. For all I know, he may take all his men and head for Leiper's Forge."

Matt set the pen down. "Maybe that's not such a bad idea. Cain and the girls could use the help."

Martin finished his drink. His hand shook so hard that the glass tipped over as he set it down. Grimacing, he placed it upright and stared at the dark stain on his desk. "Cain and the girls are as good as dead. One thing Fen and Nicholi didn't lie about, and that's the fact they're soldiers. So, if the wolves don't kill them, Fen and Nicholi will." Martin scoffed. "What chance do you think they have?"

Matt clamped his mouth shut. He hoped the Mayor was wrong, but the truth was, he didn't know. He stood. "I better get moving."

"Take the list." Martin ripped the page from the notebook and handed it to Matt. "Make sure that Allen and Josh get going too. I'll go speak with Frank."

"Do you want Allen to go with you?"

Martin shook his head. "Get out to Ben's and get back as soon as possible. I've got a feeling that when people discover what's happened, everyone will panic, and all hell will break loose."

Matt headed out the door and down the hallway —the heels of his boots rung off the stairs until he reached the first floor. A lot was left unsaid in the conversation with the mayor, but his mind filled in the details as it caught up. Frank Pickett may have already sent men out to Ben's farm. Matt was walking into a hornet's nest if that were the case.

But even if no one was there, once Matt hid the body of Frank's nephew, Matt's hands would be dirty. And the only thing more dangerous than the wolves was crossing Frank Pickett.

5

DON'T RUSH ME

Cain Haight

We reach a wide spot in the river, and I slow down so Sadie and Lucy can pull up alongside Mercy and me. Everyone looks about as spent as I feel. "There's still four or five hours of sunlight left. I figure we should sleep in shifts starting with opposite rowers. That way, we'll switch the lead canoe over, come night. Lucy will take point, watching for anything floating in the river. Then we'll switch back."

"Sounds like a plan," Sadie says. "I ain't tired right now anyway."

"I sure am." Lucy pulls up her oar and slides off her seat to lie in the middle of the canoe.

I stare at Mercy, who looks like she wants to say something. "Are you all right with steering while I sleep?"

Mercy nods but motions Sadie over. The canoes bump together. Mercy grabs the side and leans close to Sadie, so I can't hear what they're talking about.

Sadie chuckles and points at the front of the canoe. "That's what the can is for. Use it, then pitch it over the side."

The back of Mercy's neck turns as red as a summer strawberry. She glances back at me. "Can we stop on shore for just a minute?"

"Don't be a prude!" Lucy shouts from the bottom of the canoe. "Cain, close your eyes and plug your ears so Miss Modesty can use the bathroom, and we don't have to risk getting eaten."

I'm about to say something, but from the way Mercy's shoulders have risen to the bottom of her ears, it appears she's about embarrassed enough to die. Like a little kid, I stick a finger in each ear, close my eyes, and hum a tune. A couple of minutes later, something wet sprinkles my face.

Lucy laughs. "I was just letting you know you could open your eyes." Lucy, propping herself up on her elbows and smirking at me says, then waves her water bottle.

Before I can respond, a car horn splits the air. I drop my oar and pull out my shotgun. Motion up the riverbank catches my eye. Part of the road is visible, and an old car sits there. Someone inside the car is laying on the horn.

"That dang fool's gonna let every creature within five miles know where we are," Sadie says.

"It's a guy." Lucy is peering through the sight of her rifle. "I only see one. Wait. Something's moving down the road to our left. Down where the guardrail starts."

I only see bushes and a little metal peeling through from the guardrail, but I'll take her word for it.

A man jumps out of the car. He's yelling, waving his arms, and starts running toward us.

"It's gotta be at least a hundred yards to the river," Sadie says.

"One fifty." Lucy's voice is cold and hard.

My canoe suddenly changes direction, and I grab the side. Mercy's rowing us toward the bank.

"What are you doing?" I snap.

"He needs help!" Mercy says.

"We don't know who he is or if others are with him," I shoot back.

Lucy points. "Wolves! A pair of them."

Two wolves burst out of the brush near the end of a guardrail, but something is different about them. These things are even bigger than the mutant ones I'd seen before. A wide, white stripe runs the length of their backs.

The man is barreling down the bank, but the creatures are gaining on him. There's no way he'll reach the water without them catching him.

"Shoot them, Lucy!" Mercy shouts.

Lucy's rifle roars.

The bullet knocks the lead wolf's head to the side. The monster stumbles but keeps running.

Lucy swears, racks another round, and fires again.

The bullet blasts a chunk of white off the wolf's back, but it doesn't slow.

The closer it gets, I realize why. These things look to have some kind of spinal column on the outside. It's bone and acting like armor.

"I got it," Sadie says, and her 6.5mm Creedmoor sounds like a cannon when she fires.

The wolf staggers and drops.

"Aim for the throat," Sadie says.

Lucy rubs her ear against her shoulder. "What are you firing in that thing?"

"325-grain slugs."

"The other one is going to get him!" Mercy screams.

The guy is running full out. His eyes are wide, and his hands claw at the air like he's trying to pull himself forward.

The wolf is less than ten yards behind him. Another few seconds, and it'll be over.

Mercy looks at me for help, but there's nothing I can do from here.

"Take it down, Lucy!" I shout.

"Don't rush me." Lucy's voice is calm, even, and all business. She fires.

The wolf pitches forward, rolls over twice, and slides down the hill several feet.

The man splashes into the river and dives out. He goes under for a second and starts swimming toward us like sharks are chasing him now.

Mercy stares at me in disbelief. I can see the unasked question on her face — why didn't I shoot?

I hold up my Mossberg shotgun. "I can't do anything at this distance."

Mercy glances at the pistol on my hip but doesn't say anything.

I'm about to remind her that I unloaded an entire magazine from my Glock into one of those things at close range, and it didn't do anything, but Mercy turns to start paddling again.

"Wait for him to swim to us," I say, taking out my pistol.

Mercy opens and closes her mouth, then nods and sets her oar down.

Sadie and Lucy steer their canoe around, so they have a clear shot at the man in the water. It's a good feeling knowing someone's watching my back. I give Sadie an appreciative nod, and she blows me a kiss —the best ex-mother-in-law in the world.

The guy is young. Early twenties. His brown hair is on the long side, and he's got a beard. Scruffy is the '*it*' look of the apocalypse. He's wearing a black T-shirt and jeans.

"Thank you! Thank you!" He pants as he dog paddles over.

Lucy's got the SIG Sauer P238 I gave her before I left for the Army aimed at the guy's head. "He's got a pistol in a holster on his right hip."

Before the guy reaches the canoe, I'm pointing my gun at him with my right hand and holding out the oar with the other. "Far enough. Nice and slow, hold onto the oar with your right hand and hand over your weapon."

Mercy looks at me like I'm the lowest snake in the grass. It cuts, but I don't care. In the war, I'd seen men let their guard down. They ended up dead, and I didn't.

The guy stops and flounders as he hangs off the oar and tries to use his left hand to draw his gun. He hands it to me, grip first, then reaches for the side of the canoe.

"Not so fast," I say again. "What were you doing out here?"

"I came to find help. My wife is sick. My

daughter is with her. I was heading to Ridgecrest, hoping someone was there. Is that where you're from? Is there a doctor there?"

"Why'd you stop?"

"The car died. I got out to fix it but heard something in the woods and hid inside. Can I get in the boat? You've got my gun. Please?" He reaches for the side of the canoe closer to Mercy.

"Stop." I resist the urge to smack him with the oar.

"Cain." Mercy's voice is firm. "We're obligated to provide aid."

It's probably my independent temperament, but the word obligated rubs my fur the wrong way. "You may be. I'm not."

"Are you Amish?" The man asks. "My wife's a Christian. She always says do unto others as you'd like to be treated. I'd pull you up. Please let me in the boat."

Mercy stares at me with her green eyes blazing. She ain't asking. This is a stand-off I never bargained for.

"Please!" The guy's lips are trembling. "You can't leave me here."

I want to point out that I can, but whatever bit of conscience I've got left in me won't let me do it. "Swim around to the back and climb in." I think about saying something more like if you breathe wrong, I'll kill you, but that will only upset Mercy further. It's the truth, but I don't need to say it. If I have to, I'll shoot him before he gets in.

"Thanks. You all saved my life. I'm Bodhi."

After a couple of minutes of shifting, pulling, and steadying, Bodhi's sitting at the bottom of the canoe between Mercy and me. She's giving him water and a protein bar.

"Thank you." Bodhi drinks half the bottle. "My place is downstream. You can see it from the river. We're going to go right by it."

Lucy glares at me and rolls her eyes. There's no need for words. She thinks I've gone soft. Maybe she's right. It's one thing getting those wolves off the guy. It's another taking him with us. But her poor opinion of me isn't what's bugging me. It's what do I do with the guy now?

6

A GOOSE TALKED TO YOU?

Amos Yoder

Before Amos Yoder stopped his wagon, the front door of his house opened.

His wife, Sarah, ran out onto the porch, drying her hands on her apron. "Have you seen Mercy? She must have taken the children, but didn't tell me where or when. Lucy Green left late last night, too. I know she's the mayor's daughter-in-law but—What's wrong?"

"Let's go talk in the kitchen." Amos took Sarah by the elbow and led her inside. They'd been married for over twenty years, so there were times when they didn't need to speak to communicate. This was one of those times.

Sarah sat at the kitchen table, all of the color draining from her freckled cheeks.

"It's bad," Amos said, pouring himself a glass of water and staring out the window at the field. "That Fen and Nicholi took Bri and Jacob last night."

Sarah chuckled. "Don't go fooling like that, Amos. The children were here last night."

"I didn't hear anything either. Those two are military. They snuck in and snatched them. Goose saw their canoes on the river."

Sarah covered her mouth as she laughed. "You sound nuttier than a five-pound fruit cake. Don't go scaring me like that. A goose talked to you?" She waved her hand and sighed.

Amos set his glass down so hard it cracked. "I'm serious. Goose is a nickname for some fella Cain is friends with. He was fishing on a bridge and saw Fen and Nicholi taking Bri and Jacob downriver."

Sarah stood. "Why would they do that? Where are they going? They're coming back, right?"

Amos shook his head. "Sit back down." He slid the broken glass to the corner of the counter and shuffled over to the table. "Cain, Lucy, and Sadie Dawson went after the kids."

"They left town? Oh, dear Lord! It's so dangerous."

Amos reached out and took her trembling hand. "Mercy went with them."

Sarah didn't cry, cuss, or faint. She nodded and stared at him with a steady gaze.

"Mercy went with them," Amos said again. "Downriver."

"I understand. Mercy must have felt the Lord wanted her to go. Are you going after them, too?"

Amos hung his head. "I can't. There's something I haven't been telling you."

Sarah sat straighter.

"I came across Jesse Pickett down at the river a year ago. The boy was almost dead and out of his mind. He made him give him my word I wouldn't tell anyone or take him to town. He had a gun and was going to use it on himself."

Sarah blinked rapidly as she took this news in. Her foot tapped, and she gently rocked back and forth. Those were sure signs she was praying silently.

"I've done my best to nurse him back to health. Physically, he's healed, but his mind snapped. I don't know what happened to him and the hell he's been through."

"Mind your language."

"I didn't use the word as a cuss, Sarah. He mutters about what he saw. It's like Hell cracked open, and he looked inside."

Sarah rocked faster now. Her cheeks paled.

"Why didn't you tell me? Maybe I may have helped?"

"I gave my word. But there's more. Do you remember that woman Cain said he found?"

"Yes. You don't believe him, do you?"

Amos rubbed the back of his neck and swallowed.

"Whatever it is, you can tell me, Amos. You're my husband, and I love you."

"Cain was telling the truth. I saw him high tail it out of the Dixon house, and curiosity got the better of me."

"You found her? Where is she?"

"I took her to the upper meadow where I'm hiding Jesse. The minute I saw her, I recognized some connection between her and Jacob. I couldn't let anyone find her, so I took her in the carriage."

Sarah's hand smacked the table. "I knew you weren't telling me the truth about what you were doing out there. And to think you told me you were going to pray."

"I was. I've lied about a lot of things but not that. Something is happening, Sarah. Evil is coming."

Sarah stood up. "Why haven't you told anyone this? What about the other families?"

"Everyone is already on guard. I've got no specifics, but I keep having this dream. Ever since Jacob showed up. The dream is always the same.

There's a storm like none other, and I'm standing in the center of town. Cain's with me."

"Is that why you invited him to live on our property?"

Amos nodded. "In the dream, we're standing in the eye of the storm, staring at the destruction. We're in the middle of a tornado, and I'm helpless. The people I love most are caught in the wind and flying around us. You, Mercy, Jacob. There are others — Amish families and people from the town. Everyone's screaming and calling out to Cain and me for help. Out of the hurricane, these demonic creatures appear. They have jaws filled with razor-sharp teeth, and their talons claw the air."

Amos clamped his hands together, pressed them against his forehead, and shut his eyes.

"In the dream, I can't move. I want to. I want to help, but my feet are pinned to the ground. Cain charges forward, a gun in each hand, firing as fast as he can. The beasts pounce. The dream always ends there. I don't know if Cain lives or dies, but my cowardice bothers me to no end."

Sarah's gentle touch on his shoulder made Amos open his eyes. "You're no coward. It's just a dream."

Amos shook his head. "No. Jesse draws what he saw out there. The creatures in his drawing look just like the ones from my nightmare. Unless I'm losing my mind too."

Sarah slapped him across the face.

Amos stepped back. In all their years together, Sarah had never lifted a hand toward him, let alone struck him so hard his face stung.

"You're not crazy, so get that foolish notion out of your mind, Amos Yoder. God's trying to tell you something. Do you think it's a coincidence that all this happened to you? God brought Jacob, Jesse, and that woman to you, Amos. He has his reasons, and we better figure them out. The Lord gave you a warning, and we have to get ready. Something wicked is coming to Ridgecrest."

"I know." Amos took Sarah's hand. "But what can we do?"

"Pray. And then I want you to take me to speak to that woman." Sarah started out of the kitchen.

"Where are you going?"

"I'm going to get my bag."

Amos slumped in the chair. Sarah's *bag* was her version of a mobile hospital. Sarah's mother had been the go-to healer of the community as her mother before her. Sarah cared for humans and animals, but her skills were limited. Would they be enough to help Ani?

7

I'LL WATCH YOU DIE

Cain Haight

After giving Bodhi another protein bar and more water, Mercy says, "Don't worry, you're safe."

"Safe?!" Bodhi's staring at the shore. "With all those things out here?"

"The water acts as a natural barrier," Mercy explains.

"How have you survived this long out here with the wolves?" I ask.

"It hasn't been easy," Bodhi says. "My wife and I aren't even from around here. We were staying at the White Pine RV park when everything died. After waiting around for a couple of days, a few of us decided to make for the highway. My wife and daughter wanted to come, so Callie, my little girl, rode her bike. We didn't make it past the river road. We reached a garage—"

"Apex Service?" Sadie, who's been rowing beside us, calls out from the other canoe.

"That's the one. Do you know it?"

"I'm friends with the owner. Mack Gibson is the best mechanic around. Is he okay?"

"The garage was locked up. No one was inside when we broke in."

Sadie's expression hardens.

Bodhi holds both his hands up, and his voice rises. "We had no choice. Dozens of wolves came running out of the forest. Everyone ran for the building because of the fence around it. The front door was open, but besides my family, only Roy made it inside. But one of those things took off his hand. I stopped the bleeding, but he caught a fever and died. We've been hiding there ever since."

"That's horrible. I'm so sorry." Mercy said.

"Thank you." Bodhi's bottom lip trembled. "My wife, she's a Christian. She says God provided for us. The garage is a steel building, and a room was stocked with supplies. There are bars on the windows, and we barricaded the door. The wolves don't come around often, but we see them every once in a while." Bodhi stares back at me. "They're changing."

I nod. "Have you gotten a good look at them?"

"Closer than I care to." Bodhi swallows. "Along their backs, they developed bone. It's like a second skeleton. I shot one in the head, but now it's like they're wearing helmets."

"You see any other creatures?" I ask.

"The mutated squirrels. Little things with sharp teeth and a long tail with a bone tip."

"We call them bone rats," I say.

"I guess they do look more like rats than squirrels. I can't thank you enough for saving me, but Khloe needs help. She sliced her hand on some broken glass, which infected the cut. We only have some alcohol and aspirin. Do you have any medicine at Ridgecrest? Penicillin?"

"We do!" Mercy blurts out. "Doc Harmon could treat her. We can take you when we come back."

"Come back?"

"Hey." The soldier in me interrupts. We're talking too much to a guy we know nothing about. "I'm sorry to hear about your wife. I've agreed to take you to the garage. That's it. What you do then is up to you."

Lucy shouts over, "We don't have time to stop. He can swim to shore."

Bodhi starts looking between Lucy, Sadie, me, and Mercy so much that he's rocking the canoe, making it even harder to paddle. "Are you headed to

Leiper's Forge and the Army Base? Take us with you! Please?"

Mercy sets her paddle across the gunwales. "Of course, we will."

Her agreeing without asking me is like a fire chigger under my skin. "No, we won't. We've got to keep moving."

Bodhi brushes his hair back with both hands. He turns completely around to face me. "Please! You can't just leave us. She won't make it long. We're getting close to the garage. You can see it from the river. It will only take ten minutes. Tops."

"There isn't enough space in the boats for your family."

"There's a canoe in the back of the garage. Help me get Khloe to the water, and I'll take it from there. We'll follow, but won't be any trouble. If we fall behind, forget about us, but please, for the love of God, help me."

Sitting in my seat, gazing down at a man on his knees begging me for help, makes me wonder how a king ever got anything done. Bodhi's desperate. I can see it on his face. Then I glance up and meet Mercy's gaze. She's silently pleading with me, too. It's her begging that changes my mind.

Lucy paddles closer. "There's nothing for you to decide, Cain. Sadie and I voted. He jumps into the water and swims for it when we get to the garage."

I always thought it odd that Lucy referred to her mother as Sadie, not Mom. Maybe it was because they were so close in age. One look at Sadie, and I doubt there was a vote. Sadie's staring into the bottom of the canoe and won't meet my gaze.

"We're not leaving a mother and child alone," Mercy says.

"Then you jump out of the boat when he does!" Lucy's voice takes on the harsh tone she uses when she's an unhappy drunk. "Catch up to us in his canoe, but we're not stopping."

"Ten minutes," Bodhi begs. "I need help getting my wife to the river. That's it, and you can go."

Drifting downstream, the garage comes into view. It's a lot closer to the river than I thought. A dirt boat road leads up a slope from the water's edge and past a dozen rusting cars to a long building. Because of the angle of the hill, I can only see the roof and sign.

I don't know if it's the proximity or Bodhi's tears, but Sadie says, "Ten minutes, no more."

Lucy swears a blue streak that makes Mercy's ears glow red. No one is spared from Lucy's wrath, especially me. She calls me every name in the book and finishes with a promise I know she'll keep. "If they get away with Bri, I'll shoot you in the gut and watch you die."

I start paddling for the shore. There's nothing

Lucy can say that bothers me. If I lose Bri because of this foolish decision, living with myself would be far worse than anything she could do to me.

8

NOW WHAT?

Betsy Weber

Betsy crouched in the corner of her cell, blinking rapidly and rubbing her eyes. The pain and blood on her wrists confirmed she wasn't dreaming. She freed herself from her bonds, but was still trapped in her cell.

Now what?

Besides the cement cot and two buckets, the room was empty. She tried to open the steel door, but the handle didn't budge. The door was solid, and without a window, there wasn't a way to see if a guard stood outside.

Crouched in the shadows, she listened as she stared at the ceiling and the sky lightening outside.

Where an air vent once stood, her captors, who used the building as a prison, had removed the unit and covered the opening with three steel bars. The inept patch job of concrete to fasten the bars in place was visible even in the low light.

She crept forward. The ceiling was very high, and Betsy stood only five-foot-five. She reached for the bars but couldn't grab them, even on her toes and stretching. She jumped, fell short of the bars, and landed softly on the balls of her feet.

The cement cot was too far away to stand on and reach the bars. She grabbed one of the two empty five-gallon buckets. Flipping it over, the handle fell and clanged off the cement.

Betsy held her breath. Her heartbeat thumped like the background soundtrack in a horror movie.

Silence descended back into the cell. Satisfied no one was coming, Betsy climbed onto the bucket. She stretched, but her fingers still fell a few inches lower than the bars. She jumped. Like grabbing the jungle gym in elementary school, she hung onto the bar, slowly swaying above the floor.

The bucket beneath her rocked but remained upright.

Betsy pulled. Concrete cracked. Pebbles and dust fell, and her hope rose. She shifted her grip, causing her to sway back and forth. The bar in her right hand twisted a little. She jerked hard again, but it didn't move down at all.

The muscles in her shoulders burned. She twisted again, and the bar rotated a quarter of an inch. Gritting her teeth, she tried to turn it back. Sweat slickened her hands, and she lost her grip.

Betsy gasped and moved her feet out wide, not wanting to hit the bucket and send it careening across the room. She landed on her feet, but was off-balance and crashed onto her backside. Pain raced from her tailbone to the crown of her head. She bit her lip to keep from crying out. Blinking back tears, she sat there and listened.

Silence.

Hanging her head, despair washed over her. She may have freed herself from her bonds but was still trapped. Locked in a cage, she could only wait for a man in the golden mask of her husband's dead face to appear. When he did, what then? What horror would befall her as punishment for trying to escape?

Betsy set the bucket back in its place. She grabbed the rope that had bound her legs off the cot. Tears rolled down her face and landed on her bloodied hands. Should she retie her bonds? Holding an end of the rope in each hand, she pulled it taught. Her knuckles turned white as the blood drained from her fingers.

No. She wouldn't pass silently into submission. She needed to fight. For her kids. For Camila. For herself.

Faint footsteps sounded from the end of the hallway.

Betsy darted over to the cot.

The footsteps drew nearer. How many guards were coming? She may be able to fight one man, but more?

Pushing doubt aside, she wrapped the rope loosely around her ankles and then her wrists. She clutched an end of the rope in each hand, laid down, and closed her eyes.

The footsteps stopped outside the door.

One man. Alone. Keys rattled, and the lock turned. The door creaked open.

Boot heels clicked off the cement. He stopped at the edge of the slab she lay on.

Betsy cried out as he seized her hair and yanked her to a sitting position. She stared past the golden death mask of her husband at brown eyes blazing with hate.

His breath, which reeked of smoke and whiskey, seeped from the mask. "You have no idea of what you've done." The man lifted her by the hair until she was fully sitting up. "You could have had it easy. I would have been nice. Real nice. Now you have to learn. Now I have to decide."

Fear closed Betsy's throat so tightly it strangled her. But she forced herself to breathe. In. Out. Shallow breaths. Her eyes darted to the door and narrowed, pretending she'd heard something in the hallway.

The man jerked her head back and forth. "Look at me!"

She gazed back into the face of her tormentor.

"Do you know what they've asked me to do? I get to choose. You lose either your left or right foot." He chuckled. "The same with the other women. No one's going to run anymore. We'll wait until Camila has the kid, then we'll do her. But you and Gabriela get it today."

The threat made Betsy's blood cool and her breathing steady. Instead of shifting into a panic, everything slowed. Once again, she glanced at the door and knit her eyebrows together like someone was there.

Keeping his grip on her hair, the guard turned his body toward the door.

Betsy pounced. She looped the rope over his head, yanked it tight, and crossed her arms as far as possible.

The guard let go of her hair and clutched the rope around his throat. He pitched forward and toward the door with Betsy on his back.

Betsy clung to the rope like a rodeo girl atop the

meanest bull. The guard pitched and swung his arms, striking her on the side of her head. She ignored the pain and held on. The rope burned her palms, and it felt like the skin was tearing away, but she refused to let go.

The man pulled something the size of a thin flashlight from his pocket. He flicked his wrist. There was a sudden clack of metal. Like a magician's trick, the short metal cylinder extended to the size of a small wand appeared in the guard's hand. The man swung, and the rod struck her shoulder.

Betsy clenched her teeth, wrapped her legs around his waist, and pulled harder on the rope.

Twisting and turning, he charged backward toward the wall.

Betsy bent her legs, absorbing some of the impact with her feet, but her back and head crashed into the cement. Her vision darkened. Her grip slipped, and she felt herself falling, but instead of the expected smack of cold cement against her face, she landed on something soft. She opened her eyes to see what it was but —

9

TOLD YOU SO

Cain Haight

With rising dread, I watch Bodhi get out of the canoe. I lean over to Mercy and whisper. "Row back out to Lucy and Sadie. Stay on the water. Whatever you do, don't come to shore. Got it?"

"I understand. You're doing a good thing."

Her smile makes me feel like a little kid getting a valentine, but the feeling doesn't last long. Lucy and Sadie are out on the water, staring at me and shaking their heads.

I climb out of the canoe and up the muddy bank where Bodhi's waiting. I grab a branch, so I don't slip on the red clay.

"It's right up here." He jerks his thumb over his

shoulder. "I'll run right in, and we'll be gone in a minute. I promise."

I nod. I'm not agreeing or disagreeing with whatever he said. I just want him to shut up so I can hear what's happening around me. The woods are quiet, the loudest sound being Mercy paddling away.

We head up an old path toward the roof, peaking over the top of the hill. Bodhi's not a woodsman. He steps on every fallen branch and crushes every fallen leaf. I think a dead pig rolling down the slope would make less noise.

I glance back at the river, but can't see the canoes anymore because of the dense underbrush and leaf cover. As we crest the hill, we pass an old engine, and several dilapidated cars stick out of the long grass.

The one-story cement building sits about fifty yards away. Between it and us are clumps of tall brush and even more cars scavenged for parts. An old canoe rests next to the back door. Everything looks like it should, but my guts tighten up. I stop. "Call your wife. Have her come out."

"She can't walk. We have to help her." Bodhi smiles and motions me forward.

"Tell your daughter to bring her." I set my hand on the grip of my Shockwave, ready to draw.

"Don't do it." Bodhi points at me, and his smile broadens.

The windows on both sides of the garage are open. Two men appear holding rifles.

"Put your hands on your head and turn around," Bodhi says. "You flinch, and you're dead."

There are at least two shooters, and they're close enough not to miss. If they wanted to kill me, I'd already be dead. I place my hands on my head and turn around. "The world has gone to hell, and you gotta do this?"

Behind me, something metal clicks. The sound is distinct. It's a buck knife opening. I got my first buck knife when I was eight and wore it out, opening and closing it. I'd know the sound anywhere. I also realize I was wrong about Bodhi and the shooters. They didn't fire because they don't want to scare off the women.

Bodhi's about to stab me in the back.

I spin.

Bodhi lunges.

Behind me, toward the river, a gunshot rings off the hills.

Blood splatters on the side of my face.

Bodhi lurches sideways. He's screaming. His left arm hangs limp and bloody, but he's still holding the knife in his other hand.

The gun fires again, and a bullet whizzes by my head.

Bodhi raises his good arm. He's holding the buck

knife like they do in a horror movie, ready to plunge it into my chest. He lunges.

I close draw my Glock. The barrel pivots and I pull the trigger three times.

The bullets slam in a tight group into the center of Bodhi's chest. The knife tumbles from his hand. His brow knits together. He stares at me like there's something he wants to say. His mouth opens, and he falls sideways into the tall grass.

Multiple gunshots ring out, this time from the building. It ain't two people shooting. More like a dozen.

I land on my belly and glance downhill.

Mercy is crouched by a tree, the cowboy pistol shaking in her hand.

"Stay down! Stay down!" I shout as I military crawl through the high grass and toward her.

A door bashes open, and more gunshots ring out.

Crouching low, I dash to Mercy. I fire four shots at the building, grab Mercy by the arm, and sprint down the hill.

Mercy's crying. I can't hear what she's saying between the gunfire and my heart pounding in my ears, but at least she's running.

A piece of bark on the tree in front of me is blasted off. Dirt kicks up on Mercy's left.

Lucy and Sadie are sitting in their canoe in the

middle of the river. Lucy's staring through the scope of her rifle. Sadie is waving us on.

But there's no way that Mercy and I can shove off in the canoe without getting cut down. I'll have to make a stand here. We reach the bank, and I pull Mercy behind a huge old stump. My feet are slipping in the red clay as chunks of deadwood get blasted off as bullets pepper the stump.

Whoever is shooting at us is really good to be that accurate while on the move. Once they stop running, I won't want to stick my head up. I peek out. It's clear I'm about to die. Over a dozen men are charging down the hill, firing as they come. I lift my Shockwave and pull the trigger.

The front man falls screaming, but the wave continues.

I take one second to aim but slip on the red clay. My shot goes high but clips a guy farther up the slope. Dirt, wood, and sawdust hit my face as more bullets splinter off the stump.

Blinded, I make my best guess where they are, fire twice more, then wipe at my eyes.

Lucy's shooting now, and so is Sadie.

Mercy grabs my arm and shakes me but isn't saying anything. Through the dirt and blood in my eyes, I see the look of horror on her face, but she isn't looking at me. Her attention is riveted over my head.

Something big squishes the mud on the bank directly behind me.

I glance up.

A mutant wolf, larger than any I've seen, is standing so close that the drool hanging off its teeth falls on my shoulder. The creatures have changed. A bone exoskeleton covers its head and runs down its back. Black eyes shift to stare at me.

I jam my Shockwave into its open mouth and pull the trigger.

The beast drops into the mud, splattering me with bone, blood, and brains.

Up the hill, the men are screaming and shooting into the woods and no longer at us.

In the boat, Lucy and Sadie are firing as fast as they can, not at the men, but at the enormous white and grey shapes charging through the brush.

Grabbing Mercy by the arm, I drag her to the canoe, and she climbs in. Before I can push off, a bone wolf dashes out of the grass and straight toward us.

I fire once. Twice. Three times and it drops to the clay five yards away.

I shove off and hop over the side. "Paddle!" I yell, but there's no need. Mercy's paddling with all she's got in her.

Another wolf bounds forward, but skids to a stop at the water's edge.

I change my aim to the men on the hill, racing

back toward the building. Dozens of wolves are flanking them on both sides. The men don't stand a chance.

Mercy is paddling and crying. Her lips are moving, and it takes me a minute to figure out what she's saying. "I'm sorry." She keeps repeating that over and over.

Lucy and Sadie have stopped firing, and they're paddling now too. Lucy points her hand back at me like a gun and clicks her thumb. That's her way of saying I told you so. They'll be even less dealing with her now.

But I'll worry about that later. Mercy is crying so hard her paddle isn't even hitting the water. "I'm sorry." She sobs.

"There's nothing to be sorry about," I say. "You saved my life."

Mercy shakes her head. "I murdered that man. I killed him. God's curse will be on me."

"Don't be stupid," My words come out harsher than I wanted them to.

Mercy's head snaps around, and she's a sight. Her face is caked in red clay with tears cutting streaks that look like deep laugh lines on a demon mask. Her green eyes blaze like emeralds.

But instead of being scared, the irony of this angel looking like a fiend cracks me up. "He would have killed me if you hadn't shot him."

"Violence is never the answer!"

"Sometimes it's the only answer evil people hear. And it isn't murder if you're defending yourself."

"That's not what the Bible teaches."

"Actually, it is. Since your father got the whole 'thou shall not lie' thing wrong, maybe he didn't teach you that self-defense is in the Bible. Jesus told his disciples to sell their cloaks and buy a sword. You don't carry a sword if you don't intend to use it. No one's got a right to kill you. You were defending me."

"I didn't want to shoot him. I tried to fire a warning shot over his head." The angry fire in her eyes fades.

I soften my voice. "There's no point in discussing it. You didn't kill him. I did."

Mercy mumbles something, but I'm not listening anymore. Something sparkling in the water catches my attention. It could be a piece of trash. Or maybe it's a bottle that caught the sun just right.

As we get closer, the hairs on the back of my neck rise. I paddle over and lean so far out I almost tip over the canoe. A sparkly pink elephant is bobbing on the water. I snatch it up and hold it high.

"It's Pink-E! This is Bri's!" I yell over to the other canoe.

Sadie and Lucy paddle over.

"It's a stupid toy," Lucy says as the canoes bump together. "You don't know that is Bri's."

"Are you kidding me?" I'm too happy to be mad, but I'm still shouting. "I drove to every supermarket, gas station, and convenience store to get the Zoo Safari Animal Patrol Pals for Bri. I must have spent fifty bucks in quarters to get Pink-E because it's her favorite. I know it's hers!"

"So do I!" Sadie said.

"Look!" Mercy pointed. "There's another one."

Lucy picked up a white rabbit, and her lip trembled. "Why are they in the water? Did something happen to her?"

I shake my head. "No. Bri keeps them on her bracelet. She's letting us know she's okay. She's leaving a trail."

Sadie takes the plastic rabbit and holds it tight. "That's my smart little June bug."

I grab my oar. "We're catching up to them. Let's go!"

Everyone starts paddling with renewed energy. Hope lights a fire in my chest that blazes down my spine. I'm going to get those kids. And when I find Fen and Nicholi, I will make them pay.

10

HARD TO SEE THE ZIPPERS

Betsy Weber

Betsy's head felt like someone was crushing her skull. She touched the back of it and winced. A huge bump had formed. She relaxed back onto her pillow, and her eyes snapped open.

Gasping and scurrying back onto her haunches, Betsy stared in horror at the guard lying on the floor. His head lay at an odd angle. She couldn't see his face because of the mask, but his neck was visible. The rope dug into purple flesh. His chest was still.

Betsy's hand covered her mouth. She'd killed him.

Her stomach flipped, and she vomited on the

floor. Propping herself upright with her right arm, the cold cement numbed the cut on her palm. She blinked rapidly, but no tears fell. How could she have ended a human's life when she caught bugs in a cup and set them free outside?

The seconds ticked by.

"*Move.*" Someone whispered.

She lifted her head, unsure if she'd said the word aloud or if her sanity had been damaged by the blow to the back of her head. Holding onto the cot, she managed to stand. Creeping to the door, she held her breath.

Surely there hadn't been a second guard. He would have heard the commotion and come in.

Betsy turned the handle and peeked outside.

The hallway was empty.

Betsy exhaled. She opened the door farther but didn't move. She stared down at her feet, which suddenly felt stuck to the concrete.

Closing the door, she rested her aching head against the cold steel. She had to get to the others and get them out, but where were they? And where were the other guards?

Betsy's legs shook. It was impossible. The moment someone saw her, it would be over. She was in no shape to run or fight. Standing was an effort. She pressed her fist against her forehead. No. She'd fight.

Turning back to the room, she hurried over and grabbed the metal wand the guard stuck her with. It was a collapsible baton. With the press of a button, the spring-loaded metal extended like a foldable table's leg. She wriggled it out from underneath the guard's body.

The gold mask shifted, revealing part of the man's face.

Betsy's chest tightened. Brad Moore. He'd been one of Daniel's baseball coaches. Brad and his wife Tina had been over for a cookout after the team lost in the playoffs last year. They had a son and a lovely home. Brad worked in town.

Why would he be involved in something like this?

Betsy's knees trembled, and she staggered backward. She slid down the wall. From this angle, she could see behind the mask. She stared at Brad's hideously twisted face. His open eyes bulged out, and his mouth hung open.

Brad would never have made her list if you'd given her a hundred guesses for who her possible tormentors were. Neither did Nancy's brother Gary, but he was involved too.

Who else was in the cult?

Betsy shook her head. Had the Dark done this to them, or did it simply bring it out?

She stared at the golden mask of her husband's face and remembered something he'd said. Betsy's boss had been arrested on numerous embezzlement charges. It came to light that he'd been living a double life. On the surface, he was a respected businessman and married father of three. Unknown to everyone, he was a gambling addict with a sex addiction.

Betsy had felt like a gullible, naive fool that she hadn't seen the warning signs. Carl had comforted her by saying, '*when the wolves dress like sheep, sometimes it's hard to see the zippers.*'

Betsy laughed and wiped her nose. She missed her husband so badly it hurt. She'd give anything to have Carl here now. To have him lend her his strength. Betsy's hands opened wide as an idea blazed to life.

"That could work. It could!" She sat up, a newfound hope rising in her chest. But she needed to work fast. She didn't have much time.

11

ANGELS OF MERCY

Cain Haight

I pull my paddle up and lay it across the gunwales. No one has said anything for the last hour. I was starting to think that Lucy may have calmed down a bit until a water bottle sails by my head and splashes on the other side of me.

"That was full!" I glare. "I don't care if you throw a hissy fit, but don't go wasting water."

"I filled it up with river water, genius," Lucy flips me off. "Start rowing. We need to make up all the time we lost trying to be angels of mercy."

Mercy hangs her head. "I'm sorry."

"Knock it off, Lucy." I snap. "It was my call."

"I told you we should have made the guy swim for it. I can't believe you fell for his line of bull."

I feel like screaming, but I don't want to attract any more wolves, so I keep my voice down. "I admit it. You were right."

"I don't care about that." Lucy fires back. "Start paddling."

"He needs a rest, and so do I." Sadie pulls up her paddle and takes out a cigarette. "We'll catch them, but we can't burn ourselves out doing it."

Lucy grabs the canoe's sides and gets right in her mother's face. "How are we gonna do that unless we keep pushing? They have a huge lead. I'm not gonna forget you sided with him."

"Get your finger out of my face!" Sadie's hand inches toward her paddle.

"Both of you take it down a notch." I steer closer to them. I'd seen the two of them come to blows before. It wasn't a catfight. More of a mountain lioness battle, and that was the last thing we needed. "I've got a plan to make up time."

Lucy sits back and glares at the sky. "I can't wait to hear this."

"If you stopped talking," Mercy says. "Maybe you would."

Lucy holds up another water bottle. To my surprise, she doesn't fling it at Mercy's head. Instead, she opens it and takes a long swig while fixing me with a cool gaze.

"The Pintail branches off ahead, toward the dam," I say. "Fen and Nicholi most likely would have followed the main river when they came to Ridgecrest. I figure they'll head back that way seeing as how they're familiar with it. If we take the fork and head to the dam, we should be able to catch them."

Lucy's eyebrows knit together, and she sips her water. "There's a problem with your logic, Einstein. How do we get around the dam? Do we carry the canoes while the wolves are chasing us, or do we just go over the falls in a barrel?"

"Neither." Now it's my turn to smirk. "There are stairs on both sides of the dam. I fish there all the time. We can ensure the coast is clear and be down in a few minutes."

"You saw what those wolves can do in a few minutes," Lucy says. "What do we do if some are there?"

"Whatever side of the river they're on, we go to the opposite," I say. "We'll be back in the water before they get close."

Mercy raises her arm. "I vote for the shortcut."

Lucy ignores her. "What if the wolves are on both sides?"

"Then we kill them." Sadie takes a long drag off her cigarette and flicks it over the side. It lands with a hiss in the water. "There's nothing to vote on or decide. If we don't get to Bri soon, they'll be no getting her back."

All of us nod, pick up our paddles and start rowing.

But Sadie is wrong. Fen and Nicholi reaching the base won't stop me from saving my little girl. I'd take on an army for her.

12

STRIKE THREE

Cain Haight

Everyone paddled in silence as they focused on moving as fast as possible. The crushing heat and humidity pressed in from all sides. The sky was clear of birds, and the woods were silent. Besides them and the river, nothing moved. Even the bugs hunkered down.

That made it easy to hear when something scurried up a dead tree stump, sat down, and watched them pass.

A bone rat.

I've always been a fan of squirrels. I know a bunch of people hate them. Sadie shoots them for getting into her bird feeder, and Goose goes ballistic because they make nests in truck engines, but ever since I was a kid, if I saw one, it always brought a smile to my face.

As I watched the grey and white critter sitting there, I felt the corners of my lips curling up.

It dropped forward onto all fours and raised its hind quarters like Cooper does when she expects you to throw her a ball. It even wiggled its butt.

Mercy looks over and smiles. "It looks like it wants to play fetch."

The rat whips its tail around, and something flies off. It arches through the air, lands ten feet away from Lucy's canoe, and slices into the water without a splash.

"Strike one!" Lucy calls out.

The rat scurries to the edge of the stump and lets another fly. This one takes a shallower angle and hits fifteen feet away.

"Strike two!" Lucy laughs. "Loser!"

The rat turns in a circle twice. It dashes to the far end of the stump, spins around, and runs forward like a javelin thrower.

Something white gleams as it arcs through the air, and the sun reflects off it. It whizzes through the air and hits the side of Lucy's canoe with a loud thunk.

Lucy and Sadie jump.

Sadie digs whatever hit the canoe out with her

knife. “It’s a bone spike. That rotten critter shoots a bone out of its butt.”

“I think they come off its tail,” Mercy says.

The rat scurries back to the stump’s far end, looking like it’s getting ready for another throw.

Lucy grabs her rifle. “Two can play at this game. My turn, rat.”

“Don’t shoot it,” I call over. “Row toward the middle of the river, and it can’t reach you.”

Like always, Lucy ignores me and aims down the sight.

The rat charges.

Lucy fires.

I shouldn’t be surprised she hits it, but I am. It’s a heck of a shot from a moving canoe, so I gotta give her credit for that.

That rat falls off the stump, but it’s still moving. I almost feel bad until it opens its mouth. The thing has rows of pointy teeth like a shark. Its shrill call pierces the quiet of the woods.

Lucy lowers her gun.

Mercy glances back at me. “I think we better paddle.”

Before I can nod, the tops of the trees along the bank start shaking. Hundreds of shadows move, and a chittering builds until it sounds like a freight train is headed our way, and we’re standing in the middle of the tracks.

Lucy and Sadie start paddling over to my side of the river, and I'm steering toward the far bank, too — until I hear it.

The trees on the right start shaking too. The shrill chittering of bone rats grows louder.

"They're on both sides of us," I shout. "Head to the middle and paddle."

Along both banks, the rats appear. They lean forward, whipping their tails. Hundreds of bone spikes glisten in the sun and slice into the water on either side of us.

Two strike my canoe. Both are above the water line, but they punch a hole through. The spikes are hollow and only three inches long, but if they hit flesh, they'd penetrate.

"You couldn't hit the broad side of a barn!" Lucy shouts.

"Shut up and paddle!" Sadie yells back. "You got us in this mess."

"Don't you dare—"

Sadie's scream cuts off Lucy's tirade. My mother-in-law grabs her leg. Her paddle falls over the side and splashes in the water.

Lucy climbs forward, but Sadie shakes her head. "Keep paddling, or we're both gonna die!"

I slow down, trying to think how I can help.

"Move your butt, Cain!" Sadie shouts. "I ain't dead, and what do you think you're gonna do? Row both canoes?" She laughs.

Shaking my head, I start paddling. She's right. There's nothing I can do.

The bone spikes continue to arc through the air, but dwindle off after a couple of minutes. A few bone rats give chase, but soon the chittering stops, and the woods are quiet.

I glance back.

Lucy is right behind me, paddling as hard as she can. The pained expression on her face answers my unasked question. Sadie's wound is bad.

13

HOW'S YOUR HEAD?

Matt Browner

Matt Browner's horse's hooves clopped on the dirt beside the road as he passed Dr. Harmon's small Tudor house. Before the Dark, the doctor was a big-time heart surgeon in the city. You wouldn't have known it if someone didn't tell you. Rodney Woodrow Harmon, or just plain Doc to everyone in Ridgecrest, was the closest thing to an actual country doctor Matt had ever met. Drove a truck, mowed his lawn, and volunteered at the hospital.

No one could say a bad word about him or his wife Denise — but the same wasn't true about their son, Lonnie. Their only child wasn't a bad kid, but he'd drifted in with a rough group that included

Ben Pickett. Before the Dark, Lonnie had several scrapes with the law, but Doc had managed to get him out of most of those jams.

With Ben Pickett dead, the truth about what happened to Betsy Weber and Nancy Long probably died with him. But Ben was too stupid and too much of a wimp to pull something like robbing and killing all of those preppers off on his own. If someone had helped Ben, it would have been Lonnie.

Matt's job was to bury Ben's body before anyone found it, not run off on a wild goose chase. But if there was a chance those women were still alive, he needed to know.

He clicked his heels and urged the horse on. The sun gleamed off the badge on his chest, and Matt settled back in the saddle. When the Dark struck, he'd been scared out of his wits. He didn't know why, but knew immediately that whatever was happening was worse than any blackout.

And it was. Then all of the law enforcement left and never returned. The whole town was scared, Matt especially, but when the Mayor asked for volunteers, Matt raised his arm, and the people of Ridgecrest put their trust in him to act as Sheriff.

Matt trotted down the driveway and stopped at Doc's house. He dismounted and tied his horse to the rail. This shouldn't take long, and it was on the way to Ben's. He strode up the three steps, crossed the wide porch, and knocked on the door.

Doc Harmon opened the door, a handkerchief in one hand, mopping the sweat from his brow. "Sheriff. Good to see you again. Everything okay with your head?"

Matt instinctively touched the bandage circling his scalp. "It's fine. Thanks again for patching me up."

"Not a problem. Well, this humidity is about to kill me, so I was going to sit on the porch for a spell. Care to join me?"

Matt nodded, although he had no intention of staying long. "I don't want to bother you, Doc, but I'm looking for Lonnie."

"Lonnie? Why's that, Matt?" Doc moved over to a rocking chair, but didn't sit down.

"He ain't in trouble or nothing. I got a couple of questions to ask him about a friend of his."

Doc nodded and sat down. He opened a wooden box and took out two water bottles. "Wish it were cold beer, but no use crying about the lack of refrigeration."

Matt nodded again, said, "Much appreciated anyway," and took the bottle.

"Who are you wanting to talk with Lonnie about?"

Matt took a deep breath. The last thing he

wanted was to open a can of worms. Bringing up Ben Pickett was sure to do that. "I'd like to keep this between Lonnie and me."

Doc patted his face down with his handkerchief and opened his water bottle. It wasn't new, of course. Real bottled water had run out long ago, but everyone saved and reused the bottles. "Lonnie might be grown, but he's still my boy and living under my roof. I've got a right to know what this is all about."

"I don't want this growing like a hungry tick on a dog, and it's nothing to get all outta kilter over. Lonnie hasn't done anything wrong."

"You've said that, and I believe you, Sheriff. But I want to know who you want to discuss with my son. And if you don't tell me, Martin will."

Matt rolled his eyes. Doc would go over his head to the Mayor, and things would get worse from there. "Ben Pickett."

Doc swigged his water and smiled. "Lonnie hasn't had anything to do with Ben since the trouble outside the theatre, which was almost two years ago."

Matt shook his head. "I don't like being the one telling you this, Doc, but I've seen Lonnie and Ben together not a month ago. They were drinking and fishing with Brad Moore down at Deep Holler."

"Brad Moore? Why, he was Lonnie's old baseball coach. And you should know better than to think that just because you saw people fishing together doesn't mean they came or left that way. I was down at Deep Holler last week. A half dozen people had thrown out lines. It doesn't mean that I was fishing with them."

"All the same, Doc, I need to speak to Lonnie. Is he home?"

"No. For all I know, he's fishing at Deep Holler again. What is this all about, Matt?"

Matt rubbed the back of his neck. It was a mistake coming here.

"A four-wheeler has gone missing." Matt lied. "But I need you to keep it under your hat, Doc. Ben Pickett is Frank's nephew, and the owner of the four-wheeler doesn't want to start any kind of trouble. They only want it back. I'm thinking it was a drunk spur-of-the-moment kind of thing, so I'd like to keep it low-key, too."

Seemingly satisfied with that explanation, Doc Harmon started rocking in the chair. "That I understand. You should have come out and said that, Sheriff. Lonnie certainly wouldn't have anything to do with a theft."

"I know that, Doc. I was hoping that Ben may have said something about the four-wheeler. Bragging about it or something."

"If you find Lonnie, ask him. If not, I'll send him by your office when he gets home."

"I appreciate it, Doc. You have a good day."

Matt hurried off the porch and untied his horse. He waved, clicked his heels, and started back down the driveway. When he reached the road, he glanced back. The rocking chair slowly dipped back and forth, but Doc Harmon wasn't there. He was nowhere in sight.

Matt headed down Willow Street in the direction of Deep Holler. The fishing hole was on the way to Ben Pickett's farm, but the conversation with the Doc bothered him to no end. Doc was a good man, but sometimes good men will go to bad lengths to protect their children.

14

THAT'S THE WHISKEY TALKING

Cain Haight

I'm holding the two canoes together as Mercy examines Sadie's leg. The spike buried itself so deeply in her thigh that Mercy couldn't get it out. Mercy's hands are covered in blood, and she's hanging halfway into Lucy's canoe.

"It's no good." Mercy sits up. "I need to make an incision, pull it out and stitch it up."

"Then do it!" Lucy snaps.

"I can't do it in a canoe." Mercy turns to Sadie. "I'm sorry. We're rocking so much that I'm worried taking it out now will cause more damage."

Sadie presses a bloody towel against the wound.

"We'll wait for the dam. Hopefully, none of those creatures will be on it."

"We can't do it then, Mom." Lucy is rifling through a backpack as she speaks. She takes out a half-pint of whiskey and hands it to Sadie. "You and the farmer's daughter have to head back to Ridgecrest. Cain and I will go on."

"In a pig's eye!" Sadie yanks the bottle out of Lucy's hand. "There ain't no way you're keeping me from getting Bri. This thing in my leg ain't no worse than a splinter." Sadie draws her knife.

"Wait!" Mercy calls out as she leans back in their canoe. Mercy brushes the hair out of her face and tries again.

Sadie's head rolls back on her shoulders. She's swearing up a storm.

Mercy yanks the spike out. Blood pours out of the wound. I do my best to keep both boats from tipping over as Mercy tries stitching up the cut while we float down the river.

Lucy glares at me. "This is all your fault."

"Mine!" I yell so loud that it echoes off the trees. "You're the moron who shot the rat."

"What did you just call me?" Lucy's hand moves toward her gun.

Sadie takes another swig off the bottle. "Don't make me knock some sense in you, girl. There's nothing to discuss. We're going on and getting those kids back. And ain't nothing stopping us."

It takes Mercy a few minutes, but she stitches Sadie's leg and bandages it up. Mercy is washing her hands off and suddenly stiffens. "We have a big problem."

Everyone follows where Mercy is pointing.

A highway bridge spans the river up ahead, but there's something off about the guard rails.

Lucy picks up her rifle and stares down the sight. "We're all screwed now."

The shapes sitting on the guardrail move. They're not birds — they're rats —hundreds of them.

"Throw out the anchors," I say as I look around. "Give me your rifle."

Lucy hands it to me without a snide remark. That ain't a good sign.

"Don't go getting all defeated on me, darling," I say as I focus on the right bank of the river and follow the boat ramp up to a parking lot. "There are at least six or seven trucks in that lot. One of them could run."

"How do you know they haven't sat there since the Dark started?" Lucy says. "None of them could work."

Mercy tosses the line with a cinderblock tied to the end over the side. "What about trying to sneak under the bridge? Maybe we could flip the canoes and use them like a shield."

"Those spikes would shred the bottom of the canoe," Lucy says as she tosses her anchor into the water. "You might as well have a shield made of pasta."

Sadie finishes the whiskey and wipes her mouth with the back of her hand. "What about shooting our way through?"

"That's the whiskey talking, Mom. We don't have enough ammo."

I look at Sadie and don't like the lack of color in her cheeks. She's not letting on how bad her leg is, and there's no time for arguing. I pull off my boots, yank my shirt over my head and say, "Everybody stays here. It'll be quieter if I swim to shore. I'm going to see if any of those trucks are working."

"You're just gonna get yourself eaten." Lucy crosses her arms and doesn't even look at me. "See you in Hell."

I wink at my mother-in-law, but before I slip over the side, Mercy grabs my hand.

"Dear Lord, please watch over Cain and have one of those vehicles start. In Jesus' name, amen."

"You're still going to hell," Lucy calls out right before I slip into the water.

With all the heat, going for a swim is about the nicest thing that's happened to me in a week. I keep my head low and swim slowly and quietly. The end of the boat ramp is sandy and feels nice on my bare feet. I hesitate to get out.

I hate admitting it, but part of me is scared. I've got my pistol, but after seeing what those wolves and rats can do, getting torn to pieces and eaten alive is a real possibility.

But I don't have a choice. My little girl is counting on me.

I slosh out of the water and up the cement ramp.

There's a truck near the top I couldn't see from the river. It's a 1973 Ford, so there's a great chance it'll run. It's got a trailer with a bass boat attached.

As I get closer, I break out in a clammy sweat. The driver's side door is open, and some guy's body is lying a few feet away. It's in the same shape I found Gunner Pickett in. The bones are gone, but the skin is there. Judging by the skin's condition, this guy hasn't been in the Tennessee June sun longer than a few days.

I wonder if what killed him is still around.

Keeping to the shadows cast by the boat, I sneak up to the truck. I glance inside, and the ignition is empty. I look down at the body and wish I had kept my shirt on to cover my face.

Holding my breath, I flip the body over, and it's one of the weirdest experiences in my life. The skin has dried and gone rigid, so it's like flipping over a cardboard cutout of a man. But this cutout is covered in flies and stinks so bad I keep gagging.

The guy is wearing camo pants with about eighty pockets. I find a jackknife, a full 9-millimeter magazine, a lighter, and a set of keys. I glance around for the gun and notice it's stuck in the guy's mouth.

I gag again and back up. I don't need a gun bad enough to take that one. The thought of trying to clean it almost makes me vomit.

I creep back to the truck and slip into the driver's seat. There are seven keys, but the old Ford key is easy to pick out. I slip it into the ignition, give it a little gas, and the engine fires right up.

As quickly as I can, I shut it off and listen.

No chittering. No howls. The engine pings softly, and my heart is pounding in my ears, but other than that, everything is silent.

Slipping out of the truck, I stop and force myself to do something that sometimes doesn't come naturally — think. I'm a fire-the-missiles kinda guy. I like action then deciding, and in that order, but that has a way of getting me in a pile of trouble.

I've got three women out on the river and two canoes. I don't know if Sadie can walk, but there's no way she can help Lucy carry a fully loaded canoe.

Climbing back into the cab, I pull the emergency brake, shift into neutral, and steer the truck down the ramp. The trailer tires start squeaking, and I grind my teeth together. I roll back thirty yards and stop short of the water.

Pleased with my forward-thinking, my joy is short-lived. While I was getting the truck, the women paddled to shore.

"What are you doing?" I whisper as I run down and grab the bow of Mercy's canoe. "I told you to wait on the river."

"Why?" Lucy climbs out and pulls her canoe onto the sand. "You got the truck started."

"Did the rats hear it?" I ask.

The three of them exchange an I-didn't-think-about-that look.

I glance toward the road. The tops of the trees are moving. "Grab the gear!" I say, hurrying into the water and picking up my mother-in-law.

Sadie swears as I lift her, and her fingernails dig into my bare back. Ignoring the pain, I run with her to the passenger seat and unceremoniously dump her in. Jogging around the front, I climb into the cab, turn the ignition, and the engine sputters.

I try it again, but it coughs and won't turn over.

"Don't flood it!" Sadie yells through grit teeth.

"I'm not."

"You're mashing the pedal to the floor. You're giving it too much gas."

I exhale, lift off the gas a little and turn the key. The engine starts, sputters, and dies.

Now it's my turn to swear.

Lucy and Mercy are running the gear from the canoes and tossing it into the back of the truck like a bucket brigade.

"Wait!" Sadie whacks my hand off the ignition. "Half gas. Once it starts to turn over, you're gonna need to keep giving it more until it fires up."

I nod and turn the key.

The engine turns over, and I push my foot down slowly. The cab shakes and rattles as the engine sputters, but the motor keeps running.

"A little more gas," Sadie says.

A cloud of black smoke belches out of the tailpipe, and the engine roars with power.

"Yes!" Sadie and I cheer.

Over the sound of the truck, a loud chittering grows.

Sadie points at the trees nearby. Hundreds of the creatures hang onto the branches. "The rats are here!"

15

DON'T USE THE BOOZE!

Mercy Yoder

"The bone rats are coming!" Mercy shouted and pointed to the trees near the bridge, which shook like they were in a storm, but there was no wind. Mercy prayed as she dumped her bags into the truck and raced back for more. The Bible said to pray without ceasing. She never understood that verse until she left town to rescue Jacob. Now all she did was pray.

She'd always been a coward. Her greatest fear was the dark. And now it was upon her. It was filled with all the hideous creatures she imagined living beneath her bed when she was a little girl. But these beasts were real, and they wanted to kill her.

Her hands trembled so much that she dropped the bag she lifted from the canoe.

Think about someone other than yourself.

The advice her grandmother had given her steadied her shaking hands.

Sadie. Sadie's hurt. Get bandages. Medicine.

Focused, Mercy grabbed the bag she took from Doc Harmon's, and a liquor bottle.

"Good choice." Lucy nodded approvingly, then she ran toward the truck.

Mercy hoped she was talking about taking the medicine, but she doubted it.

A cloud of black smoke spewed out of the tailpipe of the truck. Mercy's heart sank, but when the engine roared to life, she triumphantly raised her arm. "THANK YOU, LORD!"

Lucy started back for another load.

Over the sound of the truck, a loud chittering grew.

Cain leaned out the driver's side window and yelled, "Get in the truck now!"

"What about the canoes?" Lucy asked, looking at the river.

"The rats are here. Get in!" Sadie called out.

Mercy ran toward the truck. A line of bone rats crested the top of the hill. Lucy grabbed Mercy's arm and pulled her toward the bass boat.

"Up and over!" Lucy said.

Mercy scrambled in behind Lucy.

The truck's tires spun, and the boat jerked forward. Mercy and Lucy clutched the sides and hung on.

Bone rats scattered. The slow ones crunched beneath the tires.

At the top of the boat ramp, the truck screeched to the left and headed for the exit.

"Rat!" Lucy pointed at Mercy's side of the boat.

Claws gripped a rope hanging off the side, and a furry head appeared.

Mercy grabbed the closest thing to her — the bottle of liquor. It struck the rat in the face and knocked it off. Mercy smiled, surprised the glass bottle hadn't broken.

"Don't use the booze!" Lucy shouted. "Hit it with something else." She raised a metal rod with a spike and hook on the end over her head and smashed another bone rat off the back of the boat. "Get the other one!"

Mercy glanced to her left.

A bone rat leaped off the bow and landed on the floor in front of her.

Mercy shrieked. Her leg shot out like she was striking a soccer ball. It felt like she kicked a brick. The creature flew up, shrieking as it sailed over the side.

THUMP! THUMP! THUMP!

Bone spikes peppered the boat.

Lucy grabbed Mercy and yanked her to the floor. "Keep your head down!"

A gunshot sounded from the cab.

The truck sped up, and the rocking stopped as they accelerated.

"Everybody okay?" Cain yelled back to them.

Lucy raised her hand and made an obscene gesture.

"We're fine!" Mercy shouted.

Lucy sat up straighter and stared toward the right side of the road. Her eyes widened. All of the color drained from Lucy's face, and her hands shook and she jerked her pistol out of the holster.

Mercy couldn't see what scared Lucy; from Lucy's terrified expression, she didn't want to.

16

EVERYBODY OKAY?

Cain Haight

I keep the gas pedal pinned to the floor. I don't know what this thing has under the hood for an engine, but it's a beast. I slow down and cut the wheel when we reach the main road. There's a tree on the corner, and a few shapes leap out of it. Two bone rats hit the hood. One flies off screaming, but the other manages to hang on.

Sadie rips out her pistol.

The bone rat raises its tail.

Sadie fires through the windshield. Glass shatters. The bullet slams into the rat and sends it flying.

As we speed up, I roll down the window and shout, "Everybody okay?"

Lucy leans out and gives me the finger.

"They're good," Sadie chuckles as she presses the towel against her thigh. Her skin is pale and her upper lip quivers.

"How are you holding up?"

"I ain't dead yet. Listen, Cain. You've got to promise me that you'll take care of my girls."

"I can't do that, Sadie. You know I'd do anything for Bri, but Lucy is a grown woman with her own mind. I'll do everything I can to keep her safe, but no one can tell your daughter what to do. You know—"

I don't finish my sentence. It all happens so fast that I think I'm seeing things. Charging out of the brush on the right side of the road is a bear as tall as a pro basketball center and as wide as an NFL lineman. Its black fur is covered with bone plates. It lowers its shoulder and slams into the front right fender of the truck.

The quarter panel crumples. The metal slices into the tire, and it blows. The steering wheel jerks out of my hand as my head bashes off the doorframe.

The truck skids across both lanes and down the embankment.

I grab the wheel but don't hit the brakes. The last thing I want is to stop with Mor'du from *Brave* chasing us.

A gunshot rings out from the back of the truck. Lucy must be trying to shoot the thing. She should be concentrating on hanging on.

The truck slides down the grass bank, and I cut the wheel to avoid hitting a giant stump. The blown tire shreds. The rim digs into the dirt. Pieces of rubber and chunks of grass fly into the air. We're going downhill and still moving so fast we don't slow much.

"Hit the brakes!" Sadie screams.

The river is below us on the left. The way I figure it, it's our only chance. I'm hoping the bass boat stays on the trailer until then.

"Aiming for the river," I manage to say as I keep the gas pedal down and steer around the few trees.

The left front tire hits a rock that kicks us into the air. For a moment, I'm flying. The steering wheel turns easily in my hands because the tires are off the ground. There's a big oak tree on the left, but we'll miss it. It's coming close, but from the angle of our arc, we'll pass right by it.

But I guess I didn't pay enough attention in Science class. Or maybe it's physics. Either way, momentum pulls the trailer with the bass boat attached around, which yanks on the truck. We start turning, and that little bit is enough to aim us straight for the tree. The front bumper strikes the base, sending bark flying.

My chest slams into the steering wheel, and the lights in my head flash white and red. On and off.

Dark and light. Dark and ... dark.

17

LUCY?

Mercy Yoder

Mercy clung to the base of the Captain's chair. The trailer jumped and hopped as they careened down a steep hill. Like a piece of popcorn in a hot pan, each jolt sent Mercy bouncing all over. The boat tipped high up. Mercy rose off the deck only to slam against it a moment later.

Lucy fired her gun again and again.

Behind them, a gigantic bear raced down the hill. It was black, but larger than a polar bear. Spiked bone plates covered its head, shoulders, and back.

The trailer bashed off something and kicked to the right.

Lucy swore. Her gun tumbled from her hand, and she rolled to the back of the boat. She hit the flat part holding the engine hard. Her head snapped back and bashed off the metal. Lucy slumped unmoving onto the floor.

The boat lifted into the air again, and so did Mercy. Her fingers slipped off the metal pole. Flying two feet above the boat, she glimpsed water below them on the left.

The river! Cain was trying to make it to the water and safety.

Mercy crashed back onto the deck. She vainly reached out for the railing on the side. Metal crunched. Momentum flung Mercy forward. Her face bashed off the Captain's seat pole. Her eyes rolled up in her head, but she managed to grab hold of the metal base.

The boat spun clockwise. Like riding a spooked horse, she strained to hold on. She tightened her grip. Her fingers burned, but she refused to let go.

A wave of water crashed over the boat. The bow kicked up, flinging her toward the stern of the boat. Her head struck something soft, and her legs slammed into something hard. She thumped down onto the deck.

The boat rocked wildly, but it was no longer airborne. Laying on her back, Mercy exhaled and stared up at the sky. She blinked rapidly and licked her lips, tasting blood. She exhaled. That horrible ride was over. Somehow, miraculously the boat had ended up in the river. They were safe.

At the front of the boat, steam rose into the air. Like a dragon hissing, it coiled high and bloated out the sun.

A can rolled past her, followed by an empty water bottle. The boat jerked forward, and the back raised into the air. Mercy slid down the center aisle of the deck until her feet struck the console. The bow was still attached to the trailer, and they were being dragged underwater.

She stared in horror as the truck sank further beneath the surface. The lights of the dashboard gleamed faintly as it disappeared into the river. Like a derailed train, the truck pulled the trailer, which tugged the boat — all sinking into the depths of the deep river.

"Cain! Sadie!" Panic gripped her. Were Cain and Sadie still inside?

Water splashed over the bow. The boat rose until it stood on its nose. Everything in the back of the boat, not tied down, fell forward. Bags, cans, and equipment bashed off of Mercy as she fought to hold on.

The huge metal cleat on the hood of the boat buckled. The rope snapped, and the boat fell backward. It slammed into the river with a huge splash.

Mercy's head smacked off the deck. Water crashed over her face like someone had dumped buckets of water over her head.

Coughing and sputtering, she rolled onto her stomach and lifted herself on her elbows.

"We're floating," Mercy mumbled as she wiped at her mouth. Blood smeared the back of her hand. "We're in the river." She glanced around. "Lucy?"

Mercy was alone in the boat.

18

I'LL BE RIGHT BEHIND YOU

Cain Haight

I open my eyes and stare at the trash floating close to my face. I'm sitting in the truck's driver's seat, and it's filling with water. We must have hit the river.

Sadie's screaming something, but my ears haven't started working yet.

I shake my head. My vision clears, and my ears open. What I see and hear isn't good. We're in the river, and the truck is sinking. Smoke streams from the engine and hisses as it rises.

Sadie's pulling on my arm. "Cain! Cain!"

I grab the steering wheel and push off, but I don't go anywhere. The broken steering column is pinning my ankle to the truck's floor. I twist, pull and yank, but I'm stuck. I grab the door and shove, but it won't open.

Sadie keeps tugging, but I don't budge.

"My foot is caught on something," I yell, pushing her toward her door. "You gotta go."

"I ain't leaving you." Sadie shakes her head.

"Both of us dyin' isn't a good plan." I grab her arm to get her to stop pulling on me. "Go save my girl."

Sadie raises her hand. I expect her to slap me in the face, but she grabs my chin and kisses my cheek. With tears in her eyes, she says, "I love ya like my own."

"I love you, too." I push her toward the door. "Now get out. I'll be right behind you."

I can tell she knows I'm lying by how her eyes narrow. She nods and swims out her window.

The engine hisses and belches smoke. I can't see because of the cloud. The water has risen to my chin. I'm pulling on my leg so hard I think I might break my foot off, but it won't budge. I plant my free foot on the floor and shove backward with all I've got. Plastic cracks, metal groans, and it feels like my muscles are gonna tear away from the bone.

I cough.

The lights from the dashboard blink, sending a rainbow of colors through the smoke, dragging a memory from when I was a kid out of the shadows of my mind.

Cigar smoke wafted across my face, and I coughed.

My father laughed. He was puffing away on a fat cigar as we stood in the middle of the barn. I musta have been six or seven. He'd caught a stray dog in a trap he'd set in the barn. It was a pup. Probably the runt since it was small enough to get caught in the trap.

I always wanted a dog and thought he would give me the pup. Why else would he have brought me out there?

He said it was a coyote full of fleas, ticks, and worms. It didn't look like any coyote I'd seen. It looked more like the neighbor's German Shepherd, but my Dad insisted it was a coyote, and when his eyes were red, and his breath stank, I knew not to speak back to him.

He picked up the trap and walked over to the rain barrel.

I shouted something. What I don't remember exactly, but I didn't want him to drown the dog, coyote or not.

He was drunk and stumbling, but still had a mean right hook. He knocked me halfway across the barn. When I woke up, the dog was lying at my feet. It turns out it was a Shepherd, after all. I don't know why my Dad let him live or why he let me keep him, but I was grateful he did.

The smoke clears, and the water crashes over my head. The trunk plunges down, taking me along for the ride. The lights on the dash flicker and go out. My world turns pitch black and upside down as the truck hits the bottom of the river and turns over.

Houston, we have a negative on that launch trajectory.

19

TOO LATE TO RUN

Betsy Weber

Betsy stared down at Brad's corpse. She hurriedly removed the white robe and pulled on his boots. They were so large she needed to stuff his socks in the toes.

She picked up the steel baton. She pressed the button on the weapon, but it didn't retract. She held the button down and pushed it against the wall. It didn't budge.

Inching the baton up her sleeve, she glanced down. The folds of cloth hid the weapon. But how could she use it? She let the baton slide through her fingers, and she grabbed it once it was clear of the sleeve. But now she held the weapon upside down.

Turning it around, she pushed it back up her sleeve, so now, when she let it slide out, she'd be holding it correctly.

Fighting back tears, she picked up the death mask of her husband. Closing her eyes, she slipped the mask over her head. Her breath came in short puffs. She didn't know if it was due to the small opening at the mouth or her growing panic. She pulled the robe hood over her head and slowly opened the door.

The hallway was deserted. In the distance, the faint hum of equipment sounded. Was it a generator? Carl explained that some electrical equipment survived the dark. Something here may still work.

Her oversized boots echoed in the cement hallway as she crept forward. The windows along the sides of the wall were the same high rectangular openings that she'd seen in the corridor door outside her cell. She reached the T intersection at the end and peered around the corner. On her left, the hallway ended at a closed door. To the right, on both sides of the hall, sat two doors, which continued until it reached another intersection.

Staying close to the wall, she took the right. Betsy made her way to the first door. It was locked. She tried the opposite door. Hinges squeaked as it swung open. Her breath caught in her throat, and she froze. A dusty room with a couch and table now stacked with boxes lay inside.

Betsy stared at the door handle in her hand as if she'd stepped on a land mine. The noise from the hinges had been so loud she expected to hear running footsteps any moment.

No one came.

Soon her heartbeat returned to normal. She opened her hand and stepped back from the door, leaving it ajar. Continuing down the long hall, Betsy decided to try to set a normal pace. That way, if someone did see her from a distance, they may believe she was one of them.

Taking a left at the end of the hallway, Betsy stopped. Her eyes widened. She recognized the area. At the far end of the hall was her cell. She was close to where they held Nancy. Hurrying, she stopped at the first door on the right and opened it a crack.

An unwashed, musty odor assaulted her nose. It was a cell similar to the one she had been kept in. Two buckets sat on the floor, and a cement slab stood against the wall. A folded, thin blanket lay on the slab, but the room was empty.

Betsy continued, stopping and checking each room. They were all deserted. She stood staring at the cell where she had been held.

Where had they taken the other women?

Betsy licked her lips. Her mouth had gone dry. Brad had said they were going to punish the women. Had they already? Did they move them somewhere else?

Doubling back the way she had come, Betsy passed the hallway leading to her new cell and where Brad's corpse lay.

She approached the double doors at the end of this corridor and listened. The only sound was her breath hissing out of the mask. She opened the door and peeked through.

Rows of tables and benches sat in the middle of the darkened room. On the left wall were several windows facing the woods. Here there wasn't a fence.

Betsy felt a sudden urge to break out the window and run for the woods. But she couldn't. Who knows what they would do to the women now? She needed to reach them so they could all escape together.

Crossing through the room, she glanced at the tables, checking for a better weapon than the steel rod in her hand. She didn't expect a gun lying around but preferred a knife or hammer to the baton. Seeing how it was expandable, she didn't know if it was a novelty gadget or if it would hold up to a few strikes.

The sound of a vehicle outside made her duck

for cover. She crouched behind a table and peered out the windows. A large pickup rumbled into view. Three men rode in the cab, and two more in the back. Because of her mask and the distance, she couldn't make out who they were. The truck circled the building and disappeared from view.

Betsy's hands shook. They were gone. That's why she hadn't run into anyone, and time had run out. She needed to find her friends now.

Opening the door, Betsy hurried into another corridor. Fifteen feet away, the hallway ended at a door. Sitting in a chair beside it was a man in a white and yellow robe holding a black mask.

"Took you guys long enough." The man said. "How's Eddie?" He rose, stretching.

Betsy froze. What could she say? Nothing. He'd know she was a woman when she spoke. Instinctively she rushed forward.

The guard pulled his mask over his face.

Betsy let the baton slide down her wrist. It reached the palm of her hand, her fingers tightening on the thick base. Her arm arced over her head as she swung the weapon.

"What the—" The guard raised his hands.

The steel baton crashed against his right forearm.

Something snapped.

Betsy worried the expandable baton had broken

until she noticed his wrist bent at an unnatural angle.

The man screamed. He doubled over, cradling his arm.

Betsy swung again. The blow caught him across the shoulders and back of his head. He pitched forward, crashed into the wall, and dropped to the floor.

Panting, Betsy yanked the door open.

On the other side stood a storage room with an actual bed in the middle. Camilla lay propped up on pillows with Nancy and Gabriela standing on either side.

Nancy stepped forward. "She hasn't had the baby yet. What do you want?"

Betsy ripped the gold mask from her face.

Tears and disbelief filled all three of their faces.

"I thought they killed you." Nancy rushed forward.

"They're coming back," Betsy said. "We have to leave now."

"We can't!" Gabriela cried. "Momma's having her baby."

"Oh, no!" Betsy ran her hands down her face. It couldn't be true, but one glance at Camilla's sweaty, pained expression and Betsy realized she was in a waking nightmare.

"Take Gabby and go," Camilla said, motioning for the door. "Run. All of you."

"No, mama!" Gabriela grabbed her mother.

Back down the hallway, in the room with the tables, a door banged open.

Betsy swallowed.

"It's too late to run." Nancy sobbed.

"But not to fight." Betsy ran back and grabbed the legs of the unconscious guard. "Help me, Nancy!"

Nancy stood there frozen in fear. "What? Why? Why bring him in here?"

"Because now we have a hostage. Help me!"

Gabriela pushed Nancy aside and seized the man's other leg. The two dragged him into the room, and Betsy slammed the steel door shut.

Betsy reached for the lock, but the bar that would have barricaded the door was missing.

"We can't lock it!" Nancy said. "They're going to get in."

Betsy jammed the baton into the place the bar was meant to go. She pulled on the door, and it didn't budge. "No, they won't. And now that we have one of their men, we've got some leverage."

20

TOP SECRET

Matt Browner

Matt rode down the trail and stopped along the bank of Deep Holler Pond. The pond was about the size of a football field, including the two end zones. A favorite spot of people fishing for catfish because the water was deep and cold. It wasn't a surprise not to see anyone swimming. There was something about the pond that bothered even the most foolhardy rednecks.

The era changed depending on who you asked, but the story remained the same. Some people thought a family of settlers drowned in the pond. Others said it was soldiers during the Civil War. Some even said a whole tribe of Chickasaw died when the sinkhole formed the pond. Either way, most people avoided going out there alone, let alone going for a swim.

Matt trotted his horse over to an enormous fallen oak tree that served as a dock of sorts for fishermen. Four rods were set in the ground next to it, along with two five-gallon buckets.

"Hello?" Matt called out, but only silence answered.

He slid off his horse and strode over to the fishing rods. One was bent over with something on the line. He glanced in the buckets. One held a good-sized catfish and the other two trout.

He cupped his hand to his mouth and hollered, "Hey! Where'd you get on to?"

Insects buzzed.

Matt picked up the flexing rod. He reeled it in a few times before whatever was on the end started fighting back. Thick, long, strong pulls made the fishing line slowly weave back and forth as Matt reeled in the catch.

A tail broke the surface, and a catfish gulped for air as Matt hoisted it out of the water. Twirling in the sun, its scales glistened. It flopped back and forth, jerking itself free. It landed with a splash and disappeared into the pond.

"Sorry!" Matt set the rod into the holder and hopped on the fallen tree. "Come on out!"

After another minute of looking around, he shrugged and headed for his horse. Before the Dark, it was common for someone to set a line and leave it overnight. But now, with horseback or foot power being the sole means of transportation, people tended to stay with their gear, not wanting to make two trips.

Climbing into the saddle, Matt headed up the slope toward Ben Pickett's place. When he reached the top, he stopped. The ground was soft here, and the prints from his horse's hooves were visible — one set heading down, another coming back up. There was also a set of boot prints — but they only headed down.

Matt trotted in a circle to make sure. Whoever went down to fish hadn't come back, and this was the only easy way out of Deep Holler.

He debated about going back down, but if someone wanted to hide, there wasn't any way Matt could find them in the Holler without a posse and dogs.

"Sheriff! Sheriff!" Someone shouted from down the road.

Matt sat up in his saddle to get a better view.

Booth Gentry raced down the road on his moped, waving his left hand over his head like his arm was on fire and he was trying to put it out. Booth pedaled that bike all over town to save the little gas he had, but he was running the engine now and really moving. He shouted, "The aliens are coming! The aliens are coming!" and whizzed right by.

"STOP OR I'LL SHOOT!" Matt shouted — why, he had no idea. He had no intention of shooting Booth, but the thought of the panic he'd cause riding around like some crazed Paul Revere made Matt not think straight.

Booth skidded to a stop and held up both hands. "Don't shoot Sheriff. I've gots to warn everybody. The aliens landed at Chapel Rock Cemetery. Someone's gots to let everyone know, and that someone's me."

Matt glanced in the direction Booth had come. Chapel Rock Cemetery was about a mile down on the right. "Hold up, Booth. I can't let you go causing a riot. What is this all about?"

"I've gots to warn people. They're here to snatch us up, and nobody wants to gets snatched by no alien!"

"I agree with you there, Booth, but we've got to warn people in the right way. So, do me a favor. Tell my brother Allen, first, and then wait for me to get back. He's at his house. And don't tell anyone else about the aliens until you talk to me."

Booth's eyes widened. "Are you sending me on a secret mission?"

Matt nodded. "Yes. Top secret."

Booth sucked in his stomach and saluted. "You can count on me, Sheriff. I'm on it."

Before Matt could say another word, Booth sat down, twisted the throttle back, and zoomed off down the road.

Matt chuckled. Booth was as crazy as a rabid fox, but he was full of good intentions. Allen would give Matt an earful later for having to babysit Booth, but Matt didn't want everyone stampeding into town believing it was *the War of The Worlds*.

Continuing, Matt caught himself reaching for his long-dead cell phone. He missed so many pieces of technology, but that phone was always at the top of his list. Before the Dark, you could speak to anyone on the planet with a video call. Now, communication was limited to face-to-face and within the confines of Ridgecrest.

Matt clicked his tongue, and his horse sped up. Hopefully, Allen could calm Booth down until Matt got back. Allen was a few M&M's shy of a whole bag, but Matt doubted he was gullible enough to believe aliens landed in Ridgecrest. But who would have thought the Dark could have happened?

Matt's curiosity got the better of him as he approached Chapel Rock Cemetery. He wanted to get to Ben's house, but something spooked Booth, and it was Matt's job to check it out. He pulled right on the reins and trotted through the wrought iron fence entranceway.

His horse huffed and skittered sideways.

Matt tightened his grip and slowed to a stop. He never understood why people felt the need to provide the dead with prime real estate, but the cemetery was set on a slight slope with a panoramic overlook of the mountains in the distance. Matt's attention wasn't on the view. The cemetery held at least a hundred graves. But a half-a-dozen new holes where graves had once been dotted the grounds.

His horse whinnied and scampered sideways.

Matt pulled him to a stop, slid down the saddle, and securely tied him to the cement post. Besides the horse and his breathing, everything was still. He crept toward the first disturbed plot. Tom Larkin had been buried there. He died two years ago. Matt hadn't known him well.

Matt peered into the hole. The pit was over ten feet deep. Fresh dirt and clumps of grass lay at the bottom. There was no coffin or body. Nothing.

Matt repeated the process at four other graves, which were all empty too. He took off his hat and brushed the sweat from his brow.

"You've got to be kidding me." He muttered.

They had enough problems trying to survive the Dark without a crazed group of murderers running around killing preppers, cutting their heads off and hearts out, possibly digging up graves, and taking the bodies.

Matt turned and marched back to his horse. He didn't care what the mayor said. After he hid Ben's body, he would have a long talk with Frank Pickett.

21

PIECES

Betsy Weber

Betsy backed away from the steel door. The three women spoke simultaneously, and Betsy couldn't understand them. Camila screamed something in Spanish, Gaby sobbed, and Nancy stood there looking terrified.

A memory from the last winter before the Dark sprang the darkness of her mind. They'd gotten an unusual snowfall, and Nadia and Daniel went sledding on the hill in the front yard. Ten minutes later, they were crying and screaming, and Carl rushed out the front door and fell down the icy steps. Betsy gathered them all into the kitchen. There was blood, tears, and shrieks, but in the middle of the chaos, like an Army field doctor, Betsy took control. All three of the cuts were superficial. Nadia cut her lip, Daniel his knee, and Carl's bald head bled all over, but small bandages and hot cocoa fixed everything.

"LISTEN UP!" Betsy shouted. "Nancy, help me get this guy tied up. Gaby, you get clean cloth and water. Camila, shut up!"

Silence descended upon the room, then both Nancy and Gaby rushed to follow her orders. Taking a moment, Nancy surveyed the room. It must have been an expansion of the cinderblock structure. Steel walls, fourteen-foot ceilings, shelves of boxes and equipment surrounding the central area that had been converted to a makeshift birthing space with a bed, chairs, and table. There were no windows, but oil lanterns and LED candles drove back the shadows.

Betsy grabbed an orange electrical cord from a shelf and tied the guard's legs.

Nancy lifted the mask and gasped. "It's Lonnie."

Betsy glanced up. She recognized the face, but not the name or from where. "His arm is broken. Let's tie the good one to his side."

Nancy shook her head. "It's Lonnie Harmon. Dr. Harmon's son. He can't be involved in this."

Camila sat up in bed. "Seeing how he's wearing a black mask and white robe, he couldn't be more involved! Kick his teeth in after you tie him up."

"Calm down, Momma," Gaby said, rushing back over with a half-gallon bottle of water.

"Hold him up," Betsy said as she grabbed Lonnie's shirt and pulled him into a sitting position.

While Nancy propped Lonnie up, Betsy wrapped the cord around his waist, tying his good arm to his side.

Nancy gently lowered the unconscious man to the floor. "This has to be a misunderstanding. Lonnie mowed my lawn. My brother coached him in baseball."

At the mention of Gary, Betsy stiffened.

"He's a monster!" Camila screamed. "He was one of the men who killed Diego." She sobbed, then grabbed her stomach in pain.

"Gaby, try to see if there's any medicine in here."

Gaby clutched her mother's hand and didn't move.

Camila whispered something to her. The young girl nodded and rushed off.

Betsy took Nancy's hand. "There's no good way to tell you this. When I escaped, I made it to your house."

Nancy's other hand covered her mouth. She shook her head. "Not Gary. He's not dead. Please tell me he's not dead."

Betsy took a deep breath. It would have been

easier to say Gary was dead than the truth. "He's alive."

Nancy cried and squeezed Betsy's hand. "Is he hurt? What's wrong?"

"He's one of them. Gary drugged me. I thought he would take me"— Nancy's stinging slap cut off Betsy's words.

"You're lying!" Nancy raised her hand again. "That can't be true!"

Betsy didn't move to defend herself. "I'm so sorry."

Tears rolled down Nancy's face. She turned to Camila, but the pregnant woman glared with hate-filled eyes.

"How could your brother be involved and you have no clue?" Camila rose on her elbows.

"Nancy didn't know." Betsy stepped between the two women.

"You may believe that. I don't," Camila said. "She's probably keeping watch on us."

Nancy's hands clutched both sides of her head. "This is crazy. You're both crazy. Gary wouldn't do that. Not my Gary."

CLANG!

The deafening sound of metal striking metal filled the room.

CLANG!

Everyone covered their ears.

CLANG!

The ringing seemed to linger for a full minute.

"Open the door!" A man shouted from the hallway. "Do it now, or after we knock it down, we'll cut multiple pieces off you."

Gaby rushed back to her mother's side. She had a small box with a red cross on the front in her hand.

"It's okay," Betsy said softly as she squared her shoulders. "They can't get in."

"How do you know?" Nancy sniffed and wiped her nose with her sleeve.

"They wouldn't be asking if they could."

CLANG! CLANG! CLANG!

Over and over, the pounding continued.

Betsy opened the emergency kit Gaby found. She gave the small package of Aspirin to Camila and then ripped open a package of cotton balls. Handing them out, she took two herself and stuck them in her ears. They did little to quiet the noise, but it did help.

Five minutes later, the hammering stopped.

The man in the hallway spewed threats and obscenities. He screamed and carried on, finally ending by promising, "If you don't open that door by the time I get back, I swear you'll wish you could die."

"Wait!" Betsy shouted.

All three women stared at her wide-eyed. Camila slowly shook her head.

"I'll open the door, but you've got to do something for us first."

"You're in no position to bargain."

"Actually, I am. You go into town and tell the mayor and sheriff we're out here, or I remove pieces of Lonnie."

"You wouldn't."

"He killed my husband. You better believe I will!" Betsy screamed. Her heart thundered in her chest. Maybe they didn't care about Lonnie. Maybe he was a bit player and not the bargaining chip she thought he'd be.

"Don't touch him." The man shouted.

Betsy smiled, and so did the other women. They were trapped but alive, and once again, there was a small hope that they may escape the nightmare.

22

DON'T YOU DIE ON ME!

Mercy Yoder

"Lucy!" Mercy grabbed the railing of the boat and sat up. "Lucy!"

The steam rising from where the truck had gone underwater had stopped. Frantically Mercy scanned the river. Debris littered the surface.

Pulling herself upright, Mercy clutched the railing as her vision darkened in and out. She brushed the hair sticking to her face aside. Blood covered the palm of her hand.

"Mercy!" Sadie shouted. "Throw a rope!"

Mercy stumbled to the left side of the boat.

Sadie swam through the floating debris using

her right arm. Her left was wrapped around Lucy, who floated behind her.

Mercy grabbed a rope tied to the railing that trailed off into the boat. She pulled up ten yards of it before it caught on something in the back. Following the line, the end was wedged between the motor and fiberglass. Planting her feet, Mercy tugged it free, then raced back to the front.

The boat had drifted farther downstream. Sadie and Lucy floated at least twenty yards away. The rope wouldn't reach them.

Stay on the boat.

Mercy's fears clawed at her mind. Pushing them aside, she yanked her dress over her head. She held the end of the rope and dove over the side.

Cold water enveloped her. She'd never been a great swimmer, but she gave everything she had now. Her arms cut through the water, but there were so many things floating in the river she couldn't see around them.

"Sadie!"

"Over here!" Sadie called weakly from somewhere on the left.

Shoving aside a plastic jug, Mercy spotted them. She swam over, scraping against a tree branch that drifted into her. The rope pulled taunt. Sadie was still too far away.

"Take Lucy," Sadie begged. Her skin was pale, and her lips trembled.

"Swim to me. I can't let go of the rope."

"I can't. My leg. Take my baby." Sadie's head dipped under the water.

Clutching the rope in one hand, Mercy kicked and swam as hard as she could. Sadie drifted closer.

"Just a little more." Mercy stretched out her arm.

"I can't hold onto you both," Sadie shook her head.

Mercy thought momentarily, then wrapped her legs around Sadie's waist. "Don't let go of Lucy!" Mercy shouted as she pulled them, hand over hand, closer to the boat.

The fiberglass rope sliced into the palms of her hands. Ignoring the pain, Mercy grit her teeth and pulled them over to the drifting boat.

"Loop the rope under Lucy's arms." Mercy said as she tread water. "I'll climb up and then help you."

"Lucy first."

"I can't lift Lucy by myself. Now shut up and focus!" Mercy shouted.

Sadie crookedly grinned. "I knew you had grit."

Using the rope, Lucy climbed over the side. By the time she turned around, Sadie had pulled herself halfway over.

"Hold onto Lucy!" Sadie said, handing the rope to Mercy.

Mercy braced her feet against the side of the boat as Sadie flopped onto the deck.

Sadie screamed in pain. Cursing and sputtering, she seized the rope. "I'll pull. You grab her."

The two women worked together to hoist Lucy up. Once Lucy's shoulders were over the side, Mercy dragged her into the boat.

Lucy smacked onto the deck like a huge fish. She wasn't breathing.

Mercy rolled her onto her back and tilted her head. "Do you know how to do chest compressions?"

Sadie shook her head. Tears streamed down her face.

Mercy checked Lucy's airway and then started CPR. The first thirty chest compressions felt like an eternity. She tilted Lucy's head back and lifted her chin. Pinching Lucy's nose shut, Mercy covered Lucy's mouth with her own and breathed.

Lucy's chest rose, and the air exited, but she didn't breathe on her own.

Mercy breathed into Lucy's mouth again, but Lucy still didn't respond.

"Please, baby. Breathe." Sadie begged. She knelt at Lucy's side and took her hand.

Mercy repeated the procedure.

Once.

Twice.

Three times.

Mercy's arms shook. She couldn't feel her fingers. They were so numb, but she tried again.

Lucy lay unmoving on the deck.

Mercy bowed her head. Sweat rolled down her brow and stung her eyes.

Sadie's hands balled into fists. Her lips pulled back. Her mouth twisted in grief and pain. "Don't you die on me!" She raised her fist over her head and brought it down like a hammer blow on Lucy's chest.

Water erupted from Lucy's mouth. She coughed, gasped in air, and curled into a fetal position.

Mercy grabbed Lucy's shoulder and rolled her onto her side. She turned Lucy's head to keep her airway clear.

Lucy vomited water.

Sadie cried and hugged her.

"Let go, Mom," Lucy muttered. "I can't breathe."

Mercy sat down, resting her back against the boat. Lucy only referred to her mother as Sadie. Maybe almost dying softened her heart a little? Mercy wrapped her trembling arms around her waist and tried to catch her breath.

Lucy looked around. "Where's Cain?"

Mercy's heart stopped beating. In all the chaos, she had assumed the man she considered invincible was somehow safe. Like Superman, he'd suddenly appear and save the day.

Sadie hung her head. "He got trapped in the truck."

"What?!" Mercy grabbed the railing and pulled herself to her knees.

A resounding, low thud sounded off the bow. The boat jerked to the right.

Mercy tumbled to the deck.

"Now what?" Sadie raised herself onto one knee and looked at the river. Her eyes went wide. "Where did the dam go?"

The boat thumped off something else and shoved Mercy to the side. They were speeding up, and the roar of rushing water grew louder.

Mercy pulled herself to her feet. All she wanted to do was look for Cain, but she couldn't take her eyes off the raging river before her. The dam was gone, and the river dropped, cascading over the broken chunks of cement and rock.

"Grab onto something now!" Sadie shouted.

Mercy turned back in the direction of the truck. The debris field had thinned, but Cain was nowhere in sight. "CAIN!"

Sadie grabbed Mercy behind the knees and yanked her down.

The boat bashed off another rock, sending everyone sliding.

Sadie looped the rope through the railing and then around the metal pole of the captain's chair. "Put it around your waist. Cinch it tight, but don't tie it in case we flip over."

Mercy stared at her. She nodded, but her arms wouldn't cooperate.

Was Cain dead? Drowned. It couldn't be.

Sadie coiled the rope around the three women and yanked it tight.

"You're killing me." Lucy snapped.

"Hang on!" Sadie shouted above the roar.

Water crashed over the side. Like a doll being swung by an angry child, Mercy was jerked every which way. The rope dug into the bare skin of her waist.

The front of the boat lifted into the air and then plummeted down.

A loud crack shuddered along the length of the boat.

Mercy's head jerked back and slammed into the fiberglass. Her vision dimmed. Water blinded her. She closed her eyes and...

23

THE DEVIL'S LAUNDRY MACHINE

Cain Haight

I've been jammed up before, but never like this.

I'm trapped in the driver's seat of a truck resting at the bottom of a river. Standing up as straight as I can and tilting my head back, my head breaks into an air pocket trapped by the truck's roof. Here, I can breathe. I don't know if the small air bubble I'm quickly draining is a miracle that'll give me enough time to figure a way out of this mess, or if it will prolong the agony of drowning.

Either way, I'm on borrowed time.

My foot is wedged tight between the crushed steering column and the gas pedal. No matter how I twist, turn, yank, and pull, it ain't coming out. My foot might be busted. I unsheathe my knife, take a deep breath and bend over. I saw the laces on my boot and cut them off. For good measure, I slice as much of the tongue of the boot off as I can too.

Then I straighten back up and try to take shallow breaths. I have to lift my chin higher now. The water is rising, or the air pocket is getting smaller.

Time is clicking.

I grab the dashboard with one hand and the roof handle with the other, plant my good foot and pull with everything I've got. After a minute, my air pocket shrinks to the point where I've got to close my mouth and breathe out my nose.

I close my eyes, and a stupid idea crams itself into my brain — *grab your shotgun*. Sometimes thoughts are funny like that. They don't seem to come from your own head. I don't know if the devil on my shoulder is whispering at me to end it all, but that's not the kind of man I am. If I'm gonna die, I ain't heading to self-checkout. The Reaper has to come get me.

I'm not sticking a shotgun in my mouth and...

I feel around the seat behind me, and the Shockwave is still crammed halfway under the seatback. I take the deepest breath I can through my nose and double up. Using my Shockwave like a crowbar, I hope the barrel is strong enough.

My fingers tighten on the stock and push. My barefoot slips out like Cinderella's after the ball. I blink twice and return to my air pocket, but it's gone. With that last piece of life support missing, I hold onto my shotgun with one hand, grab the open window and start swimming for the surface.

I glance back and see the empty trailer behind the truck. With my lungs burning, it's no time to smile, but at least the women have a boat.

My head breaks the surface, and I'm gulping in the finest Tennessee air I ever have. I expect to hear cheering and clapping, but everything is quiet. It's hard to see with all the trash in the river, but I don't see any of the women or the boat.

Nothing is on the bank either. Not even creatures.

An empty gas can bumps into the back of my head. I grab it, using it to tread water while I take my other boot off and strap my Shockwave to my thigh. An orange life preserver is caught up on a branch floating by. The current is stronger toward the middle.

The boat may have floated downstream.

I swim over to the branch and untangle the life preserver. I want to get moving so I can catch the women at the dam. Knowing Lucy, she's already trying to convince the others to go on without me.

Shoving aside some trash, I head for the middle

of the river, where the current is the fastest. After seeing that bone bear, I don't mind getting away from the shore. I still have my gun, my Shockwave, but only six extra cartridges, three spare magazines, and my survival knife, which I expect would be useless against Mor'du.

The current is speeding up, and the water sloshing becomes a roar. I round the bend and blink.

What happened to the dam?

The middle of the dam is gone. Rebar juts out of pieces of concrete like broken bones from roadkill.

The river pulls me forward, and the rush of water grows louder.

I start swimming sideways for the shore like I'm caught in a riptide. I've always been a strong swimmer, but I'd have to be Aquaman to get out of the pull. Like a dying goldfish, I'm floundering as I'm dragged toward the break in the wall.

I feel like I'm about to be dragged over Niagara Falls without a barrel until I see the spillway channel. Swimming as hard as I can, I aim for the opening in the concrete. Shooting through the gap, I drop a dozen feet until I land on the cement slope.

Sliding down the waterslide from Hell, I dodge a piece of rebar and a shattered pile of concrete. Brushing the water out of my eyes, I see a rock the size of a trashcan I'm headed straight for. I hit it feet first. My knees almost hit my face, but something gives, cushioning the impact.

It takes me a second to realize that I knocked the boulder free. It tumbles down the chute before me like a fullback clearing the way to the end zone. It smashes the cement chunks in front of it, creating a water-fueled landslide.

Until it hits a boulder that's bigger than it.

I try to repeat my perfect landing, but the back spray of water off the now-wedged rock knocks me off balance. I'm leaning forward when my feet hit, and I tumble into a summersault.

I'm flying away from the spillway and see the remnants of the dam beneath me. Giant chunks of sharp cement and rebar lay in a heap at the bottom of the falls. Flipping off that rock has put me on a trajectory where I might hit the river below.

But it ain't a guarantee. And seeing how I'm spinning through the air, I can't tell if I'll hit the water or become impaled on the twisted metal poles.

I keep my eyes open.

The bottom is rushing toward me.

I see blue sky between my bare feet, and for a moment, I remember skinny dipping with Lucy down at the rope swing at Green Holler.

Splash!

I hit the water the best way I can. Not that I had

anything to do with it, rolling out of control the way I am. My landing is kinda like a rolling cannonball, but it beats a belly flop or face plant.

I roll deep down into the water. Pressure is hammering me from all sides, and it's so loud I think my head is gonna pop. For some unknown reason, my spinning doesn't slow down — it speeds up. I'm tumbling end over end and realize that Satan's Waterfall has spit me out and into the Devil's laundry machine.

The current sucks me down, pulls me up, shoves me forward, and repeats the process.

I've got no clue how to escape from the bottom of the waterfall, but I know that you swim sideways when caught in a riptide. Making my best guess as to which way that is, I start clawing and kicking at the water. I head sideways from the path all the bubbles are headed. Bubbles mean air, and air means the water is less buoyant, so me heading away from that is a good thing, I hope.

The dragging, pulling, and deafening roar are all getting less intense, but I'm slowing down. My adrenaline is gone. My arms and legs feel like they've turned to stone. I'm so tired. I'm dog paddling now.

My fingertips hit silt. Clawing my way forward, my bare feet dig into the sand. I crawl onto the bank. My feet are still in the water, but I collapse.

Lying in the sand and mud, I gulp air. Only the automatic parts of my body are moving. I'm breathing, my heart is beating, and I blink water outta my eyes.

I'm alive, but I ain't happy. Seeing how I'm onshore, I don't know how long I've got before the wolves or the bone rats get me. I should try to get going, but my body is shutting down. I gave everything I had, and now I need to close my eyes for a minute and...

24

APPLE PIE

Amos Yoder

Amos led Sarah through the door and into the underground bunker. The hum of a generator echoed off the cement walls.

Sarah stopped, reaching out for the wall. Her legs shook, and she closed her eyes.

"What's wrong?" Amos moved to her side. "Are you all right?"

Sarah shook her head. She opened her eyes. Her steely gaze locked with his. "What is this place? I want the truth, Amos. All of it."

Amos exhaled and nodded. His wife deserved to know, even if knowing would destroy what they had.

"I'll tell you everything. But it's a long story, and this isn't the place to do it. Once we get home."

Sarah crossed her arms.

Amos grit his teeth. His wife was the stubbornest person on the planet. "I promise I will tell you, but not here. Here is not the place."

"You've been doing nothing but lying to me for the last year, Amos Yoder. Give me one reason why I should believe you now."

Her words were like a slap in the face. What could he say? That she was wrong? That he'd been lying to Sarah since he met her? No. Who knows how she'd react to that?

Amos tugged at the end of his long beard. Since the Amish don't wear jewelry of any kind, including wedding rings, men growing their beards out was the outward sign they were married.

Sarah's glare softened. Her lips pressed together, and the pain on her face clawed at his heart.

His betrayal of her trust had wounded her deeply, but now wasn't the time to explain. The unseen pressure he felt to hurry grew.

Amos turned and marched down the hallway. The corridor opened into a supply room lined with shelves filled with metal boxes and plastic crates. Motion lights flicked on as they went. The rumble of the underground river drowned out the sound of the generator it powered. His boots clinked off the metal grating as he crossed the bridge spanning the waterway. Amos opened a metal gate and entered a long hallway with a half dozen doors on each side. He passed the kitchen, the armory, and another supply room before he stopped at a door bolted and locked from the outside.

The keys shook in his hand. "You need to understand something before I open this door, Sarah. Jesse Pickett isn't the boy you remember. I know you felt bad for his mother and did what you could for them, but Jesse is bad off. Something happened to him out there that snapped his mind. You stay behind me, okay?"

Sarah nervously nodded.

Amos opened the door.

The small cement room was neat. The cot was made, the blankets were pulled tight and carefully tucked in. Jesse sat on the edge of the bed and smiled as they came in. "Hello, Amos." When he noticed Sarah, he stood. "Mrs. Yoder." His smile widened, and he gave a polite nod.

Amos felt his eyebrows rising to his hairline. Every time he'd come before, Jesse would either be hiding under the bed or cowering in the corner. Most days, he'd cry and never spoke more than a few words a month.

"Hello, Jesse." Sarah moved around Amos and sat on the wooden chair. "It's so nice to see you."

"It's nice to see you too, ma'am." Jesse sat back down on the cot. "Your husband has been very kind to me."

"I didn't know you were here," Sarah said. "If I did, I would have made you some pie."

"Apple?" Jesse licked his lips. "Momma always loved your apple pies. I wouldn't want to put you out, but I'd do anything for one of them."

Amos scratched his head and whispered. "I'm telling you, Sarah. He hasn't been like this since I found him."

"You hush." Sarah crouched in front of Jesse. "Is there anything else you need? Anything I can get for you?"

"No, ma'am." Jesse stared at the wall to his right for so long that Amos wondered if the young man had zoned out. "But you need to check on Ani. She's been asking me for help."

Amos took a step back. "How do you know Ani's name? How do you even know she's here? Did you meet her before?"

"No, sir. I met her last night. She's looking for her boy." Jesse reached out and placed his hand on Sarah's arm. "She needs a doctor. She's real sick."

"Thank you for telling me, Jesse. We'll go and see her now."

Sarah started for the door, but Amos ignored her. "How did you meet Ani last night?"

"She came to me," Jesse said.

Amos glanced at the door. "But the door was locked."

"She didn't come in that way." Jesse smiled and tapped the side of his head. "There are other ways to talk."

Sarah took a deep breath and moved closer to her husband. "We'll be right back, Jesse."

"Don't forget the apple pie." Jesse grinned.

Amos led Sarah out of the room and locked the door behind them.

"I don't understand any of this!" Sarah's cheeks flushed, and she tucked an errant strand of hair beneath her bonnet.

"Neither do I. I promise I'll explain everything once we're out of this." Amos said.

Sarah tucked her chin to her chest and stared at the floor.

Amos smoothed the front of his overalls as he waited for her to make up her mind. There was no arguing with Sarah now. They were long past that point.

Sarah looked up. "After we see her, I want the truth. Every last piece of it, Amos."

"I promise I won't leave anything out." Amos took Sarah's hand and started down the hallway. They passed by several doorways and turned down another corridor.

Amos stopped outside Ani's door.

The corridor lights flickered. Sarah didn't seem to notice, but Amos's chest tightened. Besides a tripped breaker, he'd never had an electrical issue in the bunker before. If the hydro generator developed a real problem, he didn't know how to fix it.

Sarah gave his hand a slight squeeze.

Amos entered the combination, slid back the lock, and pushed the door open to the medical room. Ani lay motionless on the bed.

Sarah crossed the room and set her bag down.

Ani turned her head. Her blue eyes searched Sarah's face and closed again.

"My name is Sarah Yoder. I'm going to examine you." Sarah said in a gentle tone.

Ani didn't respond.

Sarah glared at Amos. "Wait in the hallway. I'll call you when I'm done."

25

GOD LOVES THE MAN IN BLACK!

Mercy Yoder

Water sprinkled Mercy's cheeks, and laughter drifted on the wind. She stood at the pond's edge, the noise of a large party drifting across a grassy field. Two children splashed in the water and waved.

"Where's your father?" A voice like her own asked.

The children pointed to the pond. In the middle, rings of small waves rippled out. Smoke rose from the center of the rings, and the water bubbled and hissed. The rear end of a pickup truck rose into the air and slowly sank beneath the surface.

"Cain!" Mercy screamed. She rushed forward, her feet splashing in the water. "Cain!" The water rose to her waist, and the sand disappeared beneath her feet. She plunged into the pond, and darkness wrapped around her.

Sputtering and coughing, Mercy pushed herself onto her elbows. She lay at the bottom of the boat, the deck covered in two inches of water. Wiping her eyes, she glanced around. Sadie and Lucy were lashed together in the back of the boat. Their eyes were closed, but Sadie still gripped the rope.

Mercy crawled over to them, and Sadie opened her left eye. The right was swollen and puffy.

"We're still breathing." Sadie crookedly grinned. "Hell of a ride."

Mercy nodded but couldn't bring herself to smile back. Cain was missing. She grabbed the railing and managed to stand. Water sloshed above her ankles.

Behind them, now far away, the waterfall cascaded down. How they lived through that was nothing short of a miracle. She bowed her head, but the words of thanks wouldn't come. Tears did. Lots of them. Her shoulders rounded forward, and her frame shook with each gulp of breath.

"Don't go crying for Cain," Sadie said. "You don't know if he's dead, but if he is, he's a lot better off than us."

Mercy shook her head. "You don't know that." Guilt squeezed her chest, and she sobbed again.

"No. But I know there's a big hole in the boat, and if you don't do something, we're gonna drown." Sadie pointed to the front.

Mercy followed Sadie's outstretched, trembling arm. The bow of the boat rose and fell as they drifted. When it bobbed up, a large, jagged hole in the fiberglass was visible.

Using the deck railing for balance, Mercy walked hand-over-hand to the front. Dropping to her knees, she grabbed a duffle bag and jammed it against the hole. The boat dipped back down, and the water rushing through the gap pushed the bag aside. She tried bracing the bag with a cooler and then gathering a pile of objects, but it soon became apparent there was no way to plug the hole.

Sadie sat in the back of the boat, cradling Lucy in her arms. Lucy's eyes were closed, and she lay against her mother's chest. The women looked like war refugees. If Mercy headed to shore, how long would they last against the wolves?

The boat rocked on the waves, and the bow lifted, revealing the large hole.

Mercy grabbed the large duffle bag and dragged

it to the stern. She hurried to the front and began pushing everything not nailed down to the rear of the boat.

Sadie nodded. "You got brains and grit. I can see why Cain likes you."

The glow of Mercy's cheeks was quenched in overwhelming grief. She seized the heavy anchor and dragged it to the stern. Sweat rolled down her face, and her already weary legs trembled. She collapsed next to Sadie.

The boat's bow rode high, the hole visible and out of the water.

Mercy burst into tears once more.

"Now why are you balling?" Sadie asked. "You bought us some time."

Mercy hung her head. Shame swept over her. "I never talked to Cain about Jesus. I never invited him to Church. I didn't... And as a Christian, I believe... If he didn't... and now he's dead..."

"First off," Sadie's head reclined back until it rested on the side of the boat. "Don't count Cain out so fast. That boy's a survivor. He may have made it."

"Really?" Mercy pictured all the debris covering the river after the truck sank beneath the water. "Should we go back?"

Sadie shook her head. "If Cain did get out, he'll find us."

"And if he didn't..." Mercy wept.

"That's the thing about you religious folks I never understood," Sadie stared at the sky. "If you think Jesus is the door to heaven, why aren't you telling everyone?"

Mercy pressed her shaking hands to her face. "I should have. I should have."

"Well, good thing it ain't all up to you. Cain's a Christian in spite of the church."

Mercy shrugged, sniffed, and wiped her nose with the back of her hand. "What does that mean?"

Sadie sat up a little and winced. "I got out of prison when Cain was thirteen. He and Lucy were already an item, and when I told him I was going to church, he asked to go along. It was probably to butter me up. I didn't tell him that I was only going to make it look good for my probation officer."

"Why were you in jail?" Mercy asked, quickly adding, "You don't have to tell me."

"Murder. It wasn't, though. My ex hit me. I hit him back with a bat."

Mercy tried not to make a face.

"Anyway," Sadie continued. "I thought it would keep my probation officer off my back, so I went to church and took Cain and Sadie with me. The preacher gets behind the pulpit, but doesn't start preaching. He's staring at Cain. After a minute, he points at Cain and another boy and calls them forward. Now Cain's family didn't have no money, so he wasn't dressed in a fancy white shirt with a red tie like the other kid. Cain was wearing blue jeans and a black Johnny Cash T-shirt."

Mercy pictured a young Cain nervously standing before the congregation. The pit in her stomach grew as she wondered what happened next.

"That pastor asked Cain his name. When Cain told him, you'd have thought the Devil himself had strolled into the building. The preacher pointed at the rich kid and said, 'Tommy wanted to honor God, so today he wore his Sunday best. But who here thinks that God is happy with someone wearing a rock and roll t-shirt to His house?'" Sadie clicked her tongue. "The broken look on Cain's face just about tore my heart out. That pastor didn't understand that the Johnny Cash T-shirt was Cain's only clean shirt."

"That's horrible. God wants us to come just as we are. What happened?"

Sadie smiled down at Lucy. "The preacher asked that stupid question, and Lucy shouted, 'God loves the man in black!' Then Cain got in that pastor's face and told him that the church was God's house, not his, and everyone was welcome. All three of us got thrown out."

More tears rolled down Mercy's cheeks. "I can see why Cain never went to church again."

Sadie laughed. "I didn't say that. Cain stomped out of that church and stormed to the one down the road. He swore that no one was gonna keep him from getting to God, especially some stupid preacher."

"So, you all went?"

Sadie's smile faded, and she hugged Lucy tighter. "Not Lucy. Lucy didn't want anything to do with church or God after that." Sadie closed her eyes. "So, don't you go worrying about Cain. If he's alive, he'll find us. If he's dead, that boy found Jesus the day he got thrown out of God's house."

26

HOW AM I GONNA GET OUT OF THIS?

Cain Haight

My eyes open, and I'm staring at the blue sky. Water's lapping at my legs, but I'm breathing. The Marine in me sits up and starts a self-check. My ankle's sore, but it isn't broken. My boots are gone, but I have my Shockwave, pistol, and survival knife.

I bend over and take a long drink. The irony of being so thirsty because I almost drowned isn't lost on me. I'd laugh or at least crack a smile if another thought didn't hit me — Wolves.

I draw my Shockwave, and water pours out of the barrel. It should still fire, but I'm not testing it. That could attract the wolves, and now the only ammo

I've got is what's on me. The only sounds are the river and birds chirping. The birds are a good sign. They seem to go quiet when the wolves are around.

Scanning the empty river, I re-entertain the thought of firing my shotgun. If the women made it, they could hear the sound and.... What could they do? They can't come back in that boat. The engine wasn't new. No way it would run, and that boat would be impossible to row upstream.

I wade out into the river and check downstream — nothing, but water. Most likely, they figure I'm dead, and they'll keep going. No way any of them would give up trying to save the kids if they were alive. And seeing how there's no sign of the boat or wreckage, I think Mercy might have gotten a miracle.

But I'm literally up the creek. My only shot is the river, and not only do I not have a paddle, I don't have a boat.

I shake my head when I notice the faint trail of smoke rising over the trees. It's dark and wispy. A small fire. It could be from a house. And a home this close to the river should have a boat.

I need to get moving and catch up with them.

My feet sink into the clay on the bank as I wade out of the river and up the slope. My head is on a swivel, and I strain to hear the slightest sound of wolves or bone rats. Now I gotta add a giant freaking bone bear to that list.

Listen to me. I sound as crazy as Booth Gentry.

At the top of the slope, I stare at a little farmhouse with smoke rising from the chimney. But this is the Dark, so the field between me and the house hasn't been mowed in over a year, and someone's dug a twenty-foot-wide moat around the house. A big, old excavator sits beside the property and a horse eats the grass. There's a barn out back. It looks like they tried to get a moat around it too, but only made it halfway around.

A canoe lays on a rack attached to the barn. That's my ticket back to the river.

I'm so excited I start jogging down the hill without looking. I make it a hundred yards when the grass at the edge of the field starts moving like a crowd is pushing through it.

There's no way I can make it back to the river, and the house is too far. My only shot is a big maple tree with a rope swing hanging from the largest branch.

I take a dozen strides, and it feels like I'm racing across hot coals. The thick grass stocks are stabbing my bare feet. If I slow down, I'm gonna be lunch, so I try to shift the pain to anger.

It works. My legs are moving on autopilot, and I'm so focused on my breathing that I'm not feeling my feet. I'm so tired that the adrenaline is already starting to wear off. I start screaming, but my legs are slowing down.

Seven different columns of grass are bending over on both sides of me. They're getting closer fast.

I picture Bri with tears running down her cheeks, calling out for me. A burst of speed shoots me forward, and I dive for the single rope holding the swing. It's been years since boot camp and high-school gym, but I've always been able to climb like an acrobat. Hand over hand, I fly into the air like a monkey.

One. Two. Three wolves enter the clearing around the tree. The lead wolf pounces. It sails through the air like Michael Jordan. It's aimed at my legs. Its jaws open wide.

I pull my knees up to my chest, and the beast's teeth snap an inch beneath me.

The wolf's body hits the rope and sends me swinging like an out-of-control clock pendulum.

But I don't stop climbing until my hands reach the thick branch, and I pull myself up.

Below me, a dozen wolves circle like sharks. They snap, claw the ground and vainly jump, biting the air when they do.

I shimmy to the tree trunk and stare out at the farmhouse. It has to be a hundred yards to the moat circling it. There's no way I can outrun the wolves. I also can't wait in a tree forever. Blood from my feet drips down and lands at the tree's base.

The largest wolf, probably the Alpha, licks it off the ground and then stares at me. For a moment, I swear it smiles.

It knows I'm trapped. It knows there's nowhere I can go. It's only a matter of time before it gets its meal.

I draw my pistol, aim for the back of its head, and fire.

Bone splinters off.

The wolf staggers to the right, and they all scatter.

My hope rises until I realize they're all hiding along the edge of the clearing in the tall grass. I aim for another one and squeeze off a shot.

The bullet grazes its neck. The beast shrugs it off and darts back a few yards, disappearing into the cover of the tall grass.

I holster my pistol and then turn my back toward the tree trunk. Straddling the broad branch, I cup my hands to my mouth and holler for help until my throat is raw. Figure it won't do me any good even if whoever is in the house heard me. What could they do?

I lay my head against the bark and close my eyes.

How am I gonna get out of this?

27

A WAY WITH KIDS

Bri Haight

Bri Haight stared at the now empty leather cord around her wrist. Her beloved charms now floated behind her in the river as a signal to her father. He'd come for her. She was sure about that. He'd promised he'd always watch over her, and her Daddy always kept his word.

But the giant in the first canoe and Fenn paddled so fast. How could Daddy catch up?

"Hand me a protein bar," Fen said.

"Get it yourself." Bri didn't turn around.

Fen jabbed her paddle against Bri's back.

The blow knocked Bri off the seat and sent her

sprawling onto the gear stowed in the front of the canoe.

"Next time you disobey, I won't tap your back. I'll crack your head!" Fenn shouted.

A strange trill sounded on the bank. Farther up, another answered.

In the lead canoe, Nicholi turned around and glared. He raised his thick, long arms as if to say, *what gives*?

Fen pointed at Bri, leaned forward, and whispered, "Open your mouth again, and I'll nail it shut. Give me food."

Bri wanted to point out that Fen was the one who shouted but didn't want to get struck with the paddle again—or worse. She lifted a heavy backpack out of the way, then moved the thick sleeping bag and reached for the protein bars. Her gaze shifted to the front of the canoe and the black drain plug. She reached for it and stopped. Memaw told Bri that removing the drain plug wouldn't sink a plastic canoe.

Fen snapped her fingers.

Bri grabbed a bottle and hurried back with it.

Fen snatched it from her hand.

While the wicked woman gulped it down, Bri retreated to her seat. Up ahead, the enormous Russian continued to paddle. Like a machine, he moved from one side to the other. And Fen was somehow keeping up with him.

Bri hung her head. How was her daddy going to catch up with them going so fast? But what could Bri do? Canoes didn't have brakes. There wasn't any way Bri could slow it down.

"Stupid plastic canoe," Bri muttered.

She couldn't sink it. Even if it filled with water, it would still float.

Bri's eyes widened.

But that would slow them down!

Like she was sitting in math class, Bri raised her hand.

"What?" Fen hissed.

"Can I please get a drink of water?"

"Get me a bottle too."

Bri shot out of her seat. Her hand shook as she grabbed the drain plug. It didn't budge! She planted her feet against the bottom sides of the canoe and used both hands. She twisted as hard as she could, and the plug turned free. Bri stuffed the plug into her pocket and waited.

Nothing happened. No water rushed in.

Fen paddled. The canoe tilted forward, and water gurgled through the hole.

Biting her lip to keep from cheering, Bri grabbed a bottle and rushed to give it to Fen.

Fen stroked hard, then snatched the bottle out of Bri's hand. "I thought you wanted one."

"Oh!" Bri nodded. "I forgot."

Fen rolled her eyes.

Bri scrambled back from her seat and returned to the front. The thick sleeping bag was soaking up the water. Bri started to move it out of the way and stopped. The longer it took the water to get to the back of the canoe and Fen to realize it was flooding, the better.

Taking a bottle of water for herself, Bri used the sleeping bag, the backpack, and a gym bag filled with food to create a dam. She returned to her seat and placed her feet on the backpack, pressing it into place.

With each stroke of Fen's paddle, Bri heard water bubble up. As the bank shot by on either side, the front of the canoe slowly started getting lower. Soon, Nick's canoe began to pull away.

Bri glanced back.

Sweat dripped down Fen's face, and her shirt was soaked.

Bri looked straight ahead and grinned. Her plan was working.

Water splashed Bri's sneakers. She pressed harder on the backpack, but the water was seeping out all around it now. Soon it would pass her seat.

"The big oaf is trying to show off," Fen said.

Bri doubted Nicholi heard her, but the giant Russian looked back. The distance between the two canoes had grown considerably. He stopped rowing.

Fen said something in Chinese.

Bri didn't know what it meant, but from how Fen said it, Bri knew it was a bad word.

"What's with this water!" Fen pulled her paddle across the gunwales.

Bri shrugged as Fen crouched and made her way forward.

"Move!" Fen roughly grabbed Bri and shoved her to the back of the canoe. "We sprung a leak, and you didn't say anything?"

"I thought I spilled my bottle."

Fen dragged the soaked equipment out of the pool of water and felt around with her hand.

Bri tore the plug out of her pocket and pitched it over the side.

"The drain plug is out!" Fen glared at Bri. "Where is it?"

Bri shrugged.

Holding the gunwales, Fen charged forward.

Bri retreated as far back in the canoe as she could.

Fen grabbed Bri's shirt, balling the fabric in her hand and jerking her off her feet. Fen roughly turned out Bri's pockets and patted down her clothes.

"I didn't do nothing." Bri shook her head. "Maybe I bumped it when *you* told me to get the water."

Fen dropped Bri into the bottom of the canoe and scrabbled back to the front.

Nicholi whistled.

Fen held up her middle finger. She grabbed a water bottle floating by, poured some out, and then fiddled around in the front. After a minute of grunting and swearing, she sat on the front seat, kicked the soaked gear, and swore some more.

"What is the problem?" Nicholi asked as he paddled up next to them.

Bri stared over the side at Jacob. He lay curled up on a canvas tarp with his eyes closed.

"The drain plug came out." Fen snapped. "I jammed it up with a bottle, but the brat didn't tell me we were flooding."

Nicholi scoffed. "You can't handle a child?"

"I'd cram a pill down her throat if you hadn't given both to the boy."

"Jacob?" Bri called out. "Are you okay?"

"He's better than you're going to be if you don't shut up!" Fen snapped.

Nicholi used his paddle to pull the two canoes together. "That is your problem. You may be a woman, but you don't know how to speak to children." He held up a can and smiled at Bri. "Use this to bail the water out of the canoe." He pantomimed the action of scooping water and tossing it over the side. "Or we'll throw you out."

Fen scowled. "I already tried that."

Nicholi shrugged. "Break something. On her." He pointed at Bri for emphasis.

Bri snatched the can out of his hand and started bailing.

"See!" Nicholi grinned. "I have a way with kids. We are almost at the lake. Now get moving."

The two exchanged icy stares, and Nicholi shoved off.

Fen grabbed Bri's shirt and yanked her so close, Fen's breath blew back Bri's hair. "One more thing happens, and you go over the side."

"I didn't—"

"I don't believe you, stupid child."

Bri whipped up some fake tears and sucked in air.

Fen shoved her to the front of the canoe and then moved to her seat in the back. She picked up the paddle. "Bail! Bail!"

Bri started scooping the water, making sure she didn't fill the can too much. She smiled. She knew the canoe wouldn't sink. But she succeeded in slowing them down. Now her daddy could catch up.

28

OUT OF THE FRYING PAN

Cain Haight

One positive thing about being stuck up in a tree by a bunch of mutant wolves is that it gives you time to think and devise a plan. Of course, it's not much of a plan, but I don't have much to work with. Besides my pistol, two spare magazines, my Shockwave, a half-dozen extra shells, a survival knife, and the clothes on my back, I've got nothing but a tree to work with.

I can hear Lucy laughing at my plan and shooting it down now, but it's the only thing I can come up with.

Carefully standing up, I climb a little higher and

grab a dead branch. It must have recently died because there are dozens of dried leaves clinging to it. I've got to twist it back and forth but manage to rip it off.

Holding my prize with one hand, I climb back to the big limb and sit down. The wolves are still hiding in the grass beneath me. Two crawl forward to get a better view of what I'm doing. I whittle the smaller branches off and lay them on my lap.

Taking out my survival knife, I slide the fire starter out of the sheath. Everyone thinks it's easy to start a fire until they have to. The fire starter is just a ferrocerium rod that sparks. Don't get me wrong, that's a dream for a survivalist, but you've got to turn that spark into a fire. And sitting in a tree with only dry leaves to work with, the chances of me getting this fire going are slim. Having some dry grass for kindling would be ideal, but the only dry grass is the dead field surrounding me.

But that's when the ornery part of me comes in. If I don't like the odds — I cheat.

Next, I remove my shirt and rip a square out of it. I pluck all the leaves off the branches, crush them into a pile onto the fabric, and cover it up in case a gust of wind comes. Then I rip my shirt into strips and twirl the cloth around the sticks like small torches. I save the largest branch for one big torch. I cut a leg off my jeans and wrap the fabric around that.

The corner of my mouth ticks up when I reach for the Ace up my sleeve — two shotgun shells. Cutting them open takes a little care and finesse, but I manage and carefully pour the gunpowder onto the leaves.

I spend the next couple of minutes psyching myself up for what comes next. This plan could be brilliant, or I'll die soon after jumping out of the tree, so I think it over. I shred a few remaining pieces of my shirt to add to the kindling and realize this is my best chance.

I close my eyes, and no words come. Something about praying for myself has always bothered me. I'm okay with praying for others, but what can I say now? And to top it off, since He's God, He knows what I'm gonna ask, so why ask it?

I glare at the sky and scream, "Help the women and the kids." I quickly tack on, "Please." Then add, "I could use a hand too."

I flex my aching feet. The dried blood cracks, sending fresh pain up my legs. I pick up my knife and fire starter. Metal scratches metal, and sparks fly. They catch the fibers from the cloth and hit the gunpowder. A whoosh is followed by smoke and fire.

It's hard blowing on the embers because I'm

grinning like a fool. I pick up one of my little torches, let the fire get going, and pitch it to the left. It flips through the air, but stays lit.

I don't have time to wait to see if the grass catches as I light two more. When I glance down, I see the first torch has started a small fire on the ground. Picking my targets, I start flinging torches while trying to keep the main fire going. While straddling a tree branch, it ain't easy to do, but I fall into a rhythm.

The wolves have all moved back, but to my surprise, don't run away.

With my left hand, I'm putting twigs on the fire; with my right, I'm lighting and throwing torches. I let one fly sidearm and watch it sail through the air until a cloud of black hides it from view.

I look down and to the left. The first torch's fire had spread from a foot to almost ten yards around. Flames leap into the air, and a breeze blows my hair back. The wind fuels the fire and pushes it toward my planned escape path toward the house.

Gabbing the rest of my flaming torches in my left hand, I put the big torch in my mouth like a pirate biting his sword and swing out of the tree. It would've been a hard landing in boots, but it's brutal with bleeding bare feet. I bite down on the wood in my mouth and start running.

I don't know if the wind picked up, but the fire

grows fast. The sweat dries instantly on my skin. I'm pitching the little torches out as I run.

Something big is moving on my right.

I use the last little torch to light the big one. As the fire gets going, I draw my Shockwave and start running again.

An inhuman shriek rips the air. A wolf tears out of the grass five yards behind me on the left. I spin, but it's moving so fast I can't get a bead on it. It could have easily pounced on me, but it leaps into the air and rolls onto the ground.

Its back is on fire. The beast snarls and races away, igniting all the dead grass on its way.

My joy is short-lived as the smoke obscures my vision. With the grass trampled, and me so turned around, I'm only guessing which way is the farmhouse. I barrel ahead and break free of the tall grass.

The moat shines like an oasis.

A massive wolf emerges from the grass on my right. Its face is charred, and it looks pissed.

I lift my Shockwave and pull the trigger.

Click. Click.

The wolf crouches, ready to pounce.

I swing my torch around, and the beast slides to a stop. It growls and bites the air. I start backing toward the moat. It's about ten yards, but these creatures move so fast I won't turn my back on one.

Four more crash through the grass.

I throw my torch at Burnt Face and sprint. I draw my pistol.

Burnt Face leaps over the torch and closes in.

The four others bark and join the hunt.

Burnt Face is fast. There's no way I'm gonna make it.

I stop, turn, and fire. Bits of bone fly off the natural armor on his head, but each bullet must feel like a punch. I pull the trigger until the magazine is empty before Burnt Face turns and runs to the left.

A lean wolf, faster than the other, leaps through the air. Its mouth opens. Its claws raise.

I drop my gun and reach for my knife, knowing I won't reach it in time, but I'm too stubborn to stand here and die without trying something.

A shotgun blast roars behind me.

The wolf drops to the ground. A hole ripped in its belly.

I spin, take five long strides, and dive. The cool water wraps around me. I shoot across so fast that my fingers hit the mud of the far bank before I realize I have crossed the moat.

My head breaks the surface, and I look back at the hell I escaped on the far bank. Seven wolves howl and claw the ground. Behind them, the whole field is in flames.

I let out a loud cheer.

The sound of a shotgun breaking and closing

makes me freeze. I slowly lift my arms and turn around.

An older man is standing on the bank, staring down at me. He's holding a double-barrel shotgun, and it's pointed at my head.

Out of the frying pan...

29

THE SHORT STRAW

Betsy Weber

Betsy stared over at Camila on the bed. Gaby held her mother's hand and blotted her sweaty forehead with a cloth.

Camila grimaced.

"Her contractions are getting closer," Betsy called to Nancy, but her friend hadn't spoken a word in the last hour.

Nancy sat in a metal chair, her head in her hands and shoulders slumped.

Whether Nancy was contemplating the fact she was trapped and the fate which awaited all of them or the news that her brother was involved with the murderous group keeping them prisoner, Betsy didn't know or care. She marched over to the chair and crouched in front of her friend.

Lowering her voice to a whisper, Betsy said, "Look. Besides watching several episodes of *Call the Midwife*, I have no idea how to deliver a baby. What about you?"

Nancy peered at her with red-rimmed eyes. "I was in 4H. I delivered a calf."

Betsy placed both hands on Nancy's shoulders. "Congratulations, Dr. Long. How do we get started?"

Nancy's mouth fell open. "I couldn't. Me? No way."

"What do you want me to tell Camila? Stop? Hold on? That baby is coming whether you think you can help it or not."

"I can't do this, Betsy."

Betsy smiled. "I think this is the point where I'm supposed to slap you, but there's been too much of that today. How about I let you have a big glass of vodka when we're done?"

"Can I have that drink now?"

Betsy laughed. "Okay. That's the Nancy I know and love. What do we need to do?"

Nancy took a deep breath and stood up. "Come with me." She marched over to the bed and took Gaby's hand. "Betsy, hold Camila's other hand." Then bowed her head. After a moment of silence, she said, "God, I have no words. Help. In Jesus' name, Amen."

Gaby chuckled.

Camila looked at Nancy, laughed, then gritted her teeth. "From the look on your face, you've never done this before. I take it you drew the short straw?"

Nancy stood ramrod straight. "I did. Betsy and Gaby, I need you to gather the following things: clean towels, sterile gloves, sheets, scissors, sanitary pads, diapers, and more water." She leaned closer to Camila and said, "You and I are to get to know each other better than I ever thought. You need to trust me, and do exactly as I say, understood?"

Camila nodded.

Betsy glanced at Nancy's hands folded behind her back. They were shaking.

Nancy picked up the water bottle and moved it over to the table. She clapped her hands and said, "Get moving, you two! We need to find those supplies."

Betsy started searching through the boxes on the left side of the storeroom while Gaby took the right. Every once in a while, one of them would hit pay dirt and call out what they found.

"Scissors!" Betsy said, then hurried them over to the table and returned to her quest.

"Cloths! A whole bag!" Gaby ran them over. "I

think they're for washing a car, but they're clean. Will they work?"

Nancy nodded and gave Gaby a wink.

Betsy opened a cardboard box and let out a triumphant cheer. Judging from the toilet paper, tampons, sanitary pads, and jar of sanitizer, it contained the supplies for the woman's room, but it was just what they needed. "I struck the mother load!" She awkwardly hefted her find over and set it on the floor beside the table.

"Perfect!" Nancy clapped her on the back. "Did either of you find a wooded spoon or something similar?"

Betsy made a face. "What's that for?"

"So she can bite on it. I don't have anything for the pain."

Camila sat up groaning. A scream split the air, but not from her. Lonnie thrashed on the floor and wailed like a child.

"Stop moving!" Betsy shouted as Lonnie's broken arm flopped against his side.

"My arm! Help me. Please. It hurts. What—" His eyes rolled back in his head. His body convulsed, and he stopped moving.

Betsy held her breath until she saw his chest rising and falling. She'd taken one life today and never wanted to do it again. "Help me get him into a chair, and we'll tie him to it."

"Leave him!" Camila shouted. "He deserves to suffer."

Betsy slid over the metal chair and motioned to Nancy. Between the two of them, they hoisted Lonnie up and sat him down. Betsy used the extra length of the extension cord to fasten him to the chair.

"What are we going to do with him?" Nancy whispered.

A sense of dread rolled through the pit of her stomach. "I killed Brad Moore." She blurted out.

Nancy blinked rapidly. "When?"

"This morning. That's how I got away. I didn't mean to." Tears streamed down her face, and she collapsed into her friend's arms. "I knew him and his wife. His son. Why? Why would they do this?"

Nancy rubbed Betsy's back and rocked her as Betsy sobbed. The minutes ticked by, and the tears slowed and stopped. Nancy gently lifted Betsy's chin and stared into her eyes. "I don't know why the world's gone mad, but we'll get through this. First, we've got a baby to deliver, and I can't do it without you."

Betsy swallowed and nodded. She needed to pull herself together for everyone.

Camila cried out. "Oh, no. Oh, no. Baby's coming. He's coming. HE'S COMING NOW!"

30

I DON'T BELIEVE IN LUCK

Cain Haight

I've got my hands raised high overhead. The old man's double-barrel shotgun is pointed at my face, but his focus is on the wolves pacing back and forth on the opposite bank of the moat.

He's only three or four steps up the bank from me. I glance down at the ground. It's red clay. The odds of me slipping are too high to chance grabbing the gun, so I take a different tack.

"Hello," I work up a smile. "Thanks for saving me."

The old man shakes his head like he's just woken up from a dream and stares down at me. "You're safe now. They don't cross the water. Is anyone else with you?" He holds the shotgun lower, so it's pointed at my legs.

His hands shake so much that I'm nervous he'll accidentally pull the trigger.

"No. I'm alone. Can you stop pointing the gun at me?"

"I'm not going to shoot you. I'm trying to help you up."

I exhale and lower my arms. "I appreciate that offer, but I'll manage without grabbing the business end of that double-wide."

"Oh, that's wise. I'm not much of a gunman. Only fired a pistol before."

My eyes widen as I remember the shot zipping by me and killing the wolf. "You mean that amazing shot you just made was dumb luck?"

"Oh, I don't believe in luck." He grinned. "But I figured if I didn't shoot, the wolf would kill you, and if I did shoot and hit you, that would be kinder than letting you get eaten."

I make it up the slope and wipe my hand on my jeans. "I guess that makes sense. Either way, a heck of a shot. Thanks."

"You're the first soul I've seen in a year. Couldn't leave you out there." He glanced up at the sky and the darkening clouds. "I think the weather is gonna take care of that fire for you."

"Sorry about burning up your fields. It was the only way I could think of getting out of the tree."

"Fields are wild now. They used to be corn. Now I know two things that scare the wolves. Water and fire."

I turn toward the other bank to look for my guns and wince as I step.

"You're hurt." The old man says. "Come on inside."

I walk slowly as I examine the farmhouse. The horse I saw earlier is gone, and there's no sign of anyone else.

"This your place?" I ask.

The old man shakes his head. "It was my friend's. Ed. He's gone. My wife and I came here after we lost power. She's passed too."

"So, you're here alone?" I ask.

The old man nods. With his curved back and white hair, I'm guessing he's got to be at least eighty, but that double-barrel gives him an advantage. Visually, I start checking him for tell-tale signs of any other weapons.

What am I thinking? This guy saves my life, and now I'm wondering if he's only done it to take me inside and cook me?

I relax and follow him to the overgrown walkway leading to the house. The curtain in the window next to the front door pushes to the side and falls back down.

Ignoring the pain in my feet, I lung forward, rip the shotgun out of his hands, and step back, keeping the old man between me and the house.

"Hands up!" I shout.

The old man is startled, but he doesn't look scared.

"What for? Why would you kill me?"

"Why did you lie?" I use the barrel of the gun to point to the window. "You said you were alone. I saw the curtain move. Who's inside?"

"Pete. But I didn't lie."

Ignoring the double-talk, I shift over to keep using him as a human shield. "Tell Pete to come out."

"He can't unless I let him." The old man scratches the side of his head while giving me a look that lets me know he thinks I'm stupid.

"Come out of the house!" I shout.

The old man chuckles.

The curtain shoves aside, and the horse I saw earlier stares out the window.

"Pete is a horse?" I ask. "Why is he in the house?"

"Where else was I going to put him? The barn is on the other side of the moat, and the wolves were around."

I lower the gun. I brought Star into the Sheriff's office when it was raining. Who am I to judge? "Sorry about that," I say, giving him back his gun.

The old man nods and extends a hand. "I guess you can't be too careful. I'm Adam Wright."

"Cain Haight."

Adam cocks his head to the side like he didn't hear me correctly.

I'm used to the reaction, especially living in the buckle of the Bible belt, but I remain silent.

"Let's get your feet bandaged and some food in you." Adam climbs the front porch. "After, I'll get a room ready for you."

"I'm not staying. I'm only here to get the canoe and get back to the river."

Adam chuckles, but as he stares at me, his smile fades. "You're serious? But you only made it here by the skin of your teeth. How do you plan on getting back?"

"I'm working on that." I point at the tractor. "That still work?"

"Maybe. We ran out of diesel. You're serious?" He asks again.

I nod.

"Why do you need to get to the river so badly?"

I debate for a minute about how much to tell him. I'm about to say I don't know him from the real Adam and leave it at that. But the way he's appraising me gets me thinking he might have an idea of his own that he's debating about sharing with me, so I tell him the truth. It takes me fifteen minutes to fill him in with the Cliff Notes version of what happened with Bri and Jacob. He doesn't ask any questions. He just listens patiently.

When I'm done, Adam purses his lips together and stares at his hands. He's twisting a gold wedding band back and forth on his finger. After a minute, he nods and says, "I've got a way out of here. But to reach it, I need your help."

31

D

Mercy Yoder

Mercy poured another bucketful of water out of the boat, but it was useless. She was exhausted, and the boat kept sinking deeper. The river had run into a large lake. The joy of being farther away from the bank and the unseen creatures lurking there was overshadowed by the thought of drowning.

"We've got to make a decision," Sadie said. She was sitting in the back of the boat. The water had risen to her knees.

Lucy sat next to her mother and glared at Mercy. "Why don't you pray for a miracle?"

"What's your problem?" Sadie swatted Lucy's arm. "That girl saved your life."

"You saved my life." Lucy leveled a hate-filled glare at Mercy. "If it wasn't for her coming, I woulda been in the cab, and I woulda got Cain out."

Mercy fought back tears.

"Bull!" Sadie spat. "If you were in the cab with Cain, you two woulda been fightin' so much he woulda driven into a tree just to shut you up. Now close your trap and let me think."

Mercy turned away from Lucy's accusatory stare. Her chin trembled. The guilt of not going back for Cain washed over her again. He wouldn't have left her. She was sure of that. Wiping her eyes, she gazed out on the lake and froze. One by one, lights flicked on. They glowed red like fire and not the bright white of artificial lights.

"Torches!" Mercy shouted. "On the water!"

"Be quiet, you idiot!" Lucy snapped as she ducked down and reached for her rifle.

Sadie crouched low, and the three of them peered at the lights.

Lucy closed one eye and searched through the powerful scope of her rifle. "It's like a shanty town on the water. Someone's lashed a bunch of boats together—a lot of them. Pontoon boats mostly, but there are at least a dozen houseboats. They even have bridges going between them."

"You see anyone?"

"A thin guy is lighting the torches along the edge

of boats. He's not carrying a rifle. I don't even see a gun."

Mercy raised her hand toward the sky. "Thank you, Lord! There's your miracle, Lucy."

Lucy lowered the gun and shot Mercy a look like she thought she was the stupidest person on the planet. "I know you grew up in your little Amish bubble where everyone sits around and hugs each other, but did you ever think that maybe the rest of the world ain't that way? How do you know whoever is there won't treat you worse than the wolves? Did you already forget you almost got us all killed trying to rescue Bodhi's fake sick wife and kid?"

Mercy swallowed. The thought that whoever was on the boats might hurt them hadn't occurred to her, even after Bodhi's recent betrayal. "You're right. I'm naive."

Sadie slumped back down. "Doesn't matter. We don't have much of a choice. We're sinking, and with my leg torn up, I wouldn't last long if we went to shore. And I don't think you two would make it much longer than that."

Lucy snapped her fingers. "Why don't we steal one of their boats? We still have a chance of getting in front of Fen and saving Bri. But we've got to keep moving."

"Maybe they could help." Mercy said.

"Maybe they'll kill us and toss our bodies in the lake like gutted fish!" Lucy said.

Mercy lifted her chin. "They could. That's why I'll swim over first. If something happens to me, you two continue."

"That's the dumbest—" Lucy started to say, but Sadie smacked her in the back of the head.

"Do it. We need more than just a boat. We need food, water, and ammo."

"We can steal those, too," Lucy said.

"If Mercy's plan doesn't work, we'll go with yours."

"What's her plan? Begging for help?" Lucy said.

"Sometimes you gotta go hat in hand." Sadie turned to Mercy. "We'll get you close enough so you can swim over but try to stay far enough away that they won't see us."

Lucy rose and splashed over to the other side of the boat opposite her mother.

Sadie grabbed a long, broken piece of wood from the side of the boat and pushed it over to Lucy. "Quit sulking and paddle."

They did their best to steer the boat closer to the floating island. Mercy doubted they would be moving if it weren't for the current.

The boat rode deep in the water. It wouldn't stay afloat much longer. Mercy blinked back tears. Lucy was right. She had grown up in a bubble, but was that so bad? Most everyone she knew were honest folks who helped you if you asked. Just because the world had gone dark didn't mean all men had — did it?

Mercy didn't know anymore. She believed Bodhi, and it almost got them killed. But what choice did they have now? They'd never catch Fen without another boat and wouldn't make it long on shore on foot.

There was no way Mercy could swim that far weighed down with her dress. She took it off, gathered the fabric in her arms and grabbed the side of the boat. "I can make it from here. If I call your names, come. If not, keep going or try for shore."

Sadie held out her hand for Mercy's dress, but Mercy shook her head.

"How are you gonna swim holding a dumb dress?" Lucy snapped.

"I'll hold it in my left arm."

"Why are you taking it? It will only weigh you down." Sadie said.

"Because Miss Modesty doesn't want to show up in her underwear." Lucy scoffed.

Mercy ignored her and slipped over the side. The dress was heavy, but there was no way she'd reach the boat island half-naked. She just couldn't.

The water was cool and refreshing on her skin. The irony of it feeling different somehow to the same water in the flooded boat wasn't lost on her. Holding the dress against her side, she swam toward the light of the torches. An odd peace washed over her. As a little girl, she was afraid of all the unseen things in the water, but now, with darkness surrounding her and swimming toward the unknown, she wasn't frightened at all.

How could that be? She expected her heart to be pounding out of her chest and her hands shaking so hard she could stick them into the water, and they'd act like little motors fluttering her forward. But she breathed easily. She was so calm she turned onto her back and floated for a few minutes of rest.

Drawing nearer to the structure, she noticed that what she first thought were bridges were docks from some marina, lashed with chains and ropes. The dozen or so houseboats towered above the pontoon boats. All of these were cobbled together, creating a large, floating island.

Reaching a dock, Mercy hefted her dress up and laid it on the wood. Water poured off it and dripped back into the pond, creating little waterfalls of noise. Holding onto the rough planks, she scanned the pockets of light cast by the torches. No one was in sight, but the murmur of voices traveled on the wind. Hoisting herself up, she seized her wet dress and hurriedly pulled it over her head.

"What the... Bill! D! You better come out here." A man shouted.

The sounds of boots echoed off the docks as a dozen figures dashed past the torches' glow and raced toward her. Someone cocked a gun. Four burly men skidded to a stop beside the closest torch and stared at her wide-eyed. The shortest one, a man with a wild beard and a large belly, strutted forward. His eyes darted from Mercy to scan the lake and back again. He held a shiny, silver gun, but pointed it at the dock.

"I don't believe in freshwater mermaids, but who are you, and how'd you get out here?"

Commotion erupted all around as over a dozen men rushed in from all directions.

Before Mercy could answer, the first few cords of a loud whistled tune that Mercy didn't know came from Lucy and Sadie's boat.

The bearded man's face broke into a broad grin. He puckered his lips and whistled back the same melody, then called out, "Sweet Home Alabama! That you, Sadie?"

"It sure is D, you good for nothing hick," Sadie shouted back.

All of the men whooped and hollered.

"What the heck are you waiting for?" D yelled. "Get in here!"

Mercy cleared her throat. "The boat she and Lucy are in is sinking."

"Lucy's here, too?"

At the mention of Lucy, the men cheered, stomped their feet, and two fired their guns in the air.

D pointed at two men, "Tate and Dwight, take a boat and get 'em."

Almost two dozen men had gathered. Half of them started to run down the dock.

"You all don't need to go!" D shouted after them, but they either didn't hear him or didn't care and kept running. D turned to Mercy and smiled. "Follow me. We'll get you some towels and get you dried off."

"Thank you for your kindness, sir." Mercy inclined her head.

One of the men snickered, but D shoved his shoulder, and the crowd started walking back the way they had come.

"Hey, Bill," D called out. "Go get a case. With Sadie and Lucy here, this calls for a celebration."

Mercy shook her head. "This isn't a social call, sir. We're on a mission and must be going as soon as possible."

D stopped, and everyone else did too. "A mission? What mission? Who would send Sadie on a mission?"

"The good Lord did, sir."

D's head tipped toward his right shoulder, and he gave Mercy a sideways glance. "Like the Blues Brothers? You're telling me that you're on a mission from God?"

"I don't know who these brothers are, but yes." Mercy said. "We're on our way to save two children, and time is of the essence."

D swept his arm in a wide swath. "There's nothing out there except monsters. There's no place for you to go. It's a miracle you made it here."

Mercy was about to reply, but the hairs rising on her neck made her clamp her mouth shut. Something about the nervous way all of the men looked at each other let her know she'd already said too much.

32

DEEP BREATHS

Betsy Weber

Betsy scrubbed her hands with the antiseptic gel and started waving them. She, Nancy, and Gaby wore trash bag ponchos pulled over their heads and bandanas tied around their mouths. Gaby was struggling to pull a sterile glove over her hand. Close to tears, the young girl's lip trembled.

"The gel has to dry, or you can't get the glove on," Betsy explained. "Shake your hands off."

A minute later, Gaby pulled the gloves over her hands and gave Betsy a big blue thumbs-up.

"I'm going to need help here," Nancy said. "She's dilated. I think the baby is moving into the birth canal." Nancy's complexion was a pasty white, and she looked like she was about to pass out.

"Deep breaths," Betsy said.

Camila groaned. "I thought I was supposed to shallow breathe!"

Betsy pointed at her. "You are." Then she pointed to Nancy. "She's not."

Camila chuckled, but it was quickly replaced with a grimace. "I'm going to need that spoon."

Gaby handed the wooden spoon she'd found to her mother.

"Breath!" Nancy's hands opened like she'd be hit by lighting. "We're going to need to clear the baby's airway. We need a bulb syringe to clean out his nose and mouth."

"Can you use something else?" Betsy asked. "We're kind of limited."

Nancy thought for a moment. "What about a turkey baster?"

Gaby's eyes brightened, and she darted off to the corner of the room.

Nancy started breathing heavily. "Okay. Easy Camila. I see the baby's head."

Betsy's lip curled. "What's over it?" She whispered.

"What's over what?!" Camila shouted.

Nancy glared at Betsy. "It's perfectly normal. It's a membrane. I need to take hold of it and—"

Betsy turned away, gagging as Nancy released the amniotic fluid.

"Perfectly normal," Nancy repeated as her cheeks turned light green. "Did you find anything, Gaby?"

"Got it!" Gaby raced back, opening a sealed package.

Betsy glanced at the label and chuckled.

Camila screamed.

"Easy. Easy." Nancy said.

"I'm not a horse!" Camila shouted.

"Will this thing work?" Gaby asked as she tugged a device from the package.

"We need to sterilize it, but that's perfect," Nancy said.

Betsy grabbed the rubbing alcohol and poured it all over the bulb and tubing.

"What is it?" Camila asked.

Before Betsy could stop Gaby, the young girl triumphantly blurted out, "It's a transmission fluid siphon pump!"

"STOP!" Camila shouted, then laid back and bit on the spoon.

"Good. Good." Nancy said. "Push. Here comes the head."

"Don't use car equipment on my baby!" Camila screamed.

"It's new, and we sterilized it," Betsy said.

Camila's protests were unintelligible as she chomped down on the spoon.

CLANG! CLANG! CLANG! Three metal gongs rang through the room.

Betsy swore. "Not now!"

"Open the door!" The man in the hallway shouted.

Camila yanked the spoon from her mouth, and the stream of profanities that spewed out would make a drunken sailor sound like a prude. She called the man every curse word Betsy had ever heard and others she hadn't. She swore in English and Spanish, then switched to insulting every attribute of manliness the guard might have and continued to heap insults onto his mother and all of his ancestors as well.

Betsy chuckled. "If there was an Olympics for profanity, that was a gold medal routine."

"You're gonna regret saying that!" The man shouted.

"One more push," Nancy said. "Let him have it!"

Camila inhaled again and let fly with another verbal broadside. Machine gun fast, she ripped the man to shreds with her onslaught, then sagged back onto the bed.

Nancy took the baby into her arms and instructed Gaby what to do next. After asking for the towel and the siphon, a baby's cry split the air.

Gaby clapped.

Nancy cried.

Betsy walked nearer the door and listened.

"I don't care!" The man said to someone else on the other side. "Blow it!"

Betsy gasped.

What were they going to do? Would they really use explosives?

"HEY!" Betsy shouted. "If you try anything, I promise I'll kill Lonnie before you get through that door."

"You're a housewife, not a killer."

"That was the old me who died when you murdered my husband. I killed Brad. I'll kill Lonnie, too. Try me."

The seconds ticked by. Betsy's shirt clung to her back. She felt as if her heart had come into her throat. A heated, muffled conversation took place on the other side of the door. At least three people spoke, but she couldn't tell what was being said.

The man swore. Something metal clanked off the floor, and many departing boot steps echoed in the hall.

Betsy's shoulders slumped, and she hung her head. For the moment, they were safe, but how long could they hold out?

33

SECRETS

Amos Yoder

Sarah had spent hours cleaning Ani's wounds and redressing them. Ani opened her eyes and sipped the water offered to her, but she didn't eat anything or speak. She gave Ani an antibiotic and then motioned Amos into the hallway.

"She's running a fever," Sarah said. "We need to take her to the doctor."

Amos smoothed his hair back with his hand. "I don't know, Sarah. What are people going to say about her? What will they do when they find she's not from Ridgecrest?"

"I don't want her to die."

"Neither do I. But now I'm more worried about

Frank Pickett than ever. If he thinks that Ani knows something about Fen and Nicholi…"

"Does she?"

"I don't know." Amos crossed his arms and leaned against the wall.

Sarah leaned against the opposite one. "You need to tell me what's going on. I can't counsel you if I don't know the facts."

Amos exhaled. She was right. Besides, he owed her the truth. But what would she say?

"My name isn't Amos Yoder. He's my cousin in Pennsylvania. My name is Matthew Weber."

"You're not Amish?"

"I am. I was raised Amish. I left home when I was eighteen and joined the Army. I was in the core of engineers. I built this place."

Sarah stood there wringing her hands. "Why? What's it for?"

Amos shrugged. "I don't know. I was a low man on the pecking order. We did what we were told except… Let me back up. I'd just enlisted, and this was my first assignment. They stuck us underground and didn't tell us anything. It was all hush-hush, but we know they were building bunkers like this throughout the cave system. We were finished when a bunker farther down the line, near Cane Creek, collapsed. They ordered us to demo this one too. But we'd put in so much work we didn't think it was right. Neither did my commanding officer. Then we got orders to ship out, but I didn't want to go."

"Why?"

Amos exhaled. "Because I met someone."

Sarah's eyes widened. "You were in the Army then? Is that why you were in the field? You told me you were looking for property to buy. You dressed like you were Amish!"

"I was raised Amish. When I was sixteen, I went on my Rumspringa. My exploring the world led me away from home and community. I decided not to go back to the farm and joined the Army. But I spent months watching you out in the field. You'd come out every once in a while, and I'd sit there wondering about you. I really wanted to talk to you, but I knew you'd never speak to a soldier, so I cobbled together an outfit. I even made the hat."

Sarah chuckled and shook her head. "That was the ugliest hat I ever saw."

Amos frowned.

"But the most handsome man wore it." She added. "Why didn't you tell me the truth?"

"Because you would have run away. But you didn't. Instead, you spent the afternoon telling me all about Ridgecrest. I fell in love with you then. The problem was, we had orders to ship out the next day. That night I dreamed I shouldn't go. It was so real that I woke up and left right then."

"Didn't the Army come looking for you?"

"No. I couldn't figure out why until I went to the library and used their computer. I found a newspaper article that Matthew Weber, me, died along with my squad in a transportation accident."

"Didn't they know you left?"

"Probably not. Maybe some of my buddies were covering for me, hoping I'd return. Either way, the Army thought I was dead, and I wanted to keep it that way because I didn't think the plane crash was an accident. I knew some of the guys who worked on the other bunkers. Everyone I could remember, I looked up on the computer, and they were dead now, too. That's no coincidence."

"Are you saying they were murdered?"

"I think so. I don't know what these bunkers were for, but someone wanted to keep them secret. I never thought I'd come back here, but when I found Jesse, this was the only place to hide him.

Sarah hurried across the floor and wrapped her arms around him. "You should have told me."

"I'm sorry."

"No more secrets?"

"No more. Now what do you think we should do about Ani?"

Sarah bit her bottom lip. "Let's wait till morning. But if her fever doesn't break, we have no choice. We'll have to take her to Doc Harmon."

34

DID THAT JUST HAPPEN?

Matt Browner

Matt rode hard the rest of the way to Ben Pickett's place. He wanted to hide the body and return to town immediately. The sun was low on the horizon, sending long shadows across the grass. He slowed when he reached the open gate and let the horse trot down the road.

Ben's house was quiet. The boxy ranch had an added room on the back. The front door lay open, and so were all the windows. Matt tied his horse to the porch banister so she could munch on a clump of long grass growing out from underneath.

His boots rang off the steps as he walked up the

porch. Before checking for the body, he wanted to make certain no one was inside.

Turning on his flashlight, he scanned the living room on the left. Trash littered the floor, and blankets were heaped into a pile on the couch. A doorway in the back led to a kitchen.

Matt started to turn toward the room on the right when he froze. The blanket on the couch moved. It was only the slightest motion, but in the stillness of the place, he noticed it.

Swallowing, he reached down and unsnapped the strap on his holster. It echoed loudly in the quiet. He drew his pistol and leveled it at the couch.

The heel of his boots softly scraped the floor as he crept into the room. He leaned forward, his left hand grabbing the corner of the blanket. His mouth was so dry he couldn't swallow. His finger rested on the cold metal of the trigger.

He yanked the blanket back.

A mother and half a dozen baby possums hissed. Their beady eyes and sharp teeth gleamed in the shaking glow of the flashlight. Matt jumped and accidentally jerked the trigger. The gun fired. The bullet flew over the couch and blasted a hole in the wall.

The possum family scattered, racing off the sofa and disappearing amongst the trash on the floor.

Matt stumbled out of the room and into the hallway. His ears rang, and his bandaged head throbbed. He backed out onto the porch with his gun trained on the door. If anyone was in the house, they certainly knew he was there now too.

Sweat ran down his back. The ringing in his ears faded. A breeze rustled the dead leaves on the porch and cooled his burning cheeks. Satisfied no one was there, he holstered his weapon and returned to the front yard.

The last rays of the day disappeared behind the mountain. Using his flashlight, Matt searched the area Cain had told the Mayor he'd hidden the body. There was no sign of it — no blood, no clothes, and no body.

Matt circled the house peering in every trash can, a car rusting away, and even searching two old washing machines lying near the wood pile, but no corpse. A metal shed sat outback.

Once again, Matt drew his pistol. The palm of his hand was slick with sweat. He forced himself to keep his index finger off the trigger. They taught you that in gun safety 101, yet he almost accidentally shot a baby possum. And, if anyone had been in the house, that mistake could have gotten Matt killed.

His cheeks burned at the thought of what Cain would have said had he been there. Pushing his mistakes and humiliation aside, Matt opened the shed doors. The eight-by-ten room was packed with tarps, hoses, and welding equipment. Sitting in the back were two ten-speed bicycles.

Matt searched the little shed by shoving the canvas tarps out of the way, but there was no sign of the body. Muttering, he closed the door and turned the handle, latching it.

Clouds blocked the stars. The darkness was so thick he couldn't see a dozen feet outside his flashlight beam. It was an hour back to town, and he wanted to get moving.

He circled around to the front of the house and stopped. His horse was gone.

Matt hung his head and rubbed his left temple. Lately, it felt like he couldn't do anything right — not even tie up his horse so it didn't wander off.

He whistled and called, but the only answer was the sound of bugs. Matt opened his mouth to whistle again when his flashlight beam shined off the horse's reigns dangling off the porch's railing. He had tied her up.

Puzzled, he stepped forward, his boot splashing into something on the ground.

He panned the light down. A massive pool of blood shimmered at his feet.

"Oh, dear Lord..."

Matt had always been a Church going man. Ever since he could remember, his parents had taken him to Sunday school. Then it was Young Life in his teens and back to Church with his new wife after. He'd read the Bible from beginning to end a few times and listened to a hundred sermons. He accepted Christ, got baptized, and prayed every day. He had faith, but he'd never heard God say a word out loud or witnessed a miracle.

Matt's feet lifted off the ground. Like an angel had grabbed him underneath his arms and flung him, Matt flew up the stairs through the open front door without moving his legs. He crashed to the wooded floor in the foyer, rolled over once, and lay on his back, staring at the darkness of the open front door and the yard beyond.

He blinked rapidly.

Did that just happen? He moved so fast it couldn't be real. Was he in shock? Had he imagined the whole thing? He touched his bandaged head. Perhaps the injury was worse than he thought, and he had some brain injury. Maybe after he saw the possums and the gun fired, it hit him in the head, and walking around the house afterward was a dream.

The flashlight beam shook as he kept it trained on the doorway. It struck the toes of his boots, and fresh blood gleamed off the soles.

"Oh, no..."

The wolf leaped. It cleared the porch and slammed into the doorframe of the house. The wood cracked but held. The beast landed on the porch. It thrust its head through the front door. Its teeth clacked together as it chomped inches from Matt's feet.

Matt scurried away, screaming. Pushing with his feet and using his hands, he crab-walked backward until he felt the cold linoleum of the kitchen floor.

The wolf slammed into the doorway again. The wood cracked, and the door frame broke. The beast pushed its way inside. Its claws scraped the wood as it stepped into the hallway.

Matt scrambled to his feet and dashed out the back door. He raced across the yard toward the metal shed.

The wolf crashed through the window, sending glass and pieces of wood flying across the grass. It landed on the dirt and bounded forward.

Matt yanked the shed door open and dove inside. Spinning around, time slowed. The door clanged behind him as it shut but didn't latch. It shook and slowly opened.

The bone wolf pounced. It smashed into the door, slamming it shut again.

Matt grabbed the handle, but it wouldn't twist. The impact had bent the door too much for it to latch.

The wolf slammed into the door again. Metal crumbled, and Matt fell backward.

He raised his gun and fired. Each pull of his finger blasted a hole in the door. He'd lost count of the bullets, so he kept firing until the hammer clicked on an empty chamber.

Pointing the pistol up, he opened the cylinder, letting the casings fall out and ping off the cement. His fingers shook uncontrollably as he grabbed the quick loader from his belt. It tumbled from his hand. He snatched it up and slapped it into the cylinder.

The door was closed but, so twisted and bent, he could see outside. The yard was empty. Besides the pounding of his heart, the shed was silent.

A minute, then two passed. Insects buzzed, but nothing else moved. Keeping his gun pointed at the door, Matt crept forward. The door handle wouldn't turn, but the door itself wouldn't budge either. The impact had bent the door into the frame and jammed it shut.

Staring at the darkness, Matt immediately decided to stay inside. With the wolf still out there, there wasn't any way he'd try to make it back to town on foot at night.

His hands shook. The wolves always traveled in a pack. How many were out there?

35

HOW DARE YOU!

Mercy Yoder

Mercy sat in the crowded room of a gutted houseboat. All the walls had been removed except the four outer ones, creating a large box. There were two long tables, eight benches, and some assorted stools, but that was all. Twenty-two men stood sipping on cans of beer, staring at Sadie, Lucy, and Mercy, who sat wrapped in blankets and eating warm oatmeal. D gave both Sadie and Lucy a beer can too. When Mercy politely declined, Lucy took the can for herself.

After Sadie arrived at the boat island, she took Mercy aside. She explained that she knew the men and they wouldn't harm them, but Mercy should stick close to her to be safe. D looked to be the man in charge. Mercy thought they all belonged to the same motorcycle club from their outfits and similar patches.

Sadie had just finished explaining everything that happened since the Dark had descended on Ridgecrest and ended with Fen kidnapping the children and the pursuit. No one interrupted her until she reached the part about Cain being trapped in the pickup truck and then sinking in the river.

D shook his head, "I thought that bastard was too mean to die."

"How dare you!" Mercy jumped to her feet. "Cain was a good man. And if he was illegitimate, that is none of your business!"

D held up his hand as if calming a mad dog. "I didn't mean no offense. He and I were kinda friends. I just meant he was a tough son of a bitch."

His apology started to placate Mercy's anger until the part at the end. "Now you insult his mother?"

D cast a confused glance at Sadie who said, "Everybody take it easy. It's okay, Mercy. He liked Cain. It's just D's way of showing respect."

Mercy sat back down. She was so angry her hand shook, but she was surprised the men in the room appeared nervous when they met her gaze.

She leaned over to Lucy and whispered, "Why do they look scared of me?"

"Because my mother said the wolves ate your family right in front of you. That made you go bat-crap crazy. She said you killed two wolves with a broken knife, and if anyone gets you mad, you try to bite their face off."

Mercy's mouth dropped open. "That's not true!"

Lucy smirked. "Hey! NO biting! Easy. It's all right. NO! You can't kill anyone. Calm down!"

The men sitting nearby moved away.

Mercy tucked her chin to her chest as her cheeks flushed bright red.

"It's all right!" Sadie stood on her good leg and raised her beer. "To Cain!" Everyone except Mercy drank to the improper toast, and Sadie continued. "We're headed to get those kids back. I can't tell you how glad I am that we ran into you, D."

"Yeah." D finished his beer and grinned. "What are the odds of you ending up here, right?"

Mercy's stomach clenched tight. She may be naive, but she wasn't stupid. There was a smile on D's mouth, but he didn't look at Sadie, and his hands shook.

"Why don't you ladies sleep in here tonight?" D said. "We'll get you some clothes, bedding, and fresh bandages. We'll talk about what to do in the morning."

Sadie and Lucy nodded.

Mercy set down her spoon. "We should get going right away. We need to cut off Fen, and there isn't time to waste."

The men in the room murmured to each other in hushed voices. D held up his hands. "You shouldn't go without getting some rest and patching up Sadie's leg. At least get a couple of hours of sleep."

"He's right," Lucy said, pushing her empty bowl back. "A few hours won't kill us, and it'll give D enough time to get the boats ready."

"Exactly." D stood. "You guys crash and let me get things together."

"Agreed," Sadie said, stretching out her injured leg. "But we can't wait longer than that. Mercy's right. We need to get moving."

Mercy nodded, but she didn't want to wait. Once the men left, Mercy moved close to Sadie and whispered, "I don't want to insult your friend, but I'm worried. I think we should go — now."

Lucy laughed and rolled her eyes. "Are you freakin' kidding me? Little Miss Gullible trusts a guy like Bodhi, but not D and his crew? Listen up, Pollyanna; my mom and D go back to elementary school. They're like brother and sister. And for your information, calling someone a bastard isn't an insult, it's— "

"Will you shut up!" Sadie grabbed Lucy's arm and pushed her away. "You made your point. Now, Mercy, you need to listen to me. There ain't anyone in this world I trust more than D. He is like my big brother, and there's nothing he wouldn't do for us. Trust me. Everything is going to be fine."

Mercy took a deep breath and nodded, but the calmness she felt swimming over to the boats disappeared. Each beat of her heart thumped in her chest like a distress signal. Each chime rang out the same warning — run!

36

WHAT'S IN THE BARN?

Cain Haight

I'm eating a bowl of oatmeal at a kitchen table while Adam bandages my feet. Pete's wandering around the side yard, occasionally looking in the window like he wants to come back in.

"It's not too bad," Adam says, ripping another splinter from my heel. "I think Ed's boots will be a little big for you — which is good because they'll fit with the bandages. He's got about ten pairs, so you can have your pick. This is going to sting a bit."

I just shoveled a heaping spoonful of oatmeal into my mouth. I hold my hand up to get him to wait a second, but Adam pours rubbing alcohol over my left foot. It's all I can do not to spit oatmeal all over him.

"We'll let that dry a minute. Give me your right foot."

"You got anything to drink?" I ask through grit teeth.

Adam eyes my full water glass.

"You got something stronger?"

"Nope. Ed was a Baptist. Not a drop in the house."

I wipe the back of my mouth with my hand. I'd give anything for a drink right now. I guess I'll have to use my thirst for additional motivation to get out of here.

"What's this plan of yours?" I ask.

Adam carefully starts washing my right foot and picking out splinters. "It's not my plan. It was Ed's. This is his farm. It's been in the family for four generations."

"What happened to Ed?"

"Something got him when we were trying to get to the shed. You see, Viv, my wife, had diabetes. Her medicine ran out. We lived just down the road and came here. Ed just about went out of his mind when he saw us. He was digging the moat at the time. He said some strange wolves were coming around, but they didn't cross the water. We thought he'd gotten heat stroke until we saw the creatures ourselves."

"What keeps the moat full?"

"Ed diverted a little creek. He was right. The wolves won't cross it, and neither will the devil squirrels." Adam grabs a large pair of tweezers and tugs on a thick reed splinter sticking out of the side of my foot. He can't get it out, so he starts twisting and pulling.

My knuckles turn white, gripping the sides of the chair.

It jerks free. Adam drops it onto a towel, and his eyes well up. "We kept praying someone would come, but no one ever did. From what you told me, I can see why. I wanted to try to make it to the barn alone, but Viv begged me not to. She was so sick then. I knew she didn't have long, so I tried to comfort her the best I could. After that, what was the point of leaving? And what would I do with Pete? I couldn't bring him."

I grit my teeth. A few residents in Ridgecrest died because they ran out of medicine, oxygen, or something else that relied on electricity. I can't imagine sitting in this house, waiting for the woman I love to die.

"I'm sure Viv appreciated you staying with her." It's all I can think of to say.

"Now I've got another problem. Pete's eaten almost all the grass. I can't just let him wander off. He wouldn't make it a day with the wolves out there. So,

I need to make it to the barn anyway and get some food for him."

"What's in the barn?"

"Oats."

"Oats can't be why you and Ed were trying to get to the barn. I thought it was something to help you get away from here."

"Oh, that. We were trying to get to the dynamite."

"Dynamite," I repeat, still not following what he's talking about. "How is that going to help?"

Adam pours alcohol over my right foot, and my eyes roll back. I hold onto both sides of my head, trying to keep from cussing, bawling, or biting my tongue.

Adam puts the cap back on the bottle. "We need to blow a hole in the wall."

"You've lost me. What wall?"

"Sorry. Let me explain. You're trying to get to Fort Burgess, right? Well, we're sitting over the David Cook Caverns."

"I thought they were in Leiper's Forge. I took my little girl there."

"They start in Leiper's Forge, but they run all the way up here. Ed and his brothers used to go exploring in there as kids. They even got maps."

My mouth flops open. The only ways to Leiper's Forge I had even considered were the river or the highway. We wouldn't have to deal with the wolves if we went underground. "Great." I sit up, but Adam holds onto my ankle.

"Simmer down. I haven't finished bandaging your foot, and as I mentioned, there's the wall."

"A wall underground?"

Adam points out the window. "Jefferson Quarry is on the other side of that ridge. One of their mines hits part of the Cook Caverns. The State had a conniption, and the government made the quarry cease operation in that area. They also had to seal off the mine, so they cemented it up. But Ed thinks we could blow a hole through the cement wall and walk to Leiper's Forge. If we could reach the entrance to the Cook Caverns, we'd be a stone's throw away from Fort Burgess."

"And the dynamite is in the barn?"

Adam angles his head toward the countertop behind him. "Key to the storage box is hanging on the wall. If we can get through that wall, you got a chance to save your daughter."

I pick up my oatmeal and scrape the bowl clean as Adam finishes bandaging my foot. When he's done, I'm going to get some sleep, but come first light, I don't care what beast is in that barn — I'm going to get that dynamite.

37

WHY DON'T WOLVES EAT CLOWNS?

Cain Haight

I open my eyes, and it's still dark. Adam let me sleep in. I slip out of the bed and cross to the window. To the east, the sky is starting to lighten. I reach for the new boots I picked out and pull them on, ignoring the pain from my bandaged feet.

My little girl is out there. The river didn't sleep, so the canoes kept going. Who knows how far Fen made it last night? I've got to get moving if I'm going to catch them.

I head down the hall and into the kitchen. Adam is sitting at the table with two bowls of oatmeal. He's dressed in camouflage, and his complexion is as pale as his thin hair.

"I'm going to the shed alone," I say, sitting down and reaching for my oatmeal. "No offense, but I need to be fast and quiet."

Adam's expression hardens. "I'm not staying in here taking care of my knitting."

No real man likes sitting on the bench, no matter how old he is. But with the wolves over there, taking him with me will get us both killed. "I don't expect you to. Your job is waiting on this side of the moat. I'm not swimming back with dynamite strapped on my back. We'll rig up a raft with those two fifty-gallon drums you've got outside and attach a rope. I'll grab the dynamite, toss it in the raft, and you start pulling."

Adam breaks into a grin and nods rapidly. "But we don't need to use those barrels. Ed has an inflatable raft with his fishing gear."

I try to keep a neutral expression on my face. When I told Adam I wanted to take the canoe, he didn't mention a raft. Maybe he figured we didn't have a need if we were going through the caves. Still, I don't like not knowing.

"Does this Ed have anything else we could use?"

"Do you want to see the books?"

I think Adam is joking until he stands up and strides over to the stove. "Ed kept an inventory of everything he owns?"

Adam lifts a thick three-ring binder off the

counter. He carries the tome over and sets it down. There are dozens of color-coded tabs with section labels like MEDICINE, AUTOMOTIVE, and TOOLS.

"I've heard of people that do stuff like this, but I'd never met one." I chuckle. "Was this Ed nuts?"

Adam's smile fades. "I inventoried the equipment."

"Oh..." I rock back in my chair as I try to find a way to pull my foot out of my mouth. "Well, that's different. You didn't have a TV or anything, so taking stock of what you had available was smart. Thinking like a Marine, my drill sergeant would say."

Adam rubbed the back of his neck with one hand, but the smile returned to his face. "I was an accountant, but I thought it might be important for something."

"It is. It is." I flip open the book, and my eyes light up when I read the label of a bright red tag — GUNS.

"Ed has guns? I thought he was a Baptist."

"Some Baptists don't drink, but I don't know any round here that have a problem with guns. Especially Ed. He's got a room full."

I scan the list, and I'm drooling like a guy off his diet at the country buffet. Fourteen different pistols, five shotguns, eight rifles, a flare gun, and lots of ammo.

"Where's this room?"

~

An hour later, Adam and I take up our positions on the moat's edge. I've inflated the raft, tied a rope to it, and placed a combat shotgun and two pistols inside.

"Do you want the paddle?" Adam whispers and holds out a plastic paddle that looks like it would snap if I pulled too hard.

I would hesitate to use the boat in a pool, let alone a river. I'm not even going to risk getting in to cross the moat for fear it would pop. I shake my head and hold my finger to my lips. Adam is already breaking the rules by whispering. He nods quickly, makes a motion like a little kid locking their mouth, and holds onto the rope tied to the raft.

I slip into the water and start pulling the boat with me. The water's so warm mist is rising in the morning air. It would feel nicer and a lot prettier if I didn't have to worry about getting eaten when I reach the other side.

Pulling the raft up on the bank, I stop and listen.

Everything is quiet. Water drips off me and splashes softly. A blue jay sings somewhere off to my left. Other than that, nothing.

Sliding the large, empty backpack over my shoulders, I take the pistols I got from Ed's war room out of the boat. I slide a Desert Eagle with hollow points into the new holster on my left hip. The Sig Sauer fits nicely in the holster on my right. Holding the Benelli M4 shotgun, I start up the bank. I miss my Shockwave, but I've loaded the M4 with a mix of buckshot and flares. Ed purchased the large extension tube, so I decided on using a pattern of 2 buckshot and then a flare to fill out the 10-round capacity with the extra being a flare. Seeing how the wolves fear fire, I hope the flares scare them off.

Crawling up the slope, I lay in the mud at the crest and scan the barn. Tall grass has grown up all around and overtaken the miscellaneous equipment left outside. The barn doors are slightly open.

Crouched and stepping heel-toe, I cross the twenty yards to the barn. It feels like I'm walking into the middle of a packed football stadium alone, but there's one person hidden in the stands with a rifle trained on my head. Goosebumps rise along my arms as I imagine creatures hidden in the field staring out at me.

I reach the barn and press my back against the wall. Water pours off me. I'd be soaked with sweat if

I hadn't just gone for a swim. My heart is racing like an old Ford engine pushed too hard, too long. Forcing myself to take three deep breaths, I rack my brain for a joke and finally land on one. In the Marines, we'd use humor to keep from giving into fear. If I were on a mission, I'd say — *Do you know why the wolves don't eat clowns? They taste funny.*

Everyone would laugh. Not because it's that good of a joke, but because they're scared out of their minds. It makes me smile, but more importantly, I relax a bit. When your muscles are tight, you're slow. In combat, slow gets you killed.

Besides the water dripping off me onto the ground, it's quiet. Peeking through the open barn door, there's enough light to see. Inside looks like a thousand other barns in Tennessee — equipment, mud, dust, and scattered tools hanging on the walls.

Sweeping the shotgun left to right, I breach the room, heading for the far-right corner, and the tool cabinet Adam said held the dynamite. I don't need the keys. The doors to the cabinet are open, but I can't see inside it from here.

Moving slowly and scanning the room as I go, I stick to the right wall. Ed kept the barn neat, but there's still a hundred places to hide. A big old tractor sits in the far-left corner, along with several attachments. My focus alternates between them and the loft. Because of the deep shadows, I can't see anything up there. That bothers me.

I reach the first of several cabinets and resist the urge to open it. Whatever is inside isn't worth the noise a metal door would make. Keeping the cabinets to my back, I pass three more and stop at the open one. It's an old gun vault with steel doors. Sitting on the shelves are neatly bundled sticks of dynamite.

I slide my empty backpack off my shoulders while keeping a grip on the shotgun and one eye on the room and loft. I don't know if it's my childhood fear of the dark, but that loft is really creeping me out.

Grabbing packs of dynamite with my left hand, I load up the backpack. Reaching for the zipper, I stop.

Something's wrong.

Something is missing in this barn, and I didn't pick up on it. There are no critters. Every barn I've ever been in had all sorts of birds, mice, and whatnot, that scattered when you came in.

Except this one.

Something gleams out of the darkness of the loft like two small, blue Christmas lights.

I spin, raising the barrel.

Brilliant light blinds my vision, but it's coming from inside my head. It feels like someone is squeezing my brain in a vise. All of my muscles tighten. The shotgun in my hands seems to weigh a hundred pounds.

The lights in the loft move closer. Blue eyes stare at me, but I can't see the creature's body. Whatever it is, it is crouched down and creeping forward.

Blood trickles out of my nose. My chest feels like an elephant is stepping on it. My right hand starts to open. My body is giving up.

"CAIN!" My father's voice screams in my mind.

It can't possibly be him. He's long dead.

"Quit, you coward! Quit! Walk away! Give up!" He shouts. "That's what you do."

His words flip a switch inside me. White hot rage explodes in my gut, and a lifetime of hurt and pain is now directed at whatever is up in that loft, trying to crush my mind.

I can't see anything, but since I've got an M4 loaded with buckshot, that doesn't mean I can't hit it. I pull the trigger and start unloading. The first two rounds of buckshot roar out, and then a flare.

Something shrieks. It's high and shrill and almost sounds human.

The blinding light in my head vanishes, and I can move again. Up in the loft, something ducks behind a hay bail.

I fire two more rounds of buckshot and another flare. The flare hits a beam, bounces off the ceiling, and arcs back at me, spinning past my head.

My eyes widen as I watch it land inside the cabinet holding the dynamite.

Grabbing the backpack, I race for the door. Getting blown to bits scares me worse than being eaten, so I'm not even looking back at the loft. I'm five yards from the exit when something big drops to the ground behind me and gives chase.

I take three enormous strides, turn and fire. With the loaded backpack dangling off my left arm, aiming isn't the easiest thing to do. But with a shotgun, it's easy to hit the broad side of a barn.

The buckshot tears through the doors, and then the flare flies inside.

Turning back on my heels, I dash toward the moat. "Get ready!" I shout. I slide down the bank, heave the backpack inside the rubber raft and yell, "PULL!"

The explosion knocks me off my feet and into the water. I land on my back with my eyes open. Like gazing up while at the bottom of the deep end of a pool, the sky shimmers with brilliant reds, yellows, and streaks of black. It is beautiful. It looks like a sunset in summer, but I know it's really fire, smoke, and flying debris.

I swim underwater as long as I can before coming up for a quick breath and darting back under. Small chunks of the barn pepper the moat like meteors. My fingers sink into the mud, and my head breaks the surface again.

A piece of wood flutters down next to me, followed by a loud thump. Mud smacks me in the face and knocks me on my butt. I stare at the twisted steel door of the explosives cabinet sticking out of the clay. It would have cut me in half if it had landed two feet closer.

I glance at the edge of the water. Even with the explosion, Adam managed to pull the raft across the moat. Scrambling to the boat, I grab the loaded backpack and climb up the slope.

Adam is kneeling on the ground, the rope clutched in his hands, with a huge grin. "I've got to hand it to you, Cain. I didn't know how you were gonna handle the wolves. I didn't even think about blowing them up."

I don't know if it's pride, but I keep the fact that the explosion was an accident to myself. "Did you see what was chasing me?"

Adam shakes his head. "I was too busy pulling. I bet the wolf was big. Ed was a tough guy."

I nod, but I'm not sure that whatever attacked me in the shed was a wolf. Either way, it doesn't matter. Whatever it was is dead. Nothing behind me could have lived through that.

38

DON'T GO GETTING UPPITY

Mercy Yoder

Mercy lay on her back, staring up at the ceiling. She must have fallen asleep despite her fears. Sadie and Lucy might trust these men, but she didn't. She closed her eyes and said another prayer for Cain. He'd know how to deal with these men if he were here. If...

Tears were coming, and once again she imagined the truck sinking beneath the water with Cain still trapped inside. He would have fought. He'd do anything to save Bri and never give up. Maybe he got out.

Wood creaked. A door opened, and a breeze swept into the room.

Lucy stood in the doorway, slowly closing it. She carried a small bundle in her right hand. She hurried over to the mat on the floor and lay down.

Mercy rolled over and whispered, “Where did you go?”

“The bathroom.”

Mercy closed her mouth. She didn’t believe her, but there was no point in asking again. Lucy seemed to enjoy fighting with her. Besides, Mercy wouldn’t believe anything Lucy said without proof.

Sadie rolled over and whispered to Lucy. Mercy couldn’t hear what they said, but the conversation was intense and heated. After a minute, they both turned their backs on each other and stopped talking.

Footsteps sounded off the dock outside the room. There was more than one man. Mercy had intended to ask Sadie why there were no women on the floating island, but with Lucy hovering around her mother, she never had an opportunity.

The echo of boots clomping off the wood grew louder. Even though it was lashed to the others, the boat they were in swayed and tipped a little toward the door.

Mercy sat up.

Someone knocked. The door opened and D, followed by a steady stream of men, marched into the room. The men filed around until they stood shoulder to shoulder with their backs against the wall.

Lucy stretched. Her blanket fell, revealing she was only wearing a white t-shirt that D had given her. All of the men stared. Lucy didn't move to cover herself up.

Sadie rubbed a hand down her face. "Ain't no way it's been two hours. Why the long face, D?"

D stood staring down at Sadie, shifting his weight from one foot to the other like a nervous kid at the chalkboard, unable to answer the math equation written there.

Someone cleared their throat. None of the men were looking at Sadie. Their focus was now on D.

"The boys and I had a meeting. We, uh, got to talking, and we all think this plan of yours is never going to work. Now don't get me wrong. You know I'd go to Hell with you, but if Bri and this other boy are out there..." D gazed at the ceiling and then finally looked at Sadie. "They're dead. How you three made it here is beyond me, but nobody is gonna make it long out there."

"We have," Lucy said. "We've been living out there for a year!"

"But not out-there-out-there." Bill spoke up. "You don't know why the creatures left Ridgecrest alone. But this ain't Ridgecrest, either. They're surrounding the lake. They killed everyone."

"Not everyone," Lucy said, gathering her blanket into her lap. "You're all alive."

"And we want to keep it that way," D said. "And keep you safe. We've got enough supplies to hold out here for another year or more. There's plenty of fish— "

"My granddaughter needs me. I'm going. If you men aren't man enough to help, whatever. We're leaving." Sadie pulled her pillow closer to her side.

D said nothing. No one did. The silence of the room was broken when someone locked the door.

"Now, don't go getting uppity, Sadie." D crossed his arms. "You know me, and nothing will happen to any of you women. But we can't let you leave."

Sadie's eyes narrowed. "So not only are you saying you won't help me rescue Bri. You're not letting us go?"

"We can't," Bill said. "Say you leave, and the wolves figure out where you came from. They could come here."

"In what? Wolf boats, you dumbass?" Lucy laughed.

"The wolves could learn to swim!"

"Not out into the middle of a lake!" Lucy shot back.

"What if you make it to the base?" D said. "What then? Are you gonna take on the Army by yourselves?"

Sadie grinned.

D chuckled. "You'll try, but you'll lose. Then they'll wonder where you came from. They have boats. They could come looking for us."

Sadie shook her head. "What happened to all of you? You might have escaped from the wolves, but it looks like they ate your spines."

Four men stomped forward, but D held up his hand and they stopped. "Don't make this uglier than it needs to be, Sadie. It's decided."

Metal clinked, and two men stepped forward holding a long metal chain.

"I hate doing this, Sadie, but I know you. For everyone's safety, we gotta lock you up. It's only until we're sure you three aren't going to try anything, but like I said — we can't let you leave."

39

WON'T THAT KILL THEM?

Matt Browner

Matt spent the whole night hiding in the back of the shed. He didn't hear anything besides bugs and cicadas. But there wasn't any way he would go outside until daylight. Not with a pack of bone wolves outside.

Matt stood and stretched as the first rays of light spilled over the trees. His head ached, his back hurt worse, and he needed a large drink of water. He tried the door. It wouldn't open. He set his shoulder against it and pushed. Metal creaked and groaned. He shoved harder. The door flew open, and he stumbled out. His boots slipped on the grass, slick with dew. He slid sideways and pitched forward, landing hard on his stomach.

Laying in the dirt, he quickly lifted his head and scanned the yard for any sign of the wolves. The grass swayed in the breeze, and birds chirped as they hopped along the back-porch railing.

A faint mechanical reverberation echoed off the hills. Matt jogged around the house and stared toward the road. Dust rose in the distance. The rumble of two small engines grew louder. They could be motorcycles or side-by-sides. Whichever they were, they were coming here.

Matt stared at the space beneath the front porch. Deciding discretion was the better part of valor, he rushed over and crawled under it.

Two four-wheelers with a man apiece riding them pulled down the driveway and stopped out front.

Matt crept backward, hiding in the shadows.

"Ben! Ben!" one man yelled as they both ran onto the porch.

The men stomped around inside and suddenly dashed back onto the front porch.

"I'm telling you, a bone wolf got him! You saw the fur stuck on the kitchen window."

The other man cussed. "What do we do now? Do you think he's still alive? Maybe we should look for him?"

"Hell no. They ate him. We gotta get back and tell the others."

"Ben's the only one who knows how to use the welding gear. How else are we gonna get in the room?"

"I vote that we smoke them out." Their boots crunched the gravel as they ran back to the four-wheelers.

"Won't that kill them?"

"No. It'll be like tear gas. The cops use that because it doesn't kill people."

"But what about the baby?"

"They shoulda thought of that before. It don't matter anyway. All of those broads are gonna wish they'd never been born."

Matt's eyes widened. Was he talking about the missing women? There was a chance that Betsy and the other women could be alive.

Engines rumbled to life.

Matt needed to stop them. He crawled forward, drawing his pistol.

In a cloud of dust, the men raced out of the yard and down the driveway.

"No, no!!" Matt swore as he stood up, and his back scraped along the wooded porch. He ran forward, but they'd already driven out of sight. There wasn't any way he could catch them. Unless...

Sprinting to the backyard, he yanked the bent

doors of the shed open. He stepped over the tarps and tugged the nearest bicycle out. It had been years since he had ridden, but he was soon peddling down the driveway just like the old saying.

The sound of the four-wheelers hummed on the right — from Thompson Road. Matt gripped the handlebars tighter and peddled as fast as he could in that direction. The road gradually dipped down as it descended into another holler. He continued to gain speed until the bike began to shake. He stopped peddling and let gravity shoot him forward.

Around the bend and over the trees on the left, a trail of dust rose high into the air. There weren't any homes on that side of the hill, only two businesses — Medley Gravel and Odessa Kennels.

Zipping downhill, Matt rounded the corner. He couldn't hear the engines anymore, and the road flattened out. Tall trees towered over him, and he could no longer see the dust trail. The momentum propelling the bicycle slowed, and he was soon huffing and puffing as he peddled madly.

The road curved once again, and a gravel driveway came into view. Matt stopped at the peeling, faded sign for Odessa Kennels — a giant fiberglass statue of a German Shepherd.

Sweat stuck the bandages to his head and soaked his shirt to his back. He was so wet it felt like he'd fallen in a pool with his clothes on. Wiping his face with his shirt, he stared down at the gravel. Many fresh sets of tire tracks cut into the driveway.

Matt got off the bike, wheeled it over, and laid it behind the dog statue. He had no water and twelve bullets. Crouching in the brush, he debated about returning to town for backup. Those men had said they would try to smoke the women out. Were they trapped someplace? And with a baby?

He glanced down at the star on his chest. Everyone in town thought he shouldn't be the one wearing it. He agreed. But when the Mayor pinned it on, he swore he'd do his best to uphold the law and protect the citizens.

Matt drew his gun. He'd never forgive himself if he did nothing and the baby was hurt — or worse. He rose and started to make his way through the woods. He'd be outnumbered and outgunned, but he had no choice. Sometimes you need to do the things you fear — even if it gets you killed.

40

BURNING UP

Amos Yoder

Amos awoke in the chair with someone shaking him awake. He gulped in air and rubbed his eyes.

"Ani's burning up, Amos." Sarah's voice was tight with concern. "Her fever is bad and getting worse. We need to get her to the doctor's now."

"We'll take the gurney. We can wheel her out most of the way."

Ani moaned. Her eyes fluttered open, and she looked up at Amos. Her once bright blue eyes were hazy. They flickered like a pilot light going out and turned a dark hazel before she closed them.

Amos moved to the head of the gurney and wheeled it out the door and into the corridor. With

Sarah following, he hurried down the hallway. They turned left, and the overhead lights snapped off, plunging them into pitch dark.

Sarah gasped.

"It's all right," Amos reassured her as he fumbled along the wall, his hand traveling along the rough cement. "The generator stopped, but there's an emergency light up here."

His finger touched the metal siding of a box, and he opened the door. He felt the shaft of a fire axe, the side of an extinguisher, and the small cylinder he was searching for.

The emergency flare sparked to life in his hand, casting the hallway in a red glow. He peered inside the box for another flare, but there was only the one.

Down the hallway, a light turned on and seeped out from underneath a door.

"That's Jesse," Amos explained. "Wait in the hallway there for me. Push the gurney."

"What?" Sarah's eyes were wide. "Where are you going?"

"We must have tripped a breaker. I gave Jesse a battery lantern in case of a power failure, but it won't last more than a couple of hours. I can't leave him in the dark while we take Ani to the doctor's."

"I'm frightened, Amos."

Amos reached back into the emergency box, removed the fire axe, and handed it to Sarah. The daughter of a lumberjack, Sarah had won the axe throw at the country fair three times before they married. "You won't need it but take it. I'll be right back."

"Please hurry. Something feels so wrong." Sarah held the axe and began reciting the Lord's Prayer.

Amos clutched the flare tightly as he hurried down the hallway toward the sound of the rushing water. He hoped getting the lights working was a simple fix, like flipping a breaker. The thought of Jesse alone in pitch darkness while they took Ani to town seemed so wrong. But what else could he do? Jesse refused to leave the bunker.

His mind raced with how he was going to explain Ani to everyone. Her being there would start a panic. And now that Fen and Nicholi fled with the children, who knows what Frank Pickett would do.

The sound of the river grew louder, but some other sounds mixed with it. Amos couldn't place it.

Click. Click.

Sweat rolled down Amos's back. He licked his dry lips. His hand shook. He raised his arm, sending the flare's glow dancing off the walls.

Click. Click.

Had a piece broken in the generator?

Amos strained to make sense of the sound. It wasn't metal, and it wasn't one sound either. Several clicks joined quickly together to form the noise he heard. But what caused it?

Like flames from a campfire, the light for the flare shimmered and moved along the wall as he walked forward.

The clicking stopped.

Amos peered into the dark at the end of the hall.

Somewhere in the shadows, something moved closer.

41

WHAT SMELLS?

Cain Haight

Less than an hour after getting the dynamite, we're packed and I'm lugging two packs on my back. One's loaded with supplies, and the other is filled with explosives. Adam leads me across the yard to a well, covered with an old, metal square plate. Adam keeps looking over his shoulder at Pete grazing in the side yard.

"The Army will help me return and get him, won't they?" He asks for the fourth time.

If I had to lay odds on men risking their lives to come all the way here for a horse, I'd say there wasn't a chance of that happening. But the old guy really seems to care about Pete, so I can't tell him the truth. Still, I hate liars so I don't say anything.

"Ed's grandfather is the one who found this entrance to the caves. He was digging a well and nearly killed himself falling in. I used to go caving with Ed's father, Jim, when we were kids." He holds up a yellowed sheet of paper. "I found Jim's map when I was doing inventory."

"Are you going to be all right getting to the wall?"

"I'm not that old." Adam stopped beside the well. "I'll make it."

I slide the steel plate off while Adam puts on a headlamp. He grins and holds another out to me. I know they're practical, but I feel like an idiot as I slip the wide band over my head and flick on the light.

An iron ladder leading down is welded onto the side of the well.

"Jim's Mom was a worrier. She made his father install the ladder. If it were up to her, she'd have filled in the whole thing, but Jim was the type that would go looking for a new cave. And since this is Tennessee, you don't have to go far to find one. Jim's mom settled on a rule that we always had to tell her when and where we went caving."

I rig a rope onto the packs while Adam keeps

talking about using huge flashlights with big, heavy batteries.

"I'll go down and make sure everything's all right and then come back up," I say.

Adam grabs the side of the well. "I told you I'm not that old. There's no reason I can't go, and you lower the packs to me."

"Whatever." I give a one-shouldered shrug. How much trouble can he get in climbing down a ladder?

Adam flashes a big grin and puffs his chest up like I selected him for a moon launch. He rubs his hands together, cracks his knuckles, and goes over the side. Hand over hand, he starts his descent. He's about six rungs down when his foot slips. His light swings wildly back and forth. My breath hitches as I think he's gonna fall, but he manages to steady himself.

"The bars are slick," Adam says, his voice strained. "Watch your step."

I start pacing as I wait for him to reach the bottom. I'm surprised by how long it takes. Not that he's slow, but how deep the cave is. I'm glad I got a hundred feet of rope.

"Lower the pack!" Adam hollers up.

I lift the pack loaded with supplies over and feed it down. A few minutes later, the rope goes slack.

"Got it! Hoist it up!" Adam calls out.

I wince. Once again, he's forgotten the rule is silence. Whenever going into an unknown territory, I firmly believe in keeping quiet.

After gathering the rope, I secure the explosives and hoist them down. I go slow, more afraid of the pack catching onto something than anything else.

"Got it!" Adam shouts again.

Shaking my head, I grab the ladder's top rung and start down. The iron is cold and rusty but with a thin coat of slime. I've got to lock the heels of my boots against the bars to keep from slipping as I carefully descend.

Adam is busy checking his map as I drop down beside him. "A main tunnel runs pretty much straight to the wall. I think it was an underground stream bed that ran dry."

Gazing around, I agree with him. A limestone channel almost eight feet high and four feet wide runs into the darkness.

I move close and whisper. "Let's remember to keep our voices down. We don't know if anything is in here with us."

"Will do." Adam salutes.

I pick up the packs and try to hide my smile. From the excited grin on his face, you'd think he was a twelve-year-old Boy Scout working on his caving merit badge.

Adam lifts his chin. "Since I know these caves, it would be better if I lead the way."

"Sounds good. You take point." My quick agreement causes his mouth to open in surprise. "You're familiar with the layout, so it makes sense. But if I yell duck, you better duck."

Adam reaches for the pistol I gave him. "I have a gun."

"But you don't know how to shoot, so leave the shooting to me unless I tell you or you have to. Agreed?"

Adam nods.

"Lead the way, Arnie Saccnuson."

Adam's face lights up. "Journey to the Center of the Earth! Both Jim and I loved that Jules Verne book. I would pretend to be Otto and Jim would be Hans. You can be Otto's nephew Alex."

"Sure." I flash a crooked grin, not wanting to tell him I'd never read the book. As a kid, I'd seen the cartoon show, but only remembered the creepy bad guys.

Holding his lantern high, Adam leads us through the relatively dry cave. We go through a narrow corridor where we both have to stoop. It slowly curves back and forth like a lazy river until it opens into a larger cavern.

Light dances off the ceiling over thirty feet above. Besides an occasional loud drip, the cave is quiet. The air is colder but feels good in a strange way. Earthy.

Without checking the map in his hand, Adam keeps moving forward. The ground is surprisingly flat. The long, solid rock is worn smooth.

I smell the danger before I see anything.

Grabbing Adam by the arm, I pull him to a stop. "I smell a disturbance in the force."

His nose wrinkles. "That's not guano I'm smelling. Bat poop smells more acrid with a hint of ammonia."

"It smells like animal crap. I'm taking point." I say as I walk past him.

"Okay, but it gets really twisty up there. Lots of curves and forks. If I say stop, stop so I can check the map."

"That's fine. Tap my left or right shoulder if you want me to go that way. Tap my back twice if you want me to stop."

"Got it!" Adam gives me a thumbs up, the map crinkling in his hand.

I start forward with my shotgun raised. Something is down here with us, and I don't know what. Whatever it is, I hope it stays hidden in the dark.

We reach the end of the cavern, and the way turns back to a slowly winding tunnel. It's wide enough that Adam and I can walk side by side, but I keep him behind me. The dry river twists and turns and forks. Adam taps left or right and stops from time to time to check the map. We pass through a section so narrow I need to turn sideways to shuffle through. The pinch point is only ten feet long, but I'm soaked with sweat when I reach the other side.

Brushing the sweat from my brow with my sleeve, I fight back the wave of claustrophobia. Before I went into the Marines, I was approached by a Navy recruiter. He suggested I become a submariner. I told him where he could put that idea. I hate confined places, and the thought of being stuck under so much rock right now made my heart race and goosebumps rise on my arms. We reach a wider section, but my chest is still thumping like an old Chevy that needs a valve job.

I glance back at Adam and ask, "Did you hear about the two guys in the cave who found a bat?"

Adam's bushy white brows knit together, and he shakes his head.

"One of them says keep looking. If we find a baseball, we can take a break and play a game."

Adam's laughter is cut short by long nails scratching stone.

I swear. I broke my own rule.

Heavy steps fill the corridor. I raise the shotgun. The light from my headlamp gleams off two tiny black eyes and a bone-covered head. The mutant mole scurries forward with front paws the size of extra-large baseball mitts.

I pulled the trigger three times. Two slugs roar

out, followed by a flare. The slugs blow bits of bone off the creature's head, but the flare only bounces off and lands burning on the ground.

The mole stops three feet away from the fire and hisses.

"Run!" I turn and push Adam back the way we came.

The old man hustles forward. I think we have a chance of making it until Adam starts panting. He stumbles and grabs the wall to keep from falling. "You go ahead." He gasps.

"Just a little farther!"

Behind us, the glow fades and disappears as the flare goes out.

Bone claws on rock screech through the cave.

I grab Adam's arm. "We need to get to the narrow gap. It can't follow us through there."

Adam nods and starts moving again. He's soon gasping for air and slowing down again. In the light cast from his headlamp, I see the passage narrowing up ahead.

I turn and aim.

The mutant mole races out of the darkness. Its claws, each over a foot long, gleam like razors.

I fire two more shots.

My slugs hit their mark, but only to send bone chips flying. The impact barely slows the beast. I aim for a spot six feet in front of it and fire. The flare arches out, bounces off the floor, and flies over the creature.

I swear, spin on my heels and race for the gap.

Adam has already made it through. He's at the end and waving me on.

I don't need any encouragement as the mutant mole quickly gains on me. Turning sideways, I slip between the rocks and into the gap. My shirt catches on the stones, and all the buttons tear off and sail into the air.

Adam screams and stumbles backward.

The mole slams into the stone. Its spit splatters the side of my face. It shrieks and hisses.

I make it through and stop. My chest is all scratched up and bleeding, but I'm breathing. I stare into the black eyes glaring at me. Some scientists would have a field day examining this thing. Besides being a massive mutant mole, the bone on its head is a couple of inches thick. This thing is a breathing, digging tank.

It hisses, chomping the air and clawing the ground to get to me.

I raise the shotgun, point the barrel at its eye and pull the trigger.

The beast collapses onto the cave floor.

"Tell me there's another way around," I say.

Adam swallows, unable to take his eyes off the creature. "It almost got us."

"But it didn't. Is there another way around?"

Adam looks at the map and swallows again. "Yes, but it will set us back an hour."

"We can't lose that much time. We'll go over it." I draw my pistol and put four rounds into the mole's head. The last thing I want to happen when I crawl over its body would be if the beast was still alive and woke up when I was on it. "Are you ready?"

Adam is pale, but he nods. "Looks like we found what was making the smell. Glad it's dead."

"Me too," I say, keeping what I'm thinking to myself — Who said there's only one of these monsters down here?

42

THEY'RE BAD!

Bri Haight

Bri finished bailing out the canoe and dropped the can at her feet. Her shoulders burned, and her stomach hurt from bending over so much. On top of that, she was so hungry she'd even eat peas. They had paddled all night. The river widened until Bri could no longer see the banks on either side. Pretty lights gleamed far off. She wondered if they'd reached the lake Nicholi mentioned, but she wouldn't ask Fen. The mean woman rowed like she was possessed and hadn't said a word in hours.

The sun peaked over the trees. In the dawn light, the lake's waters sparkled all around her. Golds and whites twinkled like fireworks off the water. The lake was huge, but they were almost to the other side. Fen hurried, and soon the banks of the river closed in. Every once in a while, Bri heard something in the woods. Sometimes she'd see a bird or a squirrel, but none of the fierce creatures.

Bri stared at the homes as they passed. Most looked like no one lived in them anymore, but she wondered about a few. One had laundry outside, drying in the sun. She hoped people were there until she saw the back of the house. The windows were all smashed out, and there'd been a fire.

A big two-story farmhouse sat high on the bank on the left. An American and Tennessee State flag flapped in the breeze on poles in the front yard.

Bri's eyes widened.

A curtain in the center second-floor window moved. It wasn't like it was blown in the wind, but like someone pulled it to the side and peered out. The window was so dark she couldn't be sure, but someone might be in the house.

The side door banged open, and a man with a big beard ran out.

"Hey! Hey!" He shouted. "Stop! Hey, you! Over here!" Dressed in overalls, he raced across the yard, jumping, hooting, hollering, and waving his arms over his head. He was smiling so wide Bri could see his teeth from where she sat.

Nicholi pulled his paddle in and set it across the

gunwales. He glanced back. Fen nodded. The large Russian reached down for his rifle.

Bri leaped to her feet. The canoe rocked so much that she almost fell over the side. "They're bad! RUN! RUN!"

Fen swung her paddle around and struck Bri in the stomach. All of the air exploded out of Bri's mouth. She doubled over and fell onto her knees.

A shot rang out quickly, followed by another.

Bri peered over the side. There was no sign of the man.

"What's wrong with you?!" The man shouted from somewhere in the tall grass. "We're all in this together! We need to help one other, not kill each other!"

Nicholi scanned the yard with the scope of his rifle.

Fen whistled.

The giant Russian lowered his rifle and glared at her.

Fen pointed to the opposite riverbank.

Bri couldn't see anything. There were many trees and thick underbrush, but it all looked normal.

Something clicked and chittered. The sound rippled and grew into a river of noise. The bushes and trees shook. Leaves floated to the ground. A small gray animal hopped up on an old stump on the far bank. No larger than a fat squirrel, it had a thin, whip-like tail. It started chittering.

"Is that a monkey?" Bri wondered aloud.

Fen swore and started to paddle faster.

Dozens of other similar creatures hopped out of the brush. Like a flock of newborn chicks at the county fair, they stayed close together and moved as one. The first creature sat on its haunches, holding its hands in front of its chest like rabbits do. On the ends of its paws were long, bone-white claws. The creature opened its mouth and shrieked, revealing rows of sharp teeth.

Bri gasped.

"Get low," Fen said.

The chittering grew. The creatures ran along the bank, keeping pace with the canoes. They swung from the branches and scurried on the ground, clicking and chirping as they jumped and darted.

"What are those things?" Bri asked.

"Little demons. Bone rats. We're safe. The water is a natural barrier."

Nicholi pointed upriver. The forest thinned out, and a field with tall grass appeared.

Once the canoes passed the trees, the bone rats stopped at the edge of the field, bunching up. They appeared not to want to leave the safety of the woods.

A deep noise echoed out of the forest. The

sound was odd, like a low panting followed by a grunt. "Ummm! Ummm!"

Nicholi looked back at Fen and shrugged, opening his arms wide.

Fen shook her head.

"Ummm! Ummm!" Sounded again.

The bone rats in the rear darted forward, pushing the ones in front into the field. They disappeared into the long grass, fleeing whatever was behind them and making the noises. An enormous shadow lumbered out of the woods and vanished behind the undergrowth.

"Ummm! Ummm!" More throaty grunts sounded.

The chittering of the bone rats grew louder. The grass along the bank parted. The massive pack of rats tumbled down the bank and shrieked when they splashed in the water.

"Something is herding them," Fen said.

Bri opened her mouth, but the word *what* caught in her throat.

A gigantic black and white spiky bear lumbered out of the brush and stared at the canoe. It was way bigger than the black bear Bri saw in the backyard once. It was huge. Bigger than the polar bears at the zoo. The creature moved farther along the bank, slowly getting ahead of the canoes.

Three more bears joined the first. They all had a

similar form— black fur on their underbelly and faces and spiked bone on their backs, heads, and shoulders.

"Bears don't move in packs." Bri said. "Why are they?"

"They're not normal," Fen said, the rough edge absent from her tone. "They can't reach us."

"Can we move toward the other side — just in case?" Bri asked.

Fen nodded.

The bear in the center opened its mouth and grunted three times.

The bone rats chittered and pushed forward but bunched at the river's edge.

The bear roared.

The bone rats tried to flee, but the other bears blocked the way.

"See!" Fen smiled. "They won't willingly go in the water. We're safe."

The bear in the center reached down and scooped up a bone rat. It flung the creature toward Bri's canoe.

Bri screamed.

The rat flew over them so far it almost landed on the other bank. It plunked into the river and didn't come back up.

The bear flung another. It splashed a few feet short of the canoe, disappearing under the water.

Bri exhaled.

The rat's head broke the surface, and it swam straight toward them.

A gunshot rang out.

The rat jerked sideways and disappeared, leaving a red splotch staining the water.

"Ummm! Ummm!" All the bears howled and picked up rats.

Rats dotted the sky, tumbling end over end, but they all landed well in front of the canoes.

"Stupid American bears!" Nicholi laughed. "You missed!"

Bri stared at the river in front of them, and her eyes went wide. A dozen rats bobbed in the water, waiting for the canoes to reach them. "They're not stupid, and they didn't miss! Turn! Turn! We're heading right at them!"

Fen started paddling hard.

Nicholi did, too. But the Russian raced alongside them, using Fen and Bri's canoe as a shield.

THUNK!

A chunk of hard plastic broke off the front of Bri's canoe. A rat climbed onto the bow and hung there while its bony tail flashed like a whip and punched a hole in the side of the boat.

Fen grabbed Bri and jerked her toward the back of the canoe. Fen swung her paddle, slamming it into the bone rat. The creature shrieked as it sailed into the river.

Bri fell against the seat.

THUNK! THUNK! THUNK!

Three more rats appeared on the bow, their tails puncturing holes through the plastic.

Fen dropped her paddle and grabbed the shotgun.

Bri stuck her fingers in her ears. It didn't help quiet the noise much.

Rats screamed and flew into the water. A large portion of the canoe disappeared as well.

Bobbing in the water ahead, dozens of the floating creatures swam forward.

Fen grabbed the paddle and jammed it into Bri's hands, "You row, or we're both dead."

Bri took Fen's seat and paddled as fast as she could.

Nicholi's canoe was so far ahead that the Russian stopped rowing and turned to watch.

Fen ejected a magazine, slapped another in its place, and continued to fire.

The bears on the bank roared and flung more rats. But with all of the bears busy launching their friends into the river, the other rats fled. Soon, the bears were out of ammo.

Fen's shotgun clicked on an empty chamber. She

dropped it behind her, pulled out her pistol, and started shooting.

Water streamed through a dozen holes in the bow of the canoe. It sloshed over Bri's feet, steadily rising.

Fen reloaded. No rats clung to the boat, and the river around them was clear of the creatures. The woods were silent. Fen whistled and motioned to Nicholi to come back.

The Russian was far downstream, and it took a few minutes for him to return. His canoe appeared fine, but Fen's, while not sunk, was filled with water.

Nicholi frowned. "There is no bailing that out."

Fen nodded.

Nicholi's hand shot downward, his fingers closing on the grip of his pistol.

Bri watched in horror as the barrel of his gun cleared its holster.

Fen moved with the speed of lightning. The paddle in her hands sliced through the air and slammed against Nicholi's temple.

Nicholi's gun fired.

A piece of plastic next to Bri blasted off. It flew into the air and sliced her cheek.

Nicholi's head twisted to the right. He pitched backward and into the river.

"Grab his canoe!" Fen kicked Bri.

Bri fell forward and managed to get one hand onto the side of the other boat.

Fen crouched, her pistol sweeping over the water. Her gaze traveled up and down the river like a crane searching for a fish.

Bri hung onto the canoe with both hands. Her cheek stung and felt wet. She rubbed her face on the back of her arm. Blood smeared her skin.

A splash upstream made them turn. Nicholi's head broke the surface for a moment before he disappeared again.

Fen unloaded her pistol at the spot.

Bri held onto the other canoe with both hands and stared down at Jacob, still unconscious on the floor.

What had they done to him?

After another minute, Nicholi's head appeared and then vanished again.

"The bears will finish him," Fen said as she stepped into the other canoe.

Once she was in, Bri started to climb over.

Fen aimed her gun at Bri's chest.

Bri froze.

Fen's eyes narrowed.

Bri swallowed. "I can help paddle."

Fen's cold eyes bore into her. Her lips pressed together, and she holstered her gun. "Get in."

Bri exhaled and hurried to the front seat. She

picked up a paddle and started rowing despite her aching arms. Noises behind her made Bri glance over her shoulder.

Fen had pulled Jacob into a sitting position, trying to tug something over his head.

“Leave him alone!” Bri spun around, lifting her oar over her head, and froze.

Fen wasn’t hurting Jacob. She was putting a life preserver on him. “This boy is very important. I cannot let anything happen to him. You are expendable. I suggest you sit down and paddle.”

Bri was going to apologize until Fen said the thing about being expendable. She wasn’t sure exactly what it meant, but it sounded like Fen was thinking of tossing her overboard again.

As they continued downriver, something moved on the bank to their right. The sun was behind whatever it was, so she could only see the silhouette.

It was a man. He stood on a rock ledge watching them.

Bri looked away. She didn’t know why, but the sight of the man scared her more than the bears did.

43

I'LL DO WORSE

Betsy Weber

Betsy woke with a start.

"Water," Lonnie whispered. "Please."

Betsy rose from the canvas tarps she'd spread on the floor as a mattress and stretched. Camila slept in the bed with Gaby curled up next to her. The baby lay in the impromptu bassinet they'd made from a storage box. From the snoring from the sleeping bag, Betsy assumed Nancy was finally getting well-deserved rest.

Crossing over to the nearest shelf, Betsy grabbed a bottle of water. Their guards had done a poor job of searching the shelves or were stupid for setting the women up in here. While searching for medical supplies, Betsy had located a pallet of water and protein bars. It would be a dull meal, but they could hold out for months.

Betsy brought a chair and set it down in front of Lonnie. If they spoke quietly, they wouldn't wake the women. "Keep your voice down." She opened the bottle and held it up to his mouth.

Spilling a lot of the water down his chin, Lonnie drank like a man lost in the desert for a week. Betsy kept tilting the bottle back, but soon it was empty.

"Thank you. Can I have some more?"

"Later. Who else is out there?"

Lonnie swallowed.

Betsy set the bottle on the floor as white-hot rage flared to life deep inside her. Her lip curled, and the tightening of her chest forced her breath to hiss between her teeth.

Lonnie stared down at the floor. "I didn't kill Carl. Or the others. I swear."

Betsy leaned forward in the chair. She reached out her hand, letting it hover over Lonnie's broken arm. The skin on his wrist was swollen, bruised, and disfigured. "I don't believe you." She glanced over at the young girl sitting on the bed. "You know what they did to Gaby."

"They were going to take her whole hand! I talked them out of it."

"Lower your voice." Betsy swallowed. As she

stared into Lonnie's eyes filled with fear, she felt no pity or mercy. There was only hate. What happened to her? "Nazis used similar excuses, and I don't have the stomach or the time to listen to you. Neither do you."

Lonnie's face contorted in puzzlement.

"You have a compound fracture. It's bleeding underneath the skin. You'll lose the arm if I don't get you to your father soon. Longer, you'll be dead."

Lonnie groaned at the mention of his arm and glanced around the room. He tilted his head to the sleeping bag where Nancy lay unseen inside, snoring. "Who's the guy who attacked me?"

"I broke your arm."

Lonnie's eyes widened in disbelief. "You? Why?"

"Are you really that stupid?" Betsy's voice erupted in a strangled whisper. "You killed our husbands and kidnapped us. You mutilated a little girl."

"I didn't know they were going to do any of that."

"I don't care."

"Do you have any medicine? It hurts really bad."

Betsy retrieved the bottle of vodka and filled up his empty water bottle. She gave him a long sip.

Lonnie sputtered and coughed, but pressed his mouth against his chest to keep the noise down.

"Who else is involved? Your father?"

Lonnie shook his head. "No. I can't tell you. They'll kill me."

"I'll do worse," Betsy held the bottle up and let him take a longer gulp." "Who? I already know about Brad Moore."

Lonnie's eyes searched hers. He licked his lip, coughed, then nodded.

"Names," Betsy said, holding the bottle up again.

Lonnie sipped this time, but Betsy raised the bottle higher, forcing him to take another large gulp.

He coughed into his shirt and shook his head. "Some of the guys from the business center. Friends. It got outta hand."

Betsy's reached out and laid her fingertips on the purplish skin of Lonnie's arm. It was hot. She pressed down slightly.

Lonnie's lips pulled back, and he grimaced.

"Sorry," Betsy whispered. "I just wanted to check."

"That's okay." Lonnie exhaled, gulping in air.

"If you don't start telling me names, the next time, I'll squeeze your wrist."

Lonnie lowered his head. Tears rimmed his eyes. "Owen Lewis, Alan Copeland, Darrell Johnson, Terry Alexander, Ben Pickett and Jeff Wheeler."

"Ten, including you and Brad?"

Lonnie nodded. "It was only supposed to be for supplies. We were going to start over."

"Start what over?"

"The world. The Dark changed things. It mutated the wolves. What about man? What does it do to us?" He eyed the bottle with the vodka.

Betsy gave him another long sip. It was almost gone, so she filled it up again.

"The sun is angry. We need to move from the dark to the light. That's why we wear our masks."

"Yours is black. Others have...," Betsy swallowed down her disgust, "gold."

"I haven't made a sacrifice."

Betsy's throat tightened like a boa constrictor coiled around it and squeezed. "A sacrifice?"

"The sun is angry with man. It needs to be appeased."

Betsy forced air into her lungs. "That's why they murdered my husband? As a sacrifice to the sun?"

Lonnie nodded. "Can I have some more?" His head wobbled as he nodded to the bottle. "Please?"

Betsy rose. She crossed over to the table and picked up the scissors. Nancy had used them to cut the newborn's umbilical cord. Betsy gripped them tightly in her hand. She'd use them to end Lonnie's miserable life.

Lonnie smiled as she walked back over to him. "I'm glad you understand. I wouldn't hurt anyone. And you're right. I should have stopped them. I know that now. I can talk to them."

Betsy kept the scissors pressed against her thigh,

hiding them from his sight. She stopped in front of his chair and stared into his eyes. "I'm glad you realize that, Lonnie. But you know what? Sometimes, there does need to be a sacrifice. An eye for an eye. A life for a life."

Lonnie shook his head. "That's what they say. They're wrong. No one else has to die."

"Someone does." Betsy smiled.

"No." Gaby said as she grabbed Betsy's wrist. "You can't."

Betsy flinched as she felt the stubs of the young girl's missing fingers touch her skin. "They killed my husband. Your father. Look what they did to your hand!"

Gaby's eyes moistened, and she closed them. "If you kill him, you'll be no better."

"Do it, Betsy!" Camila shouted from the bed. "He deserves to die."

"No, Momma!" Gaby sobbed.

Nancy's head appeared as she wriggled out of the sleeping bag.

"She's a child." Camila continued. "She doesn't understand. You can't let him live. Not after what he's done."

"I didn't kill anyone!" Lonnie struggled against his bonds. "I didn't know. I swear I didn't know!" He shouted.

CLANG!

A heavy blow rang off the steel door. "Good morning, Ladies!" The man shouted. "I've got a deal for you. You open that door, or we're gonna kill Nancy's brother."

"He's serious, Nancy!" Gary shouted. "They'll kill me unless you open the door."

"GO AHEAD!" Nancy shrieked as she picked up the closest thing to her, a protein bar, and flung it at the door. It hit with a less-than-dramatic crunch and fell to the floor. "Us being trapped in here is all his fault!"

"No!" Gary shouted. "She doesn't mean that. You don't mean that, Nancy. Tell them!"

"I mean every freaking word!" Nancy stormed to the door. "Have at it. If I were out there, I'd kill him myself."

"NO!" Lonnie screamed. "Don't do it, Alan. This has gone too far. It has to end."

Silence filled the room.

Betsy closed her eyes. Lonnie didn't realize it, but he'd just doomed them all. Alan Copeland could never let the women go now. Not when they knew who he was.

"Hey!" Lonnie shouted. "Can you hear me? This has to stop. Too many people have been hurt. Let's just end this."

Betsy listened as the people in the hallway walked away without saying anything.

"They're going think about it." Lonnie smiled. "See? I told you. We can work this out. See?"

Gaby smiled, but Nancy, Camila, and Betsy exchanged knowing glances. They all realized what happened. There would be no negotiation. They were trapped in a steel box, and it was only a matter of time before their supplies would run out.

Now, what would they do?

44

KING OF THE FOOLS

Cain Haight

It's slow going getting to the end of the cave. The way is easy, but Adam needs to stop every fifteen minutes to catch his breath. He gave up apologizing, and I quit trying to make him feel better. He's old and has been stuck in a house for a year where the most exercise he'd get was sitting on the porch. I'm not one for obeying too many of man's laws, but I try to follow the golden rule — do unto others as you'd like to be treated. And one day, I might be old too.

Maybe.

I rub my face and shake my head. The stink from the mutant mole clings to my clothes.

Who am I kidding? How long will a guy like me live if I don't die rescuing Bri?

"We're almost there," Adam's hands shake as he looks at the map. "Sorry it's taking us so long."

"Stop apologizing for helping me get to my little girl." I take a swig of water. "I appreciate you coming."

Adam nods. "I understand. Viv and I didn't have any of our own. Lots of nieces and nephews. We used to volunteer at West Creek. That's our Church. I hope some folks made it there." His lips press together, and the map crumples up in his grip. "I wonder if the folks at the army base know what happened. If it matters."

"Why wouldn't it matter?"

"Everything is meaningless. Completely meaningless, like chasing the wind. Have you ever read Ecclesiastes?"

"I kind of stick to the words written in red."

"The wisest man on earth wrote Ecclesiastes."

"I don't mean any offense by this," I take another swig of water and wipe my mouth with the back of my hand. "But I got a theory about that. Solomon was the wisest man that ever lived. People are stupid. So that makes Solomon king of the fools. That's not saying much. Besides, I think Solomon's point was that trying to control your life is pointless — but life isn't."

"You sound like my Viv. She'd always say, you can make your plans, but God's in control."

I stuff my water bottle back in my pack and sling it over my shoulder. "Let's hope God is okay with Jericho part two."

Adam laughed. "With a name like Cain, I'm surprised you know so much about the Bible."

"You and me both."

We start walking, our lights bouncing off the rocks. Besides the sounds we're making, it's silent. I don't even hear water dripping.

The path dips down and opens into another big chamber. This one is two stories tall, but a cement wall blocks off the end. We approach it, walking side by side. The cement portion rises about twelve feet before it hits the natural rocks of the cave.

"This is poured cement." I lay my hand on the cold surface. "It has to be reinforced with rebar."

"Can we blow it open?" Adam sits on a large boulder.

I set the bag of dynamite down and give a wink. "Blowing a hole in the wall isn't what I'm worried about. Bringing the cave down on our heads is, so I'm gonna set off a test charge."

Adam's wide eyes shine in the darkness. "That's smart."

"I don't know. If other mole creatures are down

here, an explosion might be like ringing the dinner bell."

"I've been thinking about that." Adam stares into my eyes. "I need you to promise me something, Cain. If another one of those things comes after us, don't wait for me. You take off. I'll only slow you down."

I rub my hand down my face. "If I didn't like you so much, Adam, I'd break your nose for insulting me like that."

"What?! I didn't mean any insult."

"I'm a Marine. I don't run and leave someone to fight my fight by themselves."

Adam's mouth opens and closes a couple of times. Finally, he nods.

I know exactly what he meant, but don't say anything. I'd rather have him think I'm a little ticked off, so he doesn't bring it up again. In the end, he's right. He'll slow us both down and get us both killed. But there are some things worse than death. Running away and leaving a friend to die is one of them.

I move to the middle of the wall and pull the large hammer and cold chisel out. Each blow sends a metal echo ringing through the cavern, but the cement chips quickly. In a couple of minutes, I've got a big enough hole to place a stick of dynamite. Lighting the end, I dash back behind the boulder and crouch beside Adam.

"Did you only use one stick?" Adam asked.

"One stick will blow a small tree stump out of the ground. Let's see what it does to the wall."

Like little kids lighting off fireworks, we stick our fingers in our ears and wait. I'm starting to think something went wrong when it blows. The huge boom sends a shockwave through my chest, and a cloud of dust sweeps over us.

"That wasn't too bad." I smile as I wave away the dust.

Adam is as pale as a polar bear and shaking so much that the light on his head sparkles like a disco ball.

"Sorry," I mutter. "I must be used to stuff going boom."

"I'm glad you didn't listen to me and only used one stick."

I stand up and shine my light against the wall. There's a big pile of cement at the base, but instead of peering through to the other side of the cavern, the headlight beam gleams off metal. Confused, I march forward with Adam following me.

The dynamite blew a hole big enough for a man to fit through the now-exposed rebar, but we weren't going anywhere. On the other side of the concrete wall was a second wall. I tap it with the barrel of my shotgun, and a metallic ring echoes through the cavern.

"What in tarnation is that?" Adam asks.

"It's a steel wall." I shine my light on a series of numbers and symbols stamped on the metal. "The quarry didn't put up this wall. Do you see that stamp? That's the Army Core of Engineers. This thing is military."

"But we're still a long way from the base."

"You said the government shut down the quarry years ago, right?"

Adam nods. "But why would they put up a steel wall?"

"That doesn't matter. Is there another way around?"

"No."

45

HELLSPAWN

Amos Yoder

Amos's hand shook as he raised the flare higher.

Click. Click. Click.

The sound drew closer. The shadow at the end of the hallway darkened and moved. A dank smell burned his nose.

Amos stepped back.

A huge creature scrambled out of the darkness. The massive beast stood five feet high at the shoulder. Fine white fur covered its body. It didn't appear to have eyes or ears — at least none were visible. Paws the size of wide lawn rakes ended in razor-sharp claws that scratched the cement as it lumbered toward him.

"Back!" Amos raised the flare above his head.

The monster hissed. Its nose flared. The long tentacle-like appendages attached to its face undulated and whipped the air.

Amos screamed as he heaved the flare at the beast. It landed against the creature's shoulder, the fine fur bursting into flame.

Deafening shrieks filled the corridor. The beast rolled as it tried to extinguish the fire. The cinderblock walls splintered and cracked as it smashed into them. Dust filled the hallway.

Amos sprinted down the hall, the glow from the fire behind him casting faint shadows along the walls. He dashed past the intersection leading to his wife, praying she didn't try to come to his aide.

Claws clicked behind him. The light of the fire brightened. The creature was coming after him.

Amos shoved the first door on the left open — a motion light in the ceiling flicked on. The small room contained dozens of closed metal lockers. Yanking the closest door open, he ripped the first M16 he found off the rack.

It had been years since he'd fired one and vowed never to again. But this was different. He was no longer in the Army, and it was no man who was coming to kill him.

The creature appeared in the doorway. Patches

of hair had burned off, revealing scaly, bone-white skin.

Amos fired in bursts, aiming for the head.

The monster's left claw tore through the door-frame and the cement wall. Ceiling tiles crashed to the floor. Dust blinded him, but he kept firing.

The creature lurched away, smashing through the wall of the other room and disappearing over the rubble and into the darkness.

Amos grabbed another locker door. It opened an inch, the light inside clicking on before a chunk of cement stuck beneath it. Kicking the rocks away with his boot, he pried the door open, grabbed spare magazines, and stuffed them into his overalls. He reached up, grabbed the light, and broke it off.

Somewhere in the distance, the sound of the beast digging rumbled through the complex.

Amos raced down the hallway and returned to the other hallway and Sarah.

"Oh, Amos!" She cried. Her face was wet with tears. "What was that? Is that a gun?"

"We have to go. GO!"

Sarah pushed the gurney, and Amos covered their backs. When they reached Jesse's door, Amos stopped.

"I have to get Jesse." He said.

"But you said he wouldn't leave."

"He doesn't have a choice. We have to take him with us."

Amos opened the door.

Jesse sat in the corner, his back pressed against the wall. "They're here, aren't they?"

Amos nodded.

Jesse darted forward on his hands and knees and began crawling under the bed.

Sarah pushed past Amos and grabbed Jesse by his ankles. Like a mother dragging a wayward child from his hiding spot, she pulled him to the center of the room. "Stop that this instant, young man! You need to help me get this woman to safety. That is the behavior your mother would expect. Do you understand me?"

Amos's mouth fell open when Jesse scrambled to his feet and nodded. "Yes, ma'am."

Sarah grabbed his wrist and pulled him into the hallway. "Now help me push the gurney."

Amos took up a position behind them as they dashed down the hallway. He thought of different supplies they might need in every room they passed, but there was no time to get to them. That creature may come back.

"Amos!" Sarah yelled.

They'd reached the bridge spanning the river, and the gurney was too wide to fit.

Amos thought about handing the M16 to Sarah, but she had no idea how to fire a gun, and he doubted the devout woman would, even if that Hell spawn came after them.

"Excuse me, Mrs. Yoder." Jesse wrapped Ani in the sheets and picked her up. "I've got her."

The hallway wall to the room they'd just passed on the right shattered as a beast burst through the cinder blocks.

Amos thought it was the same creature, but this one's fur wasn't burnt, and its head was covered with bone scales. It lacked the long trunk the other monster had, and this one's gray eyes were large and visible. It marched forward, the metal railings of the bridge snapping off as it came.

Amos began firing in bursts as he backed up onto the bridge. With each press of his finger, lead spewed out of the barrel, and bright yellow and red flames danced on the water.

Each blast slowed the beast, but it didn't stop. It kept its head down, the bullets pinging off the plates on its skull.

Amos ripped a magazine out, letting it fall to the water beneath the grids with a splash, and slapped another in its place.

The monster lunged. Its enormous paw cut through the air. Its claws sliced the metal of the bridge.

The bridge buckled and snapped.

Amos fell backward, the M16 tumbling from his hand as he grabbed a bent banister.

The monster clung to the wall. It scurried forward. Its gray eyes sparkled.

Without his gun, Amos was helpless. He lay on the edge of the broken bridge and stared at the beast.

The creature lifted its head. It opened a curved, cruel mouth, revealing rows of sharp teeth, each as large as a knife.

Behind him, footsteps echoed off the bridge. Sarah yelled, but her cry wasn't one of terror — it was a battle cry.

He glanced back.

His wife charged forward, the fire axe gripped in her hands. Raising the weapon over her head, she planted her right foot. Her body arched forward. The axe flew from her grip. It spun through the air and struck the beast in the roof of its open mouth.

Shrieking and gagging, the creature dropped from the wall and crashed into the river.

Sarah rushed over, bent down, and seized him by the beard.

The pain of her yanking him up by his facial hair inspired him to scramble to his feet even faster.

Together, they dashed down the narrow corridor.

"How is this possible?" Sarah cried. "What happened to the barrier?"

Dread slammed down on Amos like a sledgehammer to his chest. The creatures had crossed the barrier. How long would it be before all of Ridgecrest fell?

46

SHUT UP, YOU BABY

Mercy Yoder

Mercy stood up. She didn't know how to fight, but she wouldn't let these men stop her from getting to those children. From the shifty way D had been acting, she hadn't expected any help from him, but she never thought he'd say they couldn't leave. Nor did she think that Sadie and Lucy would take the news sitting down. But that's literally what they were doing. Lucy sat on the floor with her blankets pulled up in her lap, and Sadie lay next to her, holding her pillow.

"I'm sorry about this, Sadie," D said. "But it's for the best."

Sadie sat up straighter. "So now you're going to chain us up like dogs?"

D stepped forward. "Please try to understand. Look, I know you want to help those kids, but there's no way they're still alive. All you're going to do is get yourself killed and us too."

Lucy jumped to her feet, pulling a boxy gun out from underneath her blankets. "DON'T MOVE!" She screamed.

"That's my P90!" D shouted, his face turning a splotchy red.

Sadie drew a gigantic silver pistol and aimed it at D. "That *was* your machine gun. Now tell your group of spineless sissies to stand down, or I'll kill you. Hands up."

"No one moves!" D shouted. "They'll do it."

Everyone froze.

Lucy menacingly waved the weapon around the room. Her eyes blazed, and her lips were pulled back so far that both rows of her teeth were visible.

"Mercy," Sadie motioned her over. "Help me up."

"Don't do this, Sadie." D pleaded. "You can't even walk."

Mercy helped Sadie to her feet.

"I can walk fine." Sadie pushed her empty pillowcase into Mercy's hands. "Everyone drop your guns in the bag. The first one of you that twitches dies, and D is next." She placed a hand on Mercy's shoulder and nudged her forward.

Mercy held out the bag as she circled the room. She didn't know what kind of gun Lucy held, but whatever it was, it scared the men. Only a few carried pistols and they all placed them in the bag.

"Move away from the door!" Lucy ordered.

The men parted out of the way.

Sadie pointed at D. "You step out first. Mercy. Take the chain."

Holding the bag in one hand, Mercy moved toward one of the men holding the chain.

He lunged forward and grabbed Mercy's wrist, which held the pillowcase.

Mercy screamed as the man jerked her arm. She pitched forward and slammed against him. Panic and pain shot through her. A fear she'd never known seized her. If this man got a hold of these guns....

The man yanked on the bag, but she refused to let go. He grabbed her other hand.

With both of her wrists trapped, Mercy shrieked and did the only thing that came to her terrified mind — she opened her mouth and bit him in the neck.

Screaming, the man let go of her arms and pushed her away.

A thunderous roar boomed through the room.

Lucy fired a burst from her gun into the ceiling, sending shiny bullet casings flying upward as chunks of wood and dust rained down.

D held his hands over his head and yelled, "I'll kill the next one of you idiots myself who try something stupid!"

Mercy wiped her mouth with the back of her hand. She picked the chain off the floor, then hurried to the door.

Sadie pushed D out, and Lucy followed, keeping her gun aimed at the men inside.

"Close the door and use that chain to lock it," Sadie said.

Mercy wrapped the chain around the handle and then around the banister.

"Lucy, you take the rear. Get moving, D," Sadie ordered.

D trudged down one dock until they reached a fork. Sadie motioned him to the left. Behind them, the men started kicking at the locked door.

Sadie jammed her gun into the small of D's back. "Stop. Hands up."

D paled. "Hold on, Sadie! Don't kill me!"

"Shut up, you baby." Sadie snapped as she yanked the large knife out of the sheath on D's belt. She handed the weapon to Mercy. "Cut the ropes on the boats on either side and behind us."

"That'll take too long," Lucy said, raising her

gun. She fired three bursts, and the large ropes securing the boats fell into the water.

"Move!" Sadie pushed D forward again. "And stop wasting ammo."

"I have two more magazines," Lucy said. "Besides, I wanted to remind the guys back there that I have a machine gun."

The four of them made their way to a large houseboat on the edge of the floating island.

"Cut the ropes, Mercy. There's one here and one at the end of the green pole," Sadie said, then motioned for D to go inside.

It took Mercy a few minutes to cut the thick ropes. Adding to her frustration, Lucy stood watching her, impatiently tapping her foot the entire time.

A big engine sputtered and started. The boat shook, and black smoke rose into the air.

Mercy and Lucy jogged to the stern. The boat bounced and jostled as someone steered it out from its berth.

Men shouted in the distance.

As they slowly sailed away, Mercy watched as men jumped into the water to catch the boats Lucy had freed.

"I'm going to keep watch out here," Lucy said. "Bring those guns into my mom."

Mercy nodded and carried the pillowcase inside.

Besides the four motorcycles filling the room, the houseboat looked like a little apartment. There was a living room, a bathroom, and a tiny kitchen.

Mercy froze. Sitting in a leather chair with a drink in his hand was D. Sadie was nowhere in sight. Mercy reached into the pillowcase and felt around for a gun.

"Before you shoot me, I'd talk to Sadie," D said. "She'll explain everything to you."

"Where is she?"

"On the upper deck driving the ship. The stairs are around the corner."

Holding the pillowcase tightly, Mercy hurried over and climbed the stairs. The boat swayed, and she grabbed the railing until she reached the top deck.

Sadie was crouched behind a steering wheel. "Stay low in case one of the morons back there tries to take a potshot."

Mercy squatted. "That man D is alone downstairs. Do you want Lucy to guard him?"

Sadie shook her head. Sweat beaded her brow, and her lips pressed together in a tight line. "Don't worry about D. He's all right. He may be the leader, but everyone else outvoted him and said we couldn't leave. He's the one who tipped me off to what the others were planning to do."

Mercy inhaled sharply and nodded. Sadie must

have had her reasons for not filling Mercy in on the plan but being left out still stung.

As if reading her mind, Sadie said, "There wasn't any way to tell you. People were listening. I'm sorry. You did great. You surprised me by taking a bite out of Bill."

Mercy wiped her mouth with the back of her hand. "It's all I could think of. Are we going to head downriver in this?"

"It's too big. And there isn't enough time. After we arrived, a lookout saw a canoe headed toward the base."

"One canoe?" Mercy's throat tightened. "Did he see who was in it?"

"A short person and a child. They were too far away to see details."

Mercy took three deep breaths to calm down, but they weren't helping.

"Don't start freaking out. The canoe was on the horizon. The other could have been out of sight, or the lookout didn't see it." Sadie frowned. "I think D's helped as much as he's going to. I don't know what they went through, but those men are a shell of the guys I knew. Trust me, it would be better if we let him take the boat back."

"How will we catch up with Fen if we don't have a boat?"

Sadie grinned. "We ride."

47

IT'S A TRICK

Betsy Weber

Betsy stared at Lonnie Harmon, passed out in the chair. Drool ran out of his mouth and onto his shirt. If it hadn't been for Gaby, she would have killed him.

"If you're not going to stab him, give me the scissors, and I'll do it," Camila said. She was sitting in bed, propped up by tarps. Her words of vengeance seemed so out of place with her newborn son in her arms.

Betsy shook her head. "Gaby is right. We'll bring him back to town and have a trial. The people need to know who was involved."

"They can't let us go," Nancy sat in the chair beside the bed. She held her head in her hands and didn't look up as she spoke. "We know who they are. We're trapped."

"We are," Betsy admitted. "But think about this. Someone has to be looking for us. And now that Lonnie is missing, his father will start a bigger search."

Nancy looked up hopefully. "If Dr. Harmon starts searching, he'll get others involved."

Betsy nodded. "They'll look in every building. They'll find us."

"But how long will that take?" Camila asked. "We could be here for days. Weeks."

"So what? We have food and water. We're safe." Betsy said.

The shelves rattled, and Betsy's legs shook. She glanced down at her feet. Another tremor rippled through the building.

"Great time for an earthquake." Nancy sarcastically chuckled.

Gaby rushed to her mother's side and excitedly whispered.

"No keeping secrets," Nancy called over.

Camila tenderly brushed her daughter's cheek. "Gabriela thought it may be the beginning of a miracle. God used an earthquake to free Peter from jail."

Gaby smiled. Innocent hope radiated in her eyes.

Betsy closed her mouth, trapping the sarcastic comment about the Lord abandoning Ridgecrest and getting ready to destroy it but plunging it to the center of the earth. Who was she to steal the young girl's lollipop? She forced a smile. "I hope you're right, Gaby."

BLAM! BLAM!

Muffled gunfire sounded in the distance.

Everyone except Camila and Lonnie hurried over to the door and listened.

"Do you think someone found us already?" Gaby asked.

"Maybe the search party is having a shootout with the cult!" Nancy said.

"Shh!" Betsy listened for any noise in the hallway, but there was only silence.

RAT-A-TAT-TAT! RAT-A-TAT-TAT! BLAM! BLAM! RAT-A-TAT- TAT!

Machine gun fire echoed along with the sounds of gunfire.

Betsy's hope rose.

Lonnie opened his eyes and glanced around the room. "Is someone shooting?"

Camila sat up in bed. "I think the calvary has arrived! Looks like your dad came looking for you after all."

"My dad? DAD! DAD!" Lonnie shouted.

RAT-A-TAT-TAT! RAT- A—

The gunfire stopped.

Everyone waited.

Boots raced down the hallway. Someone pounded on the door. "Let us in!" A man shouted; his voice filled with terror.

"Nancy!" Gary screamed. "It's me! Open the door!"

Nancy reached for the steel baton, locking the door in place.

Betsy shook her head. "It's a trick."

"Nancy, please! I'm sorry! I'm so sorry!" Gary shouted.

RAT-A-TAT-TAT! RAT-A-TAT- TAT!

A machine gun fired from the other side of the door.

A man swore. "I'm out! I'm out!"

"Please? PLEASE!" Gary cried.

Click. Click. Click.

Something else echoed in the corridor.

Click. Click.

Silence.

The door shuddered, and men screamed. Things snapped. Something wet touched Betsy's bare feet. She gazed down at a growing pool of blood seeping underneath the door.

"No!" Nancy reached for the baton.

Betsy and Gaby grabbed her and dragged her backward.

Lonnie was screaming.

Nancy sobbed and went limp in their arms. They carried her back to the chair and set her down. She covered her ears with her hands.

The sound of crunching grew louder in the hallway, and the blood continued to flow.

"What's out there?" Camila's voice was just above a whisper.

"I don't know," Betsy said. "But whatever it is, I don't think it can get through the door." Her words felt as hollow as they sounded. "Weapons. Gaby, help me find something to use as a weapon."

"There's nothing!" Nancy shrieked. "They had guns. We have nothing. We're dead! We're—"

Gaby slapped Nancy across the face and then darted behind Betsy.

Nancy sat in the chair staring. Her face was twisted in grief and fear. She burst into tears and hung her head.

"Go, Gaby!" Betsy said as she pointed to the right of the storehouse.

Betsy searched the far wall, and the only thing she found on the shelves she could even think to fashion into a weapon was a mop.

Gaby rushed up to her, holding a long length of chain. "Could we use this? Like a whip?"

Betsy nodded, but she doubted whatever was outside that door would be bothered by it.

"Hey!" Lonnie called. "I got two things. But hurt so bad. I need a drink. Please."

"Later." Betsy snapped.

"I'm in pain. Please. I got a gun, and I know where another weapon is, too."

Betsy stomped back over. "If you're lying to me—"

"I'm not. I don't want to die too. Believe me."

"Where is the gun?"

"It's in the far-right corner. It's a long handle attached to a hose connected to a white cylinder."

Betsy nodded to Gaby, who dashed off to get it. Betsy gave Lonnie more water. "Where's the other weapon?"

"In my right boot."

Betsy knelt and lifted his pant leg. Inside a holster in his boot was a snubbed-nosed pistol. "Is it loaded?"

"Yeah. Six shots. It's a Glock 43."

Betsy held the weapon up triumphantly.

"It's only a pistol," Nancy muttered. "They had a machine gun, which didn't do them any good."

Gaby came hobbling back, lugging a propane cylinder connected by a hose to a rod with a metal cup on the end. "Is this it?"

"How is that a weapon?" Betsy took the bottle away from Lonnie's mouth.

"It's a weed burner. Turn it up high, and it's a flame thrower. Not really, but if the wolves are outside, it should keep them back."

"How does it work?"

After Lonnie explained what they needed to do, Betsy took a lighter and motioned everyone back. She opened the propane valve, pulled the handle, and the hiss of gas itched her nose. She clicked the lighter and moved the fire in front of the metal cup at the end.

POP!

Flames shot out, and it sounded like a jet engine turned on. She twisted another nob, and the flames grew larger.

Betsy clicked it off. "It's not much, but if we stick it in something's face, I figure it will run away."

"I would!" Gaby nodded. "As fast as I could in the other direction."

The room rumbled and shook.

Everyone exchanged nervous glances.

Nancy leaped to her feet, one hand covering her mouth and the other pointing to a spot on the floor in front of the middle shelf. In a rough circle about five feet in diameter, the cement sunk a few inches into the floor.

SCRAPE! SCRAPE! SCRAPE!

Nancy started yelling what everyone already knew. "Something's digging! It's trying to get in!"

48

IT GETS WORSE

Cain Haight

I'm standing on a small pile of broken cement, glaring at a steel wall. If I detonated the whole backpack of dynamite, I doubt it would be enough to get through, but it could bring the entire cave down on our heads.

Adam is sitting on a rock with his head in his hands, studying the map in his lap. After a few minutes, his shoulders slump even more. "I'm so sorry, Cain. There isn't any other way."

I grind my teeth so hard that a tooth cracks in my mouth. I'm not giving up on my little girl, and I'm not turning back. Marching over to Adam, I hold out my hand, and he gives me the map. After tracing every passageway with my finger, I keep coming back to where we are standing and glaring at the large black blob representing the cavern on the other side of the steel wall. My eyes widen, and I lift my chin. "How big is the chamber on the other side of that wall?"

"It's real big." Adam scratches his chin. "Runs about as long as home plate to deep center field, I reckon."

"How high is the ceiling?"

Adam's eyes travel up and down the wall. "It's very tall on the other side. When we first found it, our flashlights barely reached the ceiling. But I don't know how far back it starts to rise."

"It's the best shot we got. The only one, for that matter." I check the bag. There are five sticks of dynamite inside. I take four out and give the bag back to Adam. "I'd get behind the rock."

I start climbing the rock wall hand over hand. The stone is dry, and the climbing is easy. I stop at a ledge a few feet from the ceiling and set the dynamite into the crevice. My hands sweat as I carefully place them as far back as possible. Once everything is rigged up, I wind out a long length of fuse and start climbing down.

Glancing back, Adam is peeking out from behind a boulder. He gives me a thumbs-up and flashes a grin.

I light the fuse and sprint to the rock Adam is hiding behind. Sticking our fingers in our ears, we both crouch down. My heart is pounding in my chest as I wait. The seconds tick by, and the doubts rise. I am tempted to look when the blast rocks me back on my heels.

Dust and concrete fly overhead. My ears and eyes are ringing, but I stand up and try to see if it worked. As the dust clears, my flashlight beam gleams off steel.

"Dadgummit!" Adam waves his hand in front of his face, sending dust swirling around us. "Maybe you should have used all of—"

The deafening screech of metal grinding against metal reverberates through the chamber. The enormous steel panel tilts forward.

"Get down!" I grab Adam's shoulder and pull him down as the panel drops forward.

The steel wall slams into the ground like a drawbridge cut from its ropes. A blast of air sweeps over us. Dirt pelts my cheeks. Something bashes into my head, and I tumble backward. I roll twice on the ground and cover my head with my hands.

Fireworks are going off in my eyes, and my vision is flickering on and off. I've been knocked out more times than I care to count, and it looks like I will be adding to that sum.

I cough. My breath clears a spot in the ground in

front of my face and sends a cloud of grey dust into the air. I touch the side of my head. My hair is wet and sticky.

"We did it, Cain!" Adam shouts, but something is wrong — he sounds far away.

I raise myself onto my knees and shake my head to try and clear my vision.

"The whole panel came down!" Adam cheers as he walks forward and climbs the pile of rubble sitting on top of the steel.

"Wait." I rub my eyes. "Part of the ceiling came down. It might not be safe."

Adam ignores me and keeps climbing. Rocks slide down underneath his feet. He's leaning forward so far that he's crawling, dragging the backpack in his right hand.

"Careful with the dynamite!" I shout, and the fireworks start again behind my eyes. I lean against the boulder, grabbing hold so I don't fall.

"We can get through." Adam stands at the top of the pile, peering into the other chamber. "If we..." His voice trails off, and he focuses his flashlight down. "There's something in there. It's moving."

I reach for my shotgun, and the world spins. "Adam! Get over here NOW!"

Adam gasps and stumbles backward. He turns around to face me, and his chest is peppered with bone spikes. Splotches of red grow until the front is covered. "Run!" Adam yells, his voice booming as blood sputters from his mouth. He flops down on the pile, pulling the backpack into his lap. "I'm dead."

From the other chamber, a chittering grows into a roar.

"There's too many!" Adam rips a lighter out of his pocket. "I miss my Viv. Run, Cain. Save Bri!"

I've got a second to assess the situation, but there's no real debate. I've seen enough wounds to know there's no way Adam will make it out of the cave alive.

My voice fails me, so I nod. It doesn't matter. There's no way of thanking someone for dying to save your life. I spin around and sprint the other way.

"Take care of Pete!" Adam shouts.

Part of me wants to look back or say something, but blood is dripping into my right eye, and my vision blurs. The chittering grows so loud I can't hear the sound of my boots pounding off the rock. My foot slips, and I stumble forward. Somehow, I manage not to fall, but as I straight up, I glance back.

A sea of bone rats swarms over the pile of rocks. For some reason, they're going around Adam, like he's a boulder in the middle of a stream, and they're the water. A human form appears atop the pile, and the rats all stop.

So, don't I.

I rub my eyes, but only succeed in smearing blood across my face. I can't tell if the person is male or female. It strolls forward until it's standing next to Adam. It raises its right arm. It's holding something in its hand.

Blinding light, fire, and flames knock me back. I land on my butt and realize Adam lit the dynamite in the bag. The rocks all around me are shaking, and they're not stopping. A large piece of the ceiling breaks free and shatters when it hits the ground.

I scramble to my feet and sprint back the way Adam and I came earlier. Behind me, the roof of the cave is giving way. It sounds like a freight train is bearing down on me. A cloud of black swirls around me. It drowns out my flashlight, but I push on, feeling my way with my right hand.

It's hard to breathe. Pulling my shirt over my mouth, I try to use it as a mask, but it's no good. Another shockwave knocks me to my knees. I crawl forward on all fours, trying to go as fast as I can.

The rumbling slows until it's as quiet as a tomb. Or maybe I punctured my eardrums and went blind, too. I'm still moving forward but being unable to see or hear anything with a possible army of bone rats behind me is quite off-putting. Since I've already got PTSD, I wonder how bad the nightmares are gonna be after this.

After a few minutes, my flashlight beam reaches a couple of feet in front of me. I start walking, and the darkness gets a little brighter with each step. The terrain is familiar, and to my amazement, I see the ladder up ahead.

My flashlight glistens off the mud at the bottom and the two sets of boot prints. Grief and doubt crash over me. I've been on a few missions where friends didn't make it back. You never get used to it, and it doesn't get easier. If anything, it gets worse.

I grab the cold steel of the rungs and start climbing. My cheeks are soaked with tears, but I don't have time to mourn. Whatever that thing was that stood next to Adam, there could be more of them. And if the cave-in didn't kill all the monsters, they'd be looking for a way out.

49

DIEGO

Betsy Weber

Betsy grabbed the scissors and a long piece of cloth off the table, then hurried over to Lonnie's chair.

"Please don't kill me. Please don't." He begged. "I've tried to help."

"Shut up." Betsy undid the cord lashing him to the chair. "We're all getting out of here. Where do they keep the vehicles?"

Nancy called over, "I don't know if Camila can be moved."

"I don't have much of a choice." Camila groaned as she slid off the bed. "Gaby, you need to carry your brother."

Gaby grabbed the little cooler, and they turned it into a bassinet holding the bottom and handle. The little girl's hands trembled, but her lips pressed into a determined tight line.

"Where are the vehicles?" Betsy cut the cloth in half and wrapped it around Lonnie's shoulder, forming a sling.

"Out in front. There's a couple of old trucks. I don't know if they're still there."

"Where do they keep the keys?"

"In the ignition. You can't take them unless you ask Alan."

Betsy rolled her eyes. "I don't think he'll mind now. Can you walk?"

Lonnie swayed when he got to his feet. He was pale, sweaty, and had a yellowish tinge to his face, but he nodded.

Betsy handed the gun to Camila. "Do you know how to shoot?"

"Diego taught me."

"Nancy, look at me!" Betsy yelled.

Nancy was gulping in air like a fish on the dock. Her eyes darted from Betsy to the circle of cement steadily sinking lower.

"You're going to walk right behind me carrying the propane tank. Stay with me. Understand?"

"Carry what?"

Betsy picked up the heavy metal cylinder and handed it to Nancy.

Pieces of cement tumbled through the floor, and a musty odor wafted out.

Betsy lit the torch. "Might as well see if this works." She moved to the hole's edge, jammed the pole inside, and pulled the lever.

Flames shot out.

Something howled in pain.

Betsy's hope rose. "Whatever these things are, fire hurts them. Ready?"

"Wait!" Nancy shouted, setting the propane down and rushing over to the table. She grabbed the vodka bottle, took a swig, and then heaved the bottle at the hole. "Light it up!"

Betsy pulled the lever and set the alcohol ablaze.

With Betsy leading the way, she pulled the baton out of the door and then jerked the door open. The hallway was something out of a horror movie. Blood and pieces of flesh clung to the wall, but whatever killed Gary and the other man was gone.

"Keep your eyes on me, Nancy," Betsy whispered as she hurried forward. "Which way to the front, Lonnie?"

"Left." Lonnie had enough sense to keep his voice down and point.

At the end of the hallway, they turned left. Halfway down the corridor, a large pool of blood and pieces of what was once a man lay on the ground.

Sweat ran down Betsy's back. Her palms were slick, and she tightened her grip on the handle. The only way forward was through the blood.

Up ahead, the hallway continued straight and branched right.

Betsy glanced back at Lonnie.

He pointed straight ahead.

As she neared the right, a noise made her slow. She crept forward.

Faint crunching echoed from the corridor on the right.

Betsy peered around the corner.

There were no windows down that way. After a half dozen yards, the shadows grew so deep she couldn't see. But something was down there. And it was eating.

Betsy motioned the others past.

Lonnie, followed by Gaby carrying the baby and Camila, silently slipped by.

Nancy gasped. The propane cylinder slipped from her left hand and dinged off the ground.

Betsy held her breath.

The crunching stopped.

CLICK. CLICK.

A beast appeared from the darkness. The size of a bloated pony, the creature filled the hallway. Its two front claws were the size of laundry baskets, with five talons as long as her arm on each hand. Its long rat-like nose had a bone platting on top that covered its skull. No eyes were visible, but blood and flesh hung off its snout.

Betsy pulled the trigger. Fire roared from the tube.

The creature shrieked.

Burnt fur filled the air and stung her eyes.

Nancy was screaming something. She grabbed Betsy by the belt around her dress and dragged her after the others.

The creature opened its mouth, revealing wicked, large teeth. It scrambled forward, its arms aflame.

Betsy pulled the trigger again.

The beast thrashed, shrieked, and backed away.

Betsy and Nancy raced toward the others.

They charged down the hallway, turned right, and stopped at the front door. The sun sat low on the horizon. An old blue pickup was parked at the bottom of the stairs.

"Does that truck run?" Betsy asked.

Lonnie nodded. His lips were pulled back and sweat poured down his face.

"I'll drive," Betsy said. "Gaby and Camila will get in the cab." She glanced at Nancy. "Unless you want to drive, and I'll ride in the bed."

Nancy chuckled. "I'm so scared, I'd drive us into a ditch."

Betsy took a shaky, deep breath. "On three. Two. One. GO!"

Shoving open the door, the ragtag group dashed down the stairs.

Betsy raced toward the truck. Camila and Gaby headed straight for the passenger side while Betsy circled around. As Betsy passed the tailgate, she noticed the driver's door stood open. Then she saw the wolf.

Hunched over the body of a man, an enormous wolf with bones protruding along the length of its back and over its skull lifted its head. Black eyes met hers. There was no white to them, and it stared unblinking as blood dripped from its sharp teeth.

Betsy lifted the torch and pulled the trigger. Flames shot forward, followed by a whoosh and silence.

The beast stepped toward her. Its head was slightly smaller than a horse's. It opened its jaw.

Betsy pulled the trigger again. Nothing happened.

The wolf lunged.

Lonnie slammed into Betsy's back, knocking her sideways into the truck.

The wolf chomped down on Lonnie's upraised arm.

Lonnie shrieked as its teeth sunk into his flesh and sheered the bone. He dropped to his knees and stared at where his arm used to be.

The beast swallowed and turned its head toward Betsy.

Betsy leaned against the side of the truck. There was nowhere to run. Her eyes widened.

Camila leaned out of the cab, thrusting the gun against the wolf's temple. She pulled the trigger.

The wolf crashed to the ground.

Nancy grabbed Lonnie and pulled him back toward the tailgate. She was screaming something at Betsy.

Betsy's ears rang so loudly she couldn't hear what Nancy was saying, but she glanced in the direction her friend pointed.

At the far end of the building, two more wolves appeared.

Betsy pulled herself up and climbed into the truck. Camila sat in the middle, and next to the passenger door, Gaby clicked the seatbelt around herself and the cooler holding the baby.

"We're in!" Nancy shouted from the truck bed. "GO! GO!"

Betsy started the truck, jammed it into drive, and pushed the gas pedal to the floor.

Gravel pinged off the undercarriage as they shot down the driveway toward the open gate.

Betsy gazed in the rearview mirror. The wolves were fast, but the truck quickly pulled away. In the truck bed, Nancy ripped off Lonnie's belt and fastened it around the stump of his arm.

Camila lay her head on Betsy's shoulder. "Can you do me a favor?"

"What?" Betsy asked as she slowed down and turned onto the main road.

"Take care of Diego and Gaby."

Betsy shook her head, trying to clear the ringing in her ears. She couldn't have heard Camila correctly. Diego was dead.

The baby cooed.

"Is that what you named the boy?" Betsy asked.

Camila nodded. "Take care of him and Gaby." Her right hand cradled her left ribs. A bone-white spike was embedded in her side. "The wolf's tail hit me."

Betsy gasped. "Hang on, Camila. Please hang on!" She jammed the gas pedal to the floor.

50

NO TEETOTALER

Cain Haight

I stumble across the yard and toward the house. The blood on my face mixed with the dirt and dried, forming a hard shell. Now I can't open my right eye and looking through my left burns like a wasp stung my pupil.

Yanking open the back door, I feel my way along the counter to the sink and the water bowl. After a few minutes of scrubbing, I can see again, but fresh blood runs from the side of my head down to my chin.

I grab a towel off the counter and press it against the wound to stop the bleeding. The floor shakes as

Pete trots onto the back porch and sticks his head inside. He glances around the room, huffs, and stares at me. I glare back at the horse. He wants to know where Adam is. Pete turns around and wanders off to the backyard. He’s searching for his owner, who's never coming back.

I grab a glass and heave it into the wall, followed by two more. Shards sparkle as they catch the light and fall to the floor. I put my fist through the cabinet and rip the door off its hinges. Screaming obscenities at the top of my lungs, I take my grief and anger out on the kitchen.

After tearing open another door and scattering the coffee cups inside across the room, I realize what I really need — a drink. Like a deranged squirrel searching for its last lost nut, I rip everything out of every cabinet before heading to the dining room.

Adam said Ed was a teetotaler, but he's got to have some kind of alcohol in here. There's nothing in the dining room, so after ransacking it, I head to the den. The office is large, and the dark wood-paneled walls and heavy black leather furniture make the room look like something out of an old English house. It's lined with shelves filled with books, a desk with drawers full of Ed's important papers, and a large framed photo of a young Ed and a beautiful woman holding a little girl.

I yank each drawer open on the desk and slam it shut when I find nothing. Knocking all of the books to the ground, hoping to discover a hidden pint, I also come up empty there. Standing in the middle of my pile of destruction, my eyes shift to the vent at the base of the wall. It has no screws holding it in place.

Dropping to my knees, I wiggle the panel off and reach inside. My fingers touch what feels like a magazine, then a box. I take both out. The magazine is emblazoned with the title Your Dream Bass Boat, and the box is half filled with cigars. I reach back inside the wall and touch cool glass.

I lift out an almost full bottle of Scotch and hold it like it's the biggest award a man's ever received. "YES!" taking everything I've found back over to the desk and laying them out.

I root around in the pile of stuff I knocked off and find a cup from Ed's 30th high school reunion. Using an old eyeglass cleaning cloth, I wipe it out and fill it with Scotch. My hands shake as I raise the glass to my lips and let the cool liquid pour down my throat. It burns a bit, and the familiar heat radiates through my chest. I pour another glass and sit down. This one, I'm going to savor. I grab a cigar, snip the butt off, and stop with the flame hovering near the end.

The little girl in the photograph is staring at me.

She's petite, with dark hair framing an angular face. She's maybe six or seven. The photo is old, and I'm wondering where she is now. I close my eyes and picture Bri riding Star. She's fearless, clutching the reigns, her blonde hair streaming out behind her.

What am I doing? My little girl is out there with monsters, and I think I'm going sit back, get blind drunk, and enjoy a cigar. But what else can I do? There's no way I can make it to the fort overland.

Bull.

There is a slim chance I can make it. The odds aren't in my favor, which is why I'm sitting here like a sissy nursing a drink and worried about dying. Why do I even care? Living, knowing I could have done something to save Bri and didn't would be a fate worse than death.

I pound back the drink and head for the bathroom. Taking out the med kit, I pour some rubbing alcohol on my cut. Soon, I'm swearing and hopping around on one foot because it feels like I lit the side of my head on fire. Grabbing a roll of gauze, I wrap the bandage around my head. I look like the Revolutionary War flute player you see in pictures on each 4th of July.

It doesn't take me long to pack another bag. Having two stiff drinks in me helps with the pain, but not with the plan. There's only one thing I can come up with, and even with the Scotch adding to my courage, I still think it ends with me ending up as something's meal.

51

NOT NOW!

Amos Yoder

Amos raced across the field with Sarah next to him and Jesse in the back of the wagon with Ani. The border had fallen, and the creatures were getting through. He needed to warn the other families.

The Longhorn's farm was the closest. Four of Paul's boys were in the field when Amos galloped up. "Listen up, boys! I've got no time to explain. You need to warn all the other families. Everyone has to get into town — now. If anyone stays behind, they'll die. Do you understand?"

The eldest stepped forward. "We'll head back and get horses, sir. You can count on us."

"I know I can, Jed. Thank you." Amos snapped the reins, and the horse started moving again.

While he headed for the road, the boys got in their wagon and sped off toward their place. Amos stopped by two other farms before continuing to the town.

In the distance, above the clatter of hooves, the town's Church bell rang out in warning.

"Amos!" Sarah tugged on his shirt sleeve and pointed.

To their left was the quarry. The once-tall peak had been mined flat and carved halfway out years ago. The yellow and red stone towered over the landscape. At the top of the sheer cliff, dozens of wolves stood silhouetted against the sky. But these creatures didn't move like any pack he'd ever seen. They rushed forward in even lines, keeping a set space between them.

"They're headed to town!" Sarah wrung her hands together. "Do you think we can hold them off?"

Amos stared at the road ahead and remained silent. There were so many beasts he didn't know if they could fight them all back. And if Ridgecrest wasn't safe, where else could they go?

"Something's wrong with Ani!" Jesse yelled from the back of the wagon.

Amos glanced over his shoulder. The poor

woman had gone into convulsions, but he couldn't stop now.

"Try to hold her still. We're almost there!"

Pecan's hooves rang off the cement as Amos urged the older horse on. The homes became closer together, and the center of town appeared. People crowded the street. He recognized families from the other sides of town. The border must have fallen all around them.

The Church bell continued to ring.

Amos slowed as they neared the doctor's office. A crowd was gathered outside. Someone recognized Jesse and gasped. People began shouting questions.

"Not now! Not now!" Amos jumped down from the wagon and helped Jesse lift Ani out. They carried her up the steps.

Sheriff Matt stood in the waiting room with Nancy and a young girl. She was alive? Did he find Betsy, too? He had many questions, but they'd have to wait. Ani was convulsing in his arms. He needed to get her to Doc Harmon.

Amos shoved open the door and stopped. The room looked like a mobile army hospital. Lonnie Harmon lay on a table, one arm missing. A woman with a stomach wound lay beside him on another table. There were other wounded sitting in chairs and lying on the floor.

"Out! Out!" Doc Harmon shouted. "I'll get to her as soon as I can."

Amos started to protest, but Ani stopped shaking. She stiffened. Her muscles felt like steel. She planted her feet and stood tall.

Jesse stepped back. So did Amos.

Ani lifted her head. Her eyes glowed a brilliant blue like twin propane flames. She stared at Amos, and he took another step back. "Nazier is coming. He brings an army with him."

Outside the house, a dozen screams filled the air.

52

BUGS IN YOUR TEETH

Mercy Yoder

Mercy stood beside two motorcycles while Sadie spoke with D. They landed the houseboat at a dock on the lake's edge. After rolling the bikes off and making sure they started, D stood at the shore, his eyes scanning the road and woods.

"I'll come with you if you need me," D said, then glanced back to the lake. "You gotta forgive the guys. They all went through hell. They weren't gonna hurt any of you."

Sadie reached forward and hugged him. "I know that D. Tell them I get it. And thanks for the offer, but they need you more than we do. We're traveling light, and that's the one thing you ain't." She patted his ample belly.

D chuckled, but it seemed forced. He opened his mouth as if to say something more, but only nodded.

Sadie kissed his cheek and then started walking toward the bikes. "Where's Lucy?"

"She said she needed something on the boat." Mercy said.

Sadie stuck her fingers in her mouth and whistled. A moment later, Lucy appeared carrying a duffel bag slung over her shoulder. She strolled down the dock, gave a one-armed hug to D, and said, "Thanks for the machine gun."

"That I didn't give freely." D frowned. "But you're welcome."

Lucy marched over to the bikes and got on one. She hadn't said a word to Mercy since they'd gotten on the boat, and that didn't look like it would change.

"You ride with me," Sadie said as she mounted a large, silver motorcycle. She hopped in the air, stomped on a lever, twisted the grip, and the engine roared to life.

It was so loud Mercy wanted to block her ears.

Sadie jerked her thumb toward the seat and yelled, "Get on!"

Mercy climbed up and hung onto Sadie's waist.

The rumble from the engine made her whole body vibrate. Even her teeth shook.

"Ready?" Sadie yelled.

Mercy smiled and nodded.

"Don't smile. You'll get bugs in your teeth."

Mercy clamped her mouth closed.

Sadie laughed and twisted her wrist. The bike surged forward and across the parking lot.

Mercy's grip tightened on Sadie's waist. At first, she felt like a child wanting to peer around Sadie's shoulder and feel the exhilaration of the wind on her face. As they sped up, her eyes stung, and she found herself ducking behind Sadie's back for cover.

The tar sped beneath the tires. Sadie planned on using the speed of the motorcycles to overtake Fen and cut her off before she reached the base. Mercy had no idea how fast they were going, but there was no doubt that this was the quickest she'd ever traveled.

To their left, Lucy straddled the seat of the other motorcycle. She'd pulled her blonde hair back into a ponytail that stuck almost straight out behind her. She glanced at Mercy, and her lip curled in disgust. She sped up, pulling slightly ahead of them.

Mercy closed her eyes. Lucy blamed her for Cain's death. Maybe she was right. Maybe Mercy shouldn't have insisted on coming. So far, all she'd been was dead weight. Was there anything she could say or do to Lucy that could ease the animosity she held? Mercy doubted it. Lucy never liked her, so what could she do to change that?

Mercy opened her eyes. Even if Lucy wouldn't accept her apology, she needed to try. She was supposed to love her enemies and be kind—

Lucy swerved.

Flickers of white gleamed in the sun and arced from the grass on the side of the road toward them.

Sadie sped up and swerved, too.

The engine roared. Mercy's stomach flipped as Sadie leaned to the side. Mercy clung to Sadie's waist as she came closer to the tar streaking by beneath her only feet away.

"Too tight!" Sadie shouted.

Mercy forced herself to lessen her grip.

On either side in front of them, a dozen bone rats rushed out of the grass and whipped their tails. White spikes sliced through the air. One pinged off the back fender, and another sank into the seat an inch beneath Mercy's thigh.

Lucy's bike shook, and she swerved again. A puff of grayish smoke appeared near her leg. The plume quickly grew darker.

"WOLVES!" Sadie shouted.

Standing in the road ahead, four wolves blocked the way.

Lucy pulled out the boxy gun. “Go left!” She fired in bursts at the farthest wolf on her side. Bullets peppered the creature. It turned and limped into the bushes.

Sadie drew her pistol, and it roared to life.

The next wolf collapsed onto the road. The third fled into the brush, but the fourth charged.

Sadie fired again and again.

Chunks of its bone hide blasted off, but the beast raced toward them. It pounced, leaping through the air and opening its mouth. Knife-sharp canines as big as spikes gleamed.

Sadie swerved.

Mercy screamed. Claws raked the air beside her face. Tires squealed. A burning smell stung her nose.

Sadie shifted her weight to the right and jerked the handlebars that way. The metal peg Mercy rested her foot on struck the tar, sending sparks streaming out behind them.

The wolf sailed past them.

Sadie straightened out the motorcycle and gunned the motor.

They quickly caught up to Lucy. Her engine spewed black smoke. She reached down and grabbed the bone spike sticking out of the side. Twisting and jerking it back and forth, she ripped it out and tossed it aside.

Sadie leaned closer, inspecting the damage to her daughter's bike. Her back stiffened.

Lucy's motorcycle shuddered. The black smoke grew thicker and darker. She twisted her wrist to give it more gas, but she was slowing down.

"Go!" Lucy waved them on. "Keep going!"

"I'm not leaving you!" Sadie shouted.

Mercy's chest felt like an elephant stepped on it. If Lucy stopped, the wolves would get her. Something splashed against Mercy's cheek.

Tears streamed down Sadie's face and whipped off in the wind. Sadie started to speed up.

Mercy reached forward and grabbed her arm. "Stop! Stop! I have an idea."

Sadie jammed on the brakes and skidded to a stop.

Lucy dismounted from her motorcycle. She held up her gun, removed a metal rectangle, and put another in its place.

Mercy waved her toward them.

"What's your plan?" Sadie asked as she whipped back tears.

"To save the children and your daughter." Mercy jumped off the back of the motorcycle, held up her dress with her left hand, and sprinted off the road.

Lucy and Sadie screamed at her to come back.

Mercy ignored them and raced through the undergrowth. It was mostly grass, but some briars ripped at her clothes and cut her legs.

The motorcycle engine revved, and the tires squealed.

Mercy's lungs burned. She debated about hiding. There weren't any rocks or trees, but maybe...

Branches snapped as something charged through the underbrush toward her.

Mercy ran faster, but her pursuers were gaining.

The roar of the motorcycle engine faded in the distance.

Mercy glanced over her shoulder. Sadie and Lucy, riding together, disappeared down the road. Her dress caught on a branch, and she stumbled. Her hand grabbed the ground. She managed not to fall, but she slowed. A chain-linked fence rose before her. Barbed wire ran along the top.

A wolf leaped out of the brush on her right.

Another slunk forward on the left.

Mercy turned around, standing with her back toward the fence.

Two more wolves stopped in front of her. A dank odor stung her nose.

Tears ran down her cheeks, and her legs shook. She sank to her knees and clasped her hands together. "Our Father who art in Heaven..."

53

THE CHARGE OF THE LIGHT BRIGADE

Cain Haight

Sitting at the dining room table, I finish re-bandaging my battered feet, pausing to look down at my letter on the table. I don't know if Adam or Ed has family that's still living, but if they come looking for them, they deserve to know what happened. I wrote everything Adam told me about Ed, Adam's wife, and what happened in the cave. I sign my name and once again find myself cursing my father.

Who names a kid Cain, especially with a last name that sounds like Hate? I can picture someone reading this, getting to my name, and then not believing a thing I said. Still, that's not my problem. I told the truth. That's all I can do.

Pete is outside, pacing back and forth. Maybe he's missing Adam, or he senses something is up. I stride out of the house carrying a huge box and set it next to the moat. I haven't seen a bird all morning. And with no breeze, the grass is completely still. There are no squirrels, rabbits, or anything else moving. So even if I don't see the wolves, I'm sure they're out there.

I deflate the raft and tie it onto Pete's saddle with my pack. I'm only taking protein bars, a few water bottles, and the cigars and the scotch I found. This is going to be the new charge of the light brigade. Pete doesn't look in the best shape, and I still doubt we will make it a hundred yards, but the lighter we are, the better.

Chomping on the end of a cigar, I pick up one of my Molotov cocktails out of the box and light the fuse. I used some antique soda bottles that fit nicely into my hand. Throwing sidearm, I manage to fling them a good distance before they shatter and set the grass on fire. Once I'm done tossing all of them, I pick up the flare gun. I've got both my shotguns loaded with a combination of buckshot and flares, so I'll use the flare gun to fire off every flare I've got left before we go.

Trying to shoot them out as far as possible with them still striking the ground takes a little doing.

But the field is soon pockmarked with flaming circles that slowly expand.

A wolf howls, and several more answer. The grass toward the barn bends over as a dozen hidden wolves move away from the flames.

That's my cue to go. I wish Mercy were here so she could say a prayer. She ain't, so when I grab Pete's reins, I bow my head and say the only thing I can think of, "God help me and this horse get outta this Hell."

Pete's eyes are wide, and he's prancing back and forth. I stroke his head as I lead him down the slope into the moat. He slides down, and we both land with a splash and start swimming. Out in the fields, the smoke is streaming straight up, and the crackle of fire is growing. I dip underneath the water to give my clothes a good soak before we reach the far bank.

Pete clamors out of the moat, and I've got to scramble to keep up. Grabbing the saddle horn, I stick my foot in the stirrup and swing up. The flames are so high behind me that I can't see the barn. Steering Pete down the driveway, the horse's hooves ring off the tar. It doesn't matter how much noise he makes. I'm sure the wolves will follow.

I urge Pete into a fast trot toward the road.

A howl rises above the flames, followed by a half dozen more.

Pete wants to break into a run, but I hold him back. I've got no idea how much gas this old horse has in him, so I don't want him exhausted right out of the gate. I'm hoping he's got at least one long sprint in him.

I'm looking everywhere when I spot the first wolf breaking through the grass near the middle of the driveway. I fire a round. Pete rears up like the Devil himself just rose out of the earth. I manage to hold onto the shotgun and the reins as Pete breaks into a sprint. He charges straight at the wolf and bashes the creature aside like a bothersome dog nipping at its legs. The wolf rolls over once, scrambling back to its feet. Pete bucks. His hind legs thrust out and smash into the wolf's ribs.

The creature whimpers and darts away.

Letting Pete have free rein, I cling to his back, looking for threats. We're almost to the end of the driveway when I see something moving next to the boxwoods. But this is no wolf. It's crouched down like a man. He turns. Half his face is charred and blackened. The other half is grayish white. His eyes are all black like the wolves, but he's wearing some kind of body armor it looks like.

I raise my shotgun, aiming for his unprotected face.

My head jerks to the side like something

punched me. But the weird thing is, it feels like whatever hit me struck me inside my head.

This is the thing that attacked me in the barn.

Everything blurs. I slump forward and wrap my arms around Pete's neck. Somehow, I manage to hold onto the shotgun, but I can't aim or fire it.

Pete cuts to the right and darts across the street. I want to steer him to the left and down the road, but my arms aren't cooperating. My left hand is still gripping the reins, but it's starting to pull back like I want the horse to stop. That's the last thing I want Pete to do, so I'm doing everything I can to keep my arm where it is, but I'm at war with myself.

Branches scrape my sides and face as Pete darts through the woods and underbrush. He's moving so fast I think we'll run straight into a tree, but like an Olympic skier going through the slalom course, Pete's weaving between the trees at full speed. The farther we go, the less my head hurts. I blink my eyes and sit up, easing Pete back a little.

The horse looks like he's still got more left in his tank, but I don't hear anything chasing us. After another couple of minutes, Pete slows to a skittish trot. The poor guy is soaked with sweat. I give him a quick once-over from atop the saddle. Besides a few scratches, he looks fine.

I don't like stopping, but unless I do, I can't tell if the wolves are running up behind us.

Pete whinnies in protest, but eventually halts.

We both listen to the forest. I can hear a couple of birds. When I see some squirrels darting up and down a tree behind us, I start breathing a little easier.

I click my tongue and get Pete moving again. Above us, I catch a glimpse of blue sky. I've seen a lot of things I can't explain in my life, but whatever that guy did to my head takes first place. Somehow, that guy attacked my mind. I felt like a puppet when it happened.

What he is and what he can do scares me. But when I realize that the guy who came out of the cavern and stood beside Adam was probably another one of them, I'm terrified.

How many of them are there?

54

BRI

Lucy Green

The moment Sadie pulled over at the scenic overlook, Lucy leaped off the back of the motorcycle. She unslung the long rifle off her shoulder and marched over to the guardrail.

Sadie sat on the bike, her shoulders slumped and her head down.

Lucy didn't have time to deal with her mother. She needed to save her girl, and they may already be too late.

To the east, Leiper's Forge lay in ruins. Burned-out buildings stretched all the way to the army base just outside town. She placed a foot on the guardrail and lifted the scope to her eye. The river snaked below, shimmering as it wound toward the distant army base.

Up and down, as far as she could see, Lucy scanned the water, but there wasn't any sign of the canoe. She checked twice more before lowering the gun.

Sadie hadn't moved. She sat on the motorcycle, slumped across the handlebars.

Lucy walked back over and pried a water bottle from the saddlebag.

Sadie's shoulders shook as she softly cried.

"What are you bawling about?" Lucy said, holding the bottle out to her mother.

Sadie slapped Lucy across the face so hard that the bottle flew from her hand.

Lucy stumbled back and yanked her knife from its sheath. She held the back of her other hand to her lip and snapped, "What the hell is wrong with you?"

"Wrong with me?" Sadie awkwardly dismounted the motorcycle with her wounded leg. The bike wobbled and fell onto the tar. "Wrong with me? How can you be so cold! Do you even have a heart?"

Lucy stared at the blood on her hand. "It's not my fault that she tried to run for it. I mean... how stupid can you be thinking that you can outrun one of those wolves."

Sadie's lip curled. "You know that wasn't what

Mercy was doing. She told me to save your sorry behind."

"Bull. That girl hated me."

"What? You can't even say her name? *Mercy*. Her name was *Mercy,* and she didn't have a hateful bone in her body."

"Why would she sacrifice herself for me?"

"Why?" Sadie lurched forward. Her hands balled into fists at her sides.

"Don't hit me again," Lucy warned, tightening her grip on the knife's handle.

"Mercy didn't want you to end up in Hell. That's why."

Lucy spat, her blood splattering on the ground. "Then she threw her life away because that's where I'm headed. And there's nothing she or Cain or you can do to stop it. But I swear that I will save my little girl before the Devil drags me there." Lucy stomped forward and snatched the water bottle off the ground. She knocked the dirt off the lip and drained it dry as she marched back to the guardrail, ignoring her mother.

How dare she accuse Lucy of not having a heart. Of course, she knew what that stupid, self-righteous Amish princess was doing. And for her? Lucy would never be so dense. She wouldn't throw her life away for anyone — except Bri.

She stared at the river, and her breath caught in

her throat. Rounding the farthest bend in the river was an object that, at this distance, was no bigger than a dot. Lucy's hands shook as she held the rifle up and stared through the scope.

Following along the river, Lucy raised the gun until... the canoe! Detail was impossible to make out clearly, but someone sat in the middle, paddling, and a child sat in the bow—a child with long sandy-blonde hair.

"BRI! It's Bri!" Lucy raced back to Sadie, who had stood the bike back up.

Fresh tears sprang up in Sadie's eyes. "Get on!"

The engine roared, and Lucy hopped on the back. "Take the highway to the next exit and double around. We can catch them."

Sadie left a trail of rubber down the highway as she pinned the throttle back and rocketed down the road.

Lucy craned her neck to scan over the guardrail and down the slope. She could still see the river and the road that followed it.

Sadie turned off the exit. The bike shook, and she hit the brakes, leaning it so far over Lucy could touch the tar. At the bottom of the off-ramp stood a traffic jam of burned-up vehicles.

"Hang on!" Sadie shouted. She cut to the left.

The motorcycle jumped over the curb and skidded across the dirt and grass. Darting between two cars, Sadie threaded the needle through the gap. Reaching the open road, she opened it up.

The road curved back and forth following the course of the river. Lucy's hope rose with each mile. Her hands were sweaty, and she wiped them on her shirt. They rounded another corner.

A line of heavy caliber bullets raked the street in front of them.

Sadie hit the brakes and swerved. The rear tire of the bike skidded to the right. They hit the dirt on the side of the road, kicking a cloud of dust high in the air.

Lucy's foot struck the ground. It felt like some beast seized her ankle and tore her off the bike. Her hands instinctively went to the sides of her head. Her hip struck the tar and then her shoulder. She spun through the air and bounced off the ground until she rolled to a stop.

Dirt and dust clouded her vision. She couldn't draw a deep breath. A metallic taste filled her mouth.

Boots sounded on the pavement. A man in camouflage gear stopped in front of her.

Lucy looked up as the butt of his rifle slammed down on her head.

55

NOT YOU TOO!

Cain Haight

I ride Pete at a slow trot until I reach another road. I decide to stick to the street, despite the loud clomp of Pete's hooves. The travel is easy, and I've got a good line of sight.

Not that I enjoy anything I'm seeing.

I've passed by six houses, and they're either burned, ransacked, or abandoned. Only one charred car sat in the remains of a garage, and all of its tires were flat. It may be safer for me to head to the river.

Pete glances over his shoulder back at me, and I look away.

What will I do with the stupid horse when I

reach the water? I can't take him in my inflatable raft, but if I let him go, he won't make it out here long with the wolves. Adam asked me to care for him, but I never said I would. How can I?

Something jingles ahead. I crest a rise in the road and see a house off to the left. A wind chime on the porch plays a haunting melody in the wind. The house is a one-story ranch that appears abandoned. It has an oversized detached boat or RV garage, and the four huge doors are shut.

That is something worth checking out.

Pete trots up the driveway, but he gets antsy as I draw my shotgun. With my free hand, I stroke his neck and remind myself when I get back to Ridgecrest to give Star extra carrots, sugar, and oats for life. There's not a better horse on the planet.

We make it up the driveway, and I slide off. Pete wanders toward the house, munching on the grass as he goes. I head to the garage and the man-sized door on the left. It's unlocked. Flicking on my flashlight, I sweep the room. There's a bus-sized RV, an F150, a cherry red 1972 Ford Mustang, and a coffee truck converted from an old milk delivery truck.

I hunt around for some keys, but there are only tools and a non-working refrigerator with soda and water. I'd kill for a beer, but I settle on some caffeine and head for the house, downing a soda. I'm tempted to add some scotch, but if I start drinking, chances are I won't stop.

The ranch house has a country vibe to it. The grass is long, and poplar saplings are now growing in the once-manicured flowerbeds. The air is filled with insects buzzing and the occasional bird chirping. There's a large nest sticking out of the hammock on the front porch. I doubt anyone is home, but I check the side door instead of heading to the front.

I knock twice, and everything except the bugs go silent. Through the window, I scan the kitchen. Some drawers are pulled out, but it doesn't look ransacked.

The door is locked, so I use the butt of my shotgun to break a pane of glass. Carefully reaching in, I unlock it while listening for any hint someone or something is inside.

"I'm coming in!" I yell, then shove the door open and stand back.

Nothing moves. My heart is pounding and sweat rolls down my back. I slowly move into the kitchen, taking a few steps at a time and peeking around corners. Aside from dust, nothing seems out of place. There's no sign of life or anything that might suggest someone has been here recently. A few dishes lay in the sink, but the thing that catches my attention is the keyring next to the microwave. I snatch it up. Whoever owned them was hyper-organized. Each key has one of those plastic-colored covers. Seeing the Ford label on two of them makes me smile.

I make my way toward the living room, gun ready in case unseen threats lurk. I scan the room, but nothing stands out as unusual. There are no strange noises, smells, or evidence of someone living here. Still uneasy, I go down the hall to check the bedrooms and bathrooms.

The floorboards creak under my boots as I creep forward. The bedroom on my right still has a suitcase on the bed, but it looks like it was left behind unpacked. Most drawers are open, and clothes lie in a pile in front of a bureau and the closet.

I turn back to the hallway, and something bangs in the closet.

Time slows. I spin—pain races up my right leg from the pressure on my cut foot. My Shockwave rises. A hanger is swaying back and forth. My finger moves toward the trigger. I'm tempted to shoot through the drywall and into the closet itself.

A black cat bounds out and leaps on the bed.

I exhale and ease my finger off the trigger, grateful I didn't fire.

The cat stays in the middle of the bed, staring at me like it's debating whether I am a friend or not.

Lowering my shotgun, I hold my hand out. The cat arches its back and hisses.

"You're welcome for me not shooting you," I mutter, continuing down the hallway.

I spend some time in each room checking if there's anything I can take. No weapons. No booze. Nothing I don't have that I want to carry.

In a small pantry, dry cat food crunches beneath my feet. The cat must have ripped open the bag, and the hard chunks are starting to get moldy. I grab a can of wet food and open it up.

The cat is purring at my feet before I set the can on the floor.

"You're welcome." I open a second can and set it down, too.

The cat is so busy eating she doesn't look up.

I grab a couple of boxes of Cheerios, some honey and almond protein bars I like, and head back outside. Pete is waiting at the door for me. He trots over and nudges me with his head. I open up the box of cereal and dump it on the ground.

Pete starts munching away.

Spinning the keys around my finger, I stroll over to the garage. Because of the Dark, I know the RV and F150 won't work, but I try anyway. The keys fit, but the cars are dead. As I walk toward the cherry red Mustang, it's all I can do not to run my hand along the doorframe. The car is pristine. I never dreamed I'd drive something as sweet as this.

The key slides in, and the engine turns over. I settle back in the leather seat that fits my body like the car was made for me. I'm picturing myself zooming down the road when Pete trots over and stares into the garage.

An image of Adam sitting on top of that pile of rubble with a backpack of dynamite flashes in my head. "Take care of Pete."

I close my eyes and rub my temples with my thumb and forefinger. There's no way I can take the Mustang and the horse. I gave Pete a box of Cheerios and got him away from the farm. Doesn't that count as taking care of him?

Pete trots over to the car and sticks his head in the open window.

I swear and shut off the engine.

"Back up! Move back." I snap as I try to get out. The RV won't run, but I haven't tried the stupid coffee truck. It looks old enough not to have a computer chip in the engine, but who knows?

I trudge over to the converted milk truck and slide the door back. The dumb thing fires right up, too. I sit there drooling over the Mustang, but I know there's no way I'm leaving the stupid horse behind. I can't do that to Adam, no matter how much I want to take the hotrod.

It takes me an hour to clean out the back of the milk truck and top off the gas tank. To my surprise, Pete gets right in.

I hop in the seat and ease the truck out of the bay.

The black cat bounds out of the grass, flies across the driveway, and jumps in the big open door.

"Not you, too! Out! Out!"

The cat ignores me and climbs up onto the counter in the back.

I hit the brakes and glare at the two animals staring back at me. The hair on my arm rises, and my skin prickles. If Bri were here, she'd have laid a gentle hand on my wrist and looked at me with those big blue eyes.

I storm out of the truck and march back inside the house. Grabbing a trash bag off the floor, I gather all the unopened cat food, cereal, and oats, sling the bag across my back like Santa, and head back to the truck.

Pete and the cat are right where I left them. If I didn't know better, they're smiling at me. I put the truck into gear and pull out onto the road. There's a chance I could outrun a wolf in this thing, but it would be close. I can't leave Pete behind, and I'm not really taking the cat with me. I'm just letting it sit in here for a while.

The main thing is I'm on my way and should get to the base by nightfall. Who knows? Most likely, I'll be dead by morning anyway.

56

YOU ARE A BAD GUY!

Bri Haight

Bri sat in the front of the boat, paddling. Jacob lay behind her, still sleeping. Fen had said that Nicholi had given the boy some pills. She wished he'd wake up.

"Paddle harder," Fen said.

They'd been going all night, and Bri's arms felt like they would fall off. She couldn't keep going, but Fen would throw her out of the canoe if she didn't. Bri's paddle caught the water at an odd angle. The water ripped it from her hand.

Fen snatched it up before it floated by. "Stupid child!" Fen hissed. "I warned you"

Bri burst into tears. She couldn't help it. She'd

been kidnapped, smacked, attacked by creatures and wanted nothing more than to sleep. And now, Fen would kill her.

Fen placed Bri's oar down in the back of the boat.

Tears rolled down Bri's cheeks as she faced her tormentor. This was it. Fen swore if Bri stopped paddling, she'd have no need for her.

Fen reached down, picked up a bag, and tossed it to Bri. "Stop crying." Fen grabbed a bottle of water and held it out. "Eat. Then sleep."

Bri suspiciously peered inside the bag. It held peanuts. She gulped down half the bottle and began shelling peanuts like she hadn't eaten in a month.

"Slow down, or you'll get sick," Fen said as she sipped from a water bottle and picked up a peanut bag for herself. "I need for you and me to reach an understanding. The bone rats killed Nicholi. The big Russian?"

Bri nodded, but she had no intention of protecting the evil woman. Once they got to wherever they were going, she would tell them what Fen had done to Nicholi.

"Listen to me. I'm not the bad guy."

"That's why you keep telling me you'll feed me to the wolves?"

Fen shook her head. "I shouldn't have said that."

"Or pointed a gun at me? Or slapped me!" Bri's

anger rose. "You even hit me with an oar! You are a bad guy!"

Fen's eyes narrowed.

Bri swallowed. She should have kept her mouth close. "I mean... I won't tell anyone."

Something slammed into the end of the canoe just behind Fen. Plastic shattered, and the canoe spun partway around and tipped over. Bri splashed into the river, the water rushing over her head. She managed to hold her breath, but a horrible thought made her eyes snap open — Jacob!

Swimming out from under the capsized canoe, Bri surfaced.

Jacob's brown head bobbed up and down as he floated downriver in his life preserver.

Gunshots rang out. Fen held onto the canoe and fired at something on the bank.

A huge bone bear stood on the bank. His arm circled like he was throwing something. What looked like a white, softball-sized rock shot through the air at Fen. It struck the middle of the canoe. Pieces splintered, scattering into the air.

Fen screamed in pain.

Bri swam after Jacob. Kicking as hard as she could, she only went a few yards before her feet touched the river's muddy bottom. She stood up. The water only reached her chest.

Behind her, the bear charged into the shallow water.

Bri wanted to swim into the deep water but couldn't leave Jacob. He was helpless. She splashed forward until she grabbed his life jacket.

"Ummm! Ummm!" The bear grunted as it barreled through the water toward her.

Bri pushed off the ground, shoving Jacob toward the middle of the river.

The bear raised its thick arms. Grey hair and bone covered its body. It opened its mouth. Its teeth were fangs like a tiger's.

Bri screamed.

The bear shrieked in pain. It spun around, creating a wave that pushed Bri and Jacob further out to the river.

Fen clung to the beast's back. The knife in her right hand plunged repeatedly into its flesh.

The bear twisted like a bull at the rodeo.

The knife tumbled from Fen's hand, but she still hung on.

The bear grabbed Fen's leg and flung her off his back.

Fen skipped once like a rock off the water and crashed onto the bank of the river. She didn't move.

The bear turned toward Bri.

Bri froze.

The hideous beast marched forward.

Bri shook. Now she was helpless. There was nothing she could do and no one there to save her.

The bear opened its mouth, and an ear-piercing, pain-filled roar filled the air. It swung its enormous head back and forth. Water flew into the air as it thrashed. It spun around and charged out of the river and up the bank.

Bri watched in disbelief as it ran away into the woods. Someone touched her shoulder.

Jacob stood in the water next to her. He was staring in the direction the bear had fled.

Bri gasped.

Jacob's eyes blazed bright blue.

Engines sounded on the shore. Three trucks raced into view and skidded to a halt. People shouted. A dozen men and women in soldier uniforms appeared and ran down to the river. Several stopped at Fen. The rest drew their guns. They aimed their weapons at Bri and Jacob.

Bri raised her hands and nudged Jacob, who did too.

A tall, broad-shouldered man waded out in the water. "You two. Come with us." He said with a thick, Russian accent.

57

DR. DOOLITTLE

Cain Haight

Sticking to the backroads, I reach the outskirts of Leiper's Forge. In the distance, the city looks destroyed. Most buildings are burned-out shells, clutching at the sky like skeletal fingers. I plan on keeping to the outer perimeter. That will hide me for as long as possible if anyone is watching from the fort.

I never thought I'd make it this far driving an old milk truck with a horse and cat along for the ride. The place looks like a war zone. Every structure I pass is heavily damaged. Buildings are charred, and the exterior walls have collapsed so you can see inside. Offices and apartments sit exposed to the elements, their contents on display as I pass.

It wasn't any of the creatures that did this, though. There are lots of destroyed pieces of military equipment all over. Tanks, transports, and even the crashed remains of a couple of helicopters sitting in the middle of the highway.

But I haven't seen any corpses — neither human nor animal. There's plenty of gear and rotting clothes scattered around. But the bodies are all gone.

Pete and the cat looked as freaked out as I feel. Everything seems off. I remember once when I was deployed, we were on patrol and came across an outdoor wedding. For some reason, the insurgents in the area targeted the wedding party. They may have thought someone was cooperating with us, or it could have been a local thing. I don't know. But we came to this beautiful field decorated with flowers, and everyone is dead. Men, women, and even the little kids were slaughtered and left where they fell. The scent of flowers and freshly cut grass mixed with death and rot. The horrors I witnessed then ended up on my mind's greatest nightmares playlist. Every few weeks, I relive seeing that in my dreams.

I drive on. The next street looks like there'd been an airstrike. The road is scorched and blackened, but passable. Farther up, some of the buildings don't look too badly damaged.

A flash of movement behind a flipped-over police car on my right catches my eye. I slow, but don't hit the brakes. I roll forward, and as I pull alongside the vehicle, a person dashes across the street away from me. They sprint toward a four-story building with shops underneath. They're small, maybe a kid, and they're carrying something.

I stop.

The kid reaches the doors and yanks on them, but they don't open. They dart further down the building and try those doors, but they're locked, too. They run again and stumble on the sidewalk. As they catch themselves from falling, I see what they're carrying — a baby.

My old drill sergeant's voice is screaming in my head to keep moving. Insurgents would use tricks like this to get a patrol to drop their guard, but this is different. There's a kid with a baby scurrying around the bones of what once was the heartland of America.

Drawing my Shockwave, I slide back the door and step out. The street is littered with crumbled cement and fifty-millimeter shell casings. They musically ping beneath my boots as I stride over to the building. Stopping about twenty feet away, I reach into my pocket and pull out a protein bar.

"Hey, kid," I call out, but not too loudly. "It's okay. I'm not going to hurt you."

Brown eyes peer out of the darkness back at me. The kid doesn't say anything.

"You hungry? This is a candy bar. I'm gonna toss it to you." I lob the protein bar underhand. It lands in the deep shadows of the doorway.

It's dark enough that I can't make out details, but the kid is crouched and holding the baby in their right arm. The kid scurries forward a foot, grabs the bar, and darts back. I reach into my pocket for another one.

"Drop the gun and put your hands up nice and slow," A woman says from the doorway.

Inside my head, my drill sergeant is swearing and calling me every name for a moron I've ever heard.

Behind me and to my right and left, people move.

"Drop the gun."

Someone chambers a round behind me.

I set the Shockwave on the ground and straighten up.

"Raise your hands!"

"Why?" I shrug as I struggle to quiet my growing anger and frustration. "If you wanted me dead, you woulda shot me already."

"Put your hands up, or I'll kill you." She shouts.

"Fine," I raise my hands. "Happy?"

From underneath a truck parked near the corner of the building, I hear someone laugh.

The woman steps out of the shadows, scowling toward the laughter. She's short, five feet tall tops, and thinly built. She's holding a Glock in her right hand, and it's pointed at my chest. Laying on the ground near the door is what I thought was a baby. It's a doll.

"Tell your friends to come out of the truck," the woman says as she pulls the sweatshirt hood off her head. She's got a hard face and cold eyes. Thin with high cheekbones, she could be in her early thirties.

A man and woman armed with assault rifles step out from the corner of the building. From underneath the truck, another man emerges with a shotgun, followed by a Marine with a combat shotgun.

"My arms are getting tired," I relax my shoulders. "I'm going to slowly lower them or hurry up and frisk me because you're not going to kill me."

The woman in the hoody marches forward and holds the gun so it's a foot in front of my face. "Keep your hands up and order your friends to come out of the truck, or my friends will open fire, and I'll shoot you in the head."

"That's an excellent Clint Eastwood impersonation, but Pete can't come out of the truck."

The woman cocks the gun.

"Hey, Pete! Come out! You know you don't have to cock the gun to fire it, right?" I smirk, but she's too busy glaring at the milk truck to notice.

"Call him again." She orders.

"Pete's a horse."

The woman turns back, notices my wise guy grin, and looks like she wants to pistol whip me. "You want me to believe you're driving around in the freaking apocalypse in a milk truck with a horse?"

"A cow would make more sense, but I got a cat in there too."

The guy who was under the truck laughs again.

"Here's the deal," I say. My arms are burning now. "I'm putting my arms down because you won't shoot me. Chuckles over there is Jerry Pace — the comedian." I turn to Jerry, "I caught your act at the Civic Center last year. You were a riot."

"Thanks, man." Jerry smiles and lowers his rifle.

I point at the man and woman at the side of the building. "They're cops. Probably partners. They've got cop belts, guns, and he's still got the shoes." I jerk my head to the guy holding the combat rifle. "He's a Marine with the 127$^{th.}$ He has their screaming hawk tattoo."

"Hold on." The cops circle me and pat me down.

"Name?" The woman with the hoodie lowers her gun.

"Cain Haight."

She rolls her eyes. "Real name?"

"If I were gonna make up a name, I'd pick something like Mr. Rodgers or I'm-not-a-threat Smith — not the first murderer and something that sounds so close to hate."

Jerry laughs again.

"Who's in the truck!" She shouts as she gets into my personal space.

Jerry grabs her arm. His eyes dart nervously around. "We better get going."

"We're taking him with us," The woman says, motioning to the cops.

They grab my arms.

"I'm not going anywhere with you." I yank my arms free. "I'm heading to the fort."

"Why?" The marine asks.

Staring at this motley crew, I'm sure they will only shoot me if one of them panics, so I opt for the truth. "A Chinese and a Russian soldier kidnapped two kids from Ridgecrest. One of them is my daughter. I'm going to get them back."

Everyone falls silent, but from the stares they're sharing, there's a whole conversation taking place that I'm not privy to.

The Marine's eyes lock with mine. His are a light blue. He squares his shoulders and sets his jaw. "If they've already reached the fort, you can't get them back."

"I'm still gonna try." I start walking for the truck.

They all start jabbering at the same time with each other. I can't make out exactly what's being said, but it doesn't sound like they're thinking of shooting me, so I keep moving.

"Hold on!" The woman with the hoodie shouts. "At least come and hear us out. Maybe it will change your mind."

"Or I can give you some intel if you insist on going." The Marine adds.

I keep walking. What the soldier says makes sense, and I need a break before continuing anyway. I open the back of the truck, and Pete and the cat hop out.

"He wasn't lying!" Jerry starts cracking up.

"You're not bringing a horse with us." The woman says.

"Pete's owner died saving my life. He asked me to look after the stupid horse. It comes with me, or I don't go."

The guy cop strides over with his hand out. Usually, Pete is scared of his shadow, but trots right over to the guy.

"What are you, a horse whisperer?" I ask.

The cop grins. "I was with the City Police in their mounted unit. The name's Bob."

"Enough, Dr. Doolittle," The woman snaps. "We need to get off the street. Everyone grab your gear. No more talking until we get downstairs."

Leaving the milk truck behind, we all start marching down the road. After a block, I realize that the cat has wandered off. "Cat!" I click my teeth.

"What part of shut up didn't you understand?" The woman with the hoodie snaps.

I'm about to say something when I see a light flash from the fifth-story window of the building ahead of us.

Jerry grabs my arm, and everyone starts running. "We've got to get inside."

The building is two blocks away, and right now, I feel foolish and guilty for bringing the horse. Its hooves ring on the tar and echo off the building. Anything within a mile knows where we are.

The building we're headed to has those roll-down metal gates. Glancing up, most of the higher windows have been barricaded, too. The center gate rises with a clatter, and everyone rushes through. I hold back.

"Cain!" The woman stretches out my name like she's strangling it.

I click my teeth, and a moment later, the black cat bounds around a chunk of concrete and darts past me into the building.

We all run deeper into the building until we

reach some stopped escalators. I don't know how Bob does it, but he manages to coax Pete down the steps. We go past another barricade and metal door until we reach a huge room that was once some big box store. There are even SALE signs still mounted on the walls. The place has been converted into an underground shelter. Dozens of sets of eyes peer out from the darkness at me.

There's commotion off to the left, and two men hurry over to the woman with the hoodie.

"Hey, Bob," I call over to the cop, but he's busy trying to fend off a group of little kids who've crept out of the darkness to catch a glimpse of the horse.

The Marine strides over and thrusts out a hand. "Tim Hall. People call me H."

The guy has a firm grip. "Who's the one with the hoodie, and why is she in charge?"

"You asking because she's female?"

I shake my head. "And here I was just starting to like you, H. No. I'm asking because you're military, and she's a civvy."

H nods, which looks to be about as much of an apology as I'm gonna get. "Angela Bowmount. Goes by Angel. She's Homeland Security, and my CO transferred command to her before he died."

That news I was unprepared for. She struck me more as someone with anger issues than a person in command.

As if sensing my thoughts, Angel marches over. The hardness in her eyes has been replaced with a neutral mask that makes my gut tighten. “Two of our lookouts spotted something at the base that we need to discuss.” She angles her head, and H, the cops, and Jerry walk away.

One of the two guys Angel just spoke with comes over and stands at attention beside her. He’s an older man with a shaved head.

Angel hands me a water bottle and asks, “Did anyone else come with you or go looking for these two kids?”

I crack open the bottle and take a sip. My throat is so dry I find myself downing half the bottle before answering. “Three women.”

Angel and the soldier exchange a glance. He folds his hands at the small of his back and says, “At approximately o-nine-thirty, my spotter and I detected two women on a motorcycle approaching the base from the road. They were apprehended by the rebels currently holding the fort.”

“Two women? What did they look like?”

“The one riding the motorcycle had grey hair pulled back in a ponytail. The passenger was blonde,” he continues, describing Lucy and Sadie.

“We left with a third woman. Are you sure you didn’t see anyone else with them?”

He shakes his head.

I wince as if someone punched me. Maybe Mercy is all right. Something could have happened, and they left her someplace. Just because she isn't there doesn't mean she's gone.

"We saw something else on the river road." The soldier drops his gaze and stares at the floor. "Three trucks. It looked like a search party. There was a boy and a girl with them. They took the children to the fort."

My back stiffens. "It looks like I'll have to fight an army after all."

JOIN THE FREE PREFERRED READER PROGRAM

Visit ChristopherGreyson.com to sign-up!

ALSO BY CHRISTOPHER GREYSON

The Girl Who Lived 1

The Girl Who Lived 2

One Little Lie

The Woman Beneath the Stairs

Pure of Heart

The Detective Jack Stratton Mystery-Thriller Series

Kiku - The Rogue Assassin Series

The Dark - A Post-Apocalyptic Thriller Series

The Adventures of Finn and Annie - A Mini Mystery Series

ACKNOWLEDGMENTS

I would like to thank all the wonderful readers out there. It is you who make the literary world what it is today—a place of dreams filled with tales of adventure! Word of mouth is crucial for any author to succeed. If you enjoyed the novel, please consider leaving a review at Amazon, even if it is only a line or two; it would make all the difference and I would appreciate it very much.

I would also like to thank my amazing wife for standing beside me every step of the way on this journey. My thanks also go out to Laura and Christopher, my two awesome kids, and my dear mother and the rest of my family.

ABOUT THE AUTHOR

My name is Christopher Greyson, and I am a storyteller. Since I was a little boy, I have dreamt of what mystery was around the next corner, or what quest lay over the hill. If I couldn't find an adventure, one usually found me, and now I weave those tales into my stories.

My love for tales of mystery and adventure began with my grandfather, a decorated World War I hero. I will never forget being introduced to his friend, a WWI pilot who flew across the skies at the same time as the feared, legendary Red Baron. I love to hear from my readers. Please go to Christopher-Greyson.com and sign up for my mailing list to receive periodic updates on new book releases. Thank you for reading my novels. I hope my stories have brightened your day.

Sincerely,

THE DARK 2
Copyright: Christopher Greyson
Published: November 1st 2023

Find out more about the author and upcoming books online at www.ChristopherGreyson.com.

V.1.11.1.23

Printed in Great Britain
by Amazon

57379229R00209